The Big Lie

by

Richard Johnston

To E J with hopes for a better world

Richard Johnston

Bloomington, IN   Milton Keynes, UK

authorHOUSE®

AuthorHouse™
1663 Liberty Drive, Suite 200
Bloomington, IN 47403
www.authorhouse.com
Phone: 1-800-839-8640

AuthorHouse™ UK Ltd.
500 Avebury Boulevard
Central Milton Keynes, MK9 2BE
www.authorhouse.co.uk
Phone: 08001974150

First published by AuthorHouse 3/22/2007

ISBN: 978-1-4259-7368-1 (e)
ISBN: 978-1-4259-7367-4 (sc)
ISBN: 978-1-4259-7366-7 (hc)

Library of Congress Control Number: 2006909353

Printed in the United States of America
Bloomington, Indiana

This book is printed on acid-free paper.

Photo Credit:
Shadows, Quai de Bourbon   Mary Alice Johnston

Dedication

For: Mary Alice Johnston

I am indebted to my wife Mary Alice, an experienced editor, who has read every word in this novel plus an impressive number that were excluded. And I thank these friends who read and responded to various drafts of the manuscript: Michele Ferrand, Mario Ivanoff, Don and Erika Johnston, David Nicholas and Judy Walden.

Foreword

From times of old warriors with their wives and chattel would come to gather around the confines of captured territory, keeping the nights ablaze with their campfires and the natives restrained from unwise adventure in the wake of defeat. And just as conquering hordes once moved across land and water to reap the fruits of victory, so did Americans flow into Europe after V.E. Day.

In Paris—well Paris was different. France was not an occupied country, a fact the French always remembered and the Americans sometimes forgot as they joined the "Little America" already present with its American Cathedral.

They frequented the American Library; they picked up copies of *The Paris Herald Tribune* and browsed in the Shakespeare & Company bookstore along the banks of the Seine; they were served by the American Hospital in *Neuilly sur Seine* and the American Express Bank and Travel Bureau at *Place de l'Opéra;* they ordered their hamburgers and banana splits in the United States Embassy restaurant and a few cast ballots in a straw vote for president every four years after drinking Bloody Marys at Harry's New York Bar.

Some came hoping to stay. Others arrived for a tour of duty or a period of study. And when they departed they left something of themselves. *Partir c'est mourir un peu* (to go away is to die a little) the French say and the Americans left behind them a fraction of their lives—some of their years, some of their hopes, some of their regrets.

Paris: 1953

Part One: Opening Day

Chapter 1

Bill Helmer awoke that morning earlier than was his habit. As if impelled by some inner force, he was out of bed and standing by the big double windows before he was fully awake. There was little traffic along the quay and no boats moving on the Seine past *l'île Saint-Louis*. The arches of *le pont Marie* were veiled in morning mist drifting upriver with the breeze. Across the river two men were sleeping on the stone parapet. Above them he made out the letters splashed in red *AMERICAINS EN AMERIQUE.*

Eastward bound traffic on the *quai des Célestins* frightened a flock of sparrows into rising from the parapet along the river wheeling in a graceful arc toward the towers of Notre Dame.

Bill stood there for a moment fighting the urge to crawl back into bed but also trying to discover the source of his feeling that this was no ordinary beginning. Sitting on the windowsill he shoved his feet into his slippers. Sleep was gone as he remembered. This was opening day.

Pulling himself away from the scene he went into the kitchen and placed leftover coffee on a low flame while he shaved and showered. Even the needles of hot water on his back failed to give him the usual feeling of relaxation. He rummaged for his clothes as he dressed, gulped down his coffee and departed.

The traffic on the Left Bank was light. While responding to the demands of driving he tried to concentrate on the day ahead. *Place St. Michel, la Chambre des Députés, Trocadero*—these familiar landmarks had only a shadowy substance this morning.

1

He rolled down his window as he entered his favorite shortcut through the *Bois de Boulogne*. Following a winding road he passed a column of French soldiers marching briskly behind a sergeant. This brought to mind Captain Murphy and he tromped down on the pedal. Bill could see Murphy's eyes. *"Coming back next year, Mr. Helmer? I hope you can get the school under better control than last year."*

Arriving at school he found two buses unloading students. Officers and enlisted men from the Transportation Section dashed about carrying clipboards, confirming with military precision the confusion of opening day.

"Good morning, sir," the transportation sergeant at the gate greeted him. "All set for the stampede?"

"As ready as we'll ever be I guess. How are the bus runs shaping up?"

"One hell of a mess. We're picking up students who didn't register, kids and mothers on every corner. We already got two drivers out on second runs. Where do all these people come from?"

Bill smiled. "Cheer up, sergeant. It'll all shake down in a few weeks." Again he had that tight feeling in his stomach as he walked on toward the office.

"Morning, Mr. Helmer." The transportation officer stepped along with him. "It's these damn French drivers who are screwing up the works. They all made trial runs last week but they don't know up from down. Every time some mother yells at them in English they go four or five blocks off the route to pick up her brats."

A driver came up waving his arms indignantly.

"Monsieur le directeur, what am I to do? Captain says to park here the bus. The major says to park there the bus. *Je veux bien faire mon travail.* Everybody says me something different. *Merde alors. Merde!"*

A group of children waiting for a transfer bus to the elementary school were chanting:

Peas porridge hot, peas porridge cold,
Peas porridge in the pot, nine days old

Pausing to watch them Bill could feel their excitement. He found the nursery rhyme turning around and around in his head and he recalled another first day of school. So gripping was the memory that the blood rushed to his forehead.

Peas porridge hot, peas porridge cold...

He was trudging across the schoolyard of Spring Valley School in new knee-pants and button shoes. A group of little girls were chanting.

Peas porridge hot, peas porridge cold...

He had stopped to watch some third-graders playing marbles.

"Hey, look, fellas. Look at the girls' shoes. Ain't they purty?"

"Whatcha wearin' girl shoes for? Whatchur name, kid?"

"Billy Helmer."

"Hey, that's the Helmers down by the railroad tracks. My pop said old man Helmer don't believe in God. They're poor white trash."

Peas porridge hot, peas porridge cold...

Egged on by the older boys a group of third-graders gathered around and pranced in a circle pointing, "Look at the girls' shoes. Where's your skirt, Billy? Little girl wants her mommy."

As the circle closed tighter he had a dizzy impression of leering faces, unfriendly eyes.

Some like it hot, some like it cold...

An eighth-grader came up to watch the fun and called out, "Bet he doesn't know whether to stand or squat when he goes to piss."

Miss Miller, his first-grade teacher, rescued him when the bell rang. Gathering all the children in the first three grades she marched them into the classroom. He sat, isolated from the world by a wall of hurt ego and baffled pride. He tried to hide his shoes under the desk while studying the tennis shoes and low cut laced shoes that other boys wore. His were the only button shoes. He saw a boy in the next row snickering and nudging his neighbor as he pointed to Billy's shoes.

When he left the building after school his third-grade friends were waiting for him. He tried to ignore them and walk with dignity across the dusty playground. His uneaten lunch in the new tin lunchbox and his book bag felt heavy. He was tired and wanted to cry.

Some fourth-graders had joined the group. Led by a boy named Hank they gathered around, escorting him convoy fashion as he started down the hill toward home.

"Let's take the little boy home to his mommy."

"No, Hank, it's a little girl. Look at her shoes."

"He's got no religion," said Hank. "Come on, fellas, Let's show him how to pray." They were pressing closer now running to keep up with him.

Billy was gripped by sheer terror as hands struck him in the back, pushing him off balance. Lunchbox and books rolled away from him as he fell. Clawing wildly at the mass of faces he dimly felt a blow to his face, tasted blood running from his nose over his lip. Abandoning books and lunch pail he scrambled to his feet and ran with all his might.

Peas porridge hot, peas porridge cold...

Bill was standing there clenching his fists when the secretary came up and spoke to him. She had to speak twice before he realized she was there.

"Mr. Helmer," she repeated sharply.

"I shouldn't have run." He stood staring at her.

"I beg your pardon?"

"Those damn button shoes," he said. "But it wasn't so bad after I had a fight with Hank."

"I'm afraid I don't understand. Did some of the youngsters get into a fight already?"

"Uhm...No. Good morning, Mrs. Stepanovic." He stifled an impulse to feel and be reassured there was no blood on his shirt. "I guess I was thinking about something else."

"Oh, is that it? Anyway, I'm glad that you are here. First, you should call Captain Murphy. He has already phoned twice, something important. Then..."

"Just a minute, Maria. When I have done that, I'm going over to the cafe for breakfast no matter what happens. I'll be back by eight o'clock if anybody wants me."

In the little cafe, *Chez Maurice*, the day was getting off to a leisurely start. There were no customers to disturb the two dogs sleeping by the corner stove and the cat curled up on one of the tables. Maurice was washing bottles behind the bar.

"*Bonjour, monsieur le directeur. Comment allez-vous?*" he offered his wrist.

"*Bonjour, Maurice. Bien, merci.*" He shook the wet wrist; then took his habitual table in the corner by the stove. The dogs stirred uneasily. The cat stretched, arched her back and jumped resentfully to the next table. Maurice finished rinsing the bottles, wiped his hands on his apron and came over. Bill ordered *un grand café et une tartine.*

"*Un grand crème et une tartine beurrée pour monsieur le directeur,*" Maurice called out to the kitchen.

Bill began to feel a little more relaxed. The respect accorded him as *monsieur le directeur* by the French was surprising and always gratifying. Today it helped to restore his sense of dignity by putting a comfortable partition of time between the present and those button shoes. I wonder, he asked himself, how much I've really learned since then. I'll be damned if I know to this day the best thing to do. Is it better to run away, or should you brawl with a bunch of numbskulls to show them you can't be pushed around? He took a deep breath and stretched. This year will be different.

"Good morning, Mr. Helmer. I've been looking for you." The assistant principal pulled up a chair.

"Morning, Hal. Have a cup of coffee. And lay off the 'Mister' angle. It's Bill to you."

"Don't like formality myself. *Garçon,*" he called, "*un café au lait, s'il vous plaît.*"

"How are things across the street?" Bill buttered a slab of crusty bread.

"So far it looks to me like one hell of a mess."

"Ah. Things are running normally then."

"I'm worried about the enrollment. We're way over the estimates. What if we don't have enough teachers?"

"That worries me a little, too. Did you count heads this morning?"

"Yes, We're only two short. The typing teacher came in this morning. Corson still hasn't showed so I checked with Civilian Personnel. He had orders to report at Westover Field for air transportation ten days ago. No news of him since."

"You're new here, Hal. Sometimes teachers don't show up for weeks. They get lost in some military point of debarkation like soldiers do."

"Just like a casual company in the Army. My infantry training may come in handy here."

"This is no picnic, my friend. Teachers hired in all parts of the forty-eight states are dumped here with a principal who didn't hire them and whom they don't know. Back in the U.S. they were assigned to locations and perhaps did not choose to come to Paris. Many of them would probably prefer Germany. So by some miracle not defined in civil service regulations the school is supposed to run smoothly. And our School Officer can't help much even if he wants to, which he usually doesn't."

"The School Officer," Hal said. "That reminds me. Captain Murphy called and left a message with the secretary. Did you know that they're going to paint all the blackboards today?"

"The hell they are. I'll bet that's Murphy's idea. No wonder I couldn't get him on the phone."

"That was sprung on me about ten minutes ago."

"That's all we need the first day of school. I doubt that regular paint will work on slate boards and anyway I won't tolerate workers in the classrooms during school hours. They can't do that."

"Maybe they can't, but about five Frenchmen with paint buckets and brushes showed up a few minutes ago. A sergeant is in charge of them."

"Over my dead body." Bill gulped the last of his coffee and rose to his feet.

"Maybe they can go out and paint 'Americans Go Home' signs instead. There sure are enough of them around. Why do they want us to leave?"

"The Communists are demanding it. They have a big block of votes in the *Assemblée nationale.* A lot of people agree with them that we are taking over their country. Our time here could be limited. But we have to stay out of their affairs."

"What do you think of all that? I'm not much into politics."

"Maybe our faculty can play a tiny role in improving relations. We may be forced to leave, but right now I just want to keep intruders from disturbing classes. I'll get the painters out of the building. I don't care what they do so long as it isn't in my school."

"If you have trouble I'll be along in a minute," Hal said.

"Well, here's where we take on the U.S. Army."

"Give them a good fight, boss," Hal called after him.

Bill paid for his breakfast and strode out the door. The Assistant Principal watched him leave. This job, he was thinking, might prove to be even more amusing than he had imagined.

6

Chapter 2

As Bill hurried back across the school yard an army staff car pulled into the parking lot. The driver jumped out and opened the door for his passenger. He took several suitcases from the car, piling them on the sidewalk.

"Hello, Mr. Helmer. Got a teacher for you." He slid under the steering wheel and started the motor.

"Just a minute, Corporal. We may want you to take this baggage to a hotel."

"Sorry, Sir, I got orders to get right back to the Motor Pool. The captain expects some big-shot general and he's all in a sweat. Call in if you want a car later." He drove off in a shower of gravel.

Bill looked at the teacher. She was young, not more than twenty-two or three he guessed, standing tall despite a rumpled appearance of overnight travel. Her wide-set hazel eyes, almost at a level with his own, radiated an expression of good humor.

"Are you the principal?"

"Yes." He loaded the suitcases under his arms. "Let's get your baggage inside. Then we can introduce ourselves properly."

"I'm Irene Young," she said when they were in the office. "I think I'm assigned to your school."

"I'm Bill Helmer." He shook hands with her. "Sorry you had to arrive at the last minute in this madhouse. First days in our school are always wild but it will settle down. Happy to have you with us."

"What do I do now?"

"Have you had breakfast?"

"I ate at the railway station."

"Do you have a place to live?"

"No. I just arrived about an hour ago."

"Want us to get a hotel room for you?"

"That would be wonderful."

"I'll have our secretary make a reservation. Your baggage will be sent down to the hotel. Are you game to jump right in and take over a homeroom this morning?"

"If you tell me what to do."

"I'll have my secretary introduce you to Mr. Evans, our Assistant Principal. He can take you on a quick tour of the building and show you where your homeroom will be. When you've done that come back and see me."

"Maria," he asked his secretary, "have you tried to get a substitute for Corson?"

"That won't be necessary." A man stepped out from the inner office. "Corson will play himself in the first act."

"Hi, John. We were beginning to think they had you locked up at Ellis Island. When did you get in?"

"This morning about eight o'clock. Commercial flight. We sat around Westover Field for eight days chewing our nails and waiting for space on a plane. It's good to be back, Bill."

"Here's your schedule, John. Two sections of physics and three of advanced Math but we'll probably tear that all to hell before the day is over. We're way over our estimated enrollment and kids are still pouring in."

"Same old story." Corson studied his schedule. "Let me know if you want me. I'll probably be here late tonight getting the lab set up."

Bill sat down at his desk. "Let's see. What next? Oh, yes. Blackboards. Where is Michael Murphy?" Bill jumped to his feet and started for the door. Just then Irene Young came back into the office.

"Did you see the building?"

"Yes. Do I just go up to my room when the bell rings?"

"No. The day starts with an orientation assembly in the auditorium. All the students and teachers will be there. We'll...Good Lord! What's that noise?"

"Oh, some girls are cheering out in the hall."

"Just a moment, please." Bill stepped out of the office and was back almost immediately. "Where were we? Oh, yes. Teachers will be introduced and then leave, one at a time with their homerooms."

"I've got the general idea."

"Now, if you will excuse me I have to see the school officer."

A bell rang.

"That's for the assembly. Let's go. I'll come up afterward," he said as they walked into the auditorium, "and help you get started."

After the assembly he introduced Miss Young to her students.

"Seniors, this is Miss Young, your homeroom teacher. She arrived in Paris about an hour ago so she hasn't had much opportunity to study our class schedule. I ask your cooperation this morning in getting our courses lined up as quickly as possible."

Miss Young turned to write a list of senior elective subjects on the blackboard when her stick of chalk broke. As she stooped to pick it up from the floor one of the boys gave out with a loud, sharp whistle. Remembering that the principal was in the room he cut it short and sat looking innocently ahead at the board. There was an uncomfortable silence as the students waited to see what would happen. Bill walked over to the student.

"Miss Young," he placed his hand on the boy's shoulder, "this is Tony Mosca. He's a well-meaning young man but a bit uncivilized. He has just expressed his admiration for you in a rather unrefined way. Until this morning I was unaware of the fact that he was such a talented whistler. I call your attention to him in case you need a solo artist for your first homeroom program."

Tony flushed and bent his head, studying the top of his desk. The other students sat quietly waiting. It was a first test and Bill was anxious to see how the new teacher would handle the situation.

"Glad to know you, Tony. I'm pleased to find talent in my room. Now that the ice is broken it might be a good idea for all of us to introduce ourselves. We'll be working together all year."

"Miss Young," Bill stood in the door, "if you have any questions don't hesitate to call on me. If Tony should want to practice his whistle solo, you can send him down to my office where he can work undisturbed. I am an excellent dramatic coach."

As Bill walked down the corridor, automatically searching out possible trouble spots, he heard Jackson's big voice from the junior homeroom.

"Most of you probably labor under the illusion that you speak English, but you will change your minds in a hurry. By the Grace of God and the efforts of Jackson some of you may be able to express yourselves clearly and correctly in the English language by the end of this year."

Down the hall Ellen Neilson, the typing teacher, was waving at Bill.

"Oh, Mr. Helmer, come and help me. My room is a terrible mess."

He followed her into the classroom. The workmen had put a scaffolding of heavy planks along the chalk tray of the blackboard. Two of them were sitting on the plank and a third man was mixing paint. Delighted with the show the students gathered around and some of them who spoke French tried to talk with the smiling workers.

"You'll have to get your equipment out of here immediately," Bill told them.

"Sorry," the man said, "we were ordered to come here to paint blackboards. A sergeant brought us over. You will have to see *monsieur le directeur*."

"I am the director."

"Yes, sir." The man slid down from the scaffolding.

"Who is in charge of your group?"

"The sergeant, monsieur. I do not know his name."

"Who is the French person in charge?"

"I am, *monsieur*."

"Look, please get all the workmen and their equipment out of the building in the next ten minutes. You understand, we have classes in session."

"*Oui, monsieur*. Take it away," he told the other two.

"Where shall we go now, *monsieur le directeur*?"

"Take your equipment outside and stack it by the corner of the building. There's a cafe, *Chez Maurice*, across the street. That would be a pleasant place for you to wait and see what the United States Army wants to do with you today."

"I will have the men out immediately."

"Mr. Helmer," a teacher called as he walked by her door, "come here quickly. You would never believe what is happening in my room."

"Don't try to tell me that some French workers came in and started to paint your blackboards right in front of your class."

"How on earth did you guess?"

"I'm psychic. They'll be out of your room in ten minutes."

"Thanks," she flung at his back as he left.

Mr. Bennett, in the bus dispatcher's office, was sticking colored pins in one section of a huge map that covered his desk and trailed across the floor. A sergeant was sitting there behind a copy of the *Stars And Stripes*, with his feet on the map, his heels resting on the outskirts of Versailles.

"Captain Murphy around?" Bill asked as he came into the room.

"No," Mr. Bennett answered, "but the sergeant here is from his section."

"Are you in charge of the blackboard painting detail?"

"Yes, sir."

Bill noticed that the sergeant had looked up from his newspaper and started to get up. Then he settled back in his chair.

"Who ordered that detail in here during school hours?"

"The captain, sir. The Old Man made a military inspection of the building yesterday to see if it was ready for school and he didn't like the looks of the blackboards. Captain Murphy got an ass-eating but good. Never saw the captain move so fast. Got a work order early this morning. He don't like having his ass et."

"Nobody is going to paint blackboards while school is in session. I've ordered the men out of the building."

Something in his tone raised the sergeant to his feet.

"You can't order them out, sir. The captain sent me in here with them. I'm in charge of them and I'm under military orders."

"Maybe I can't but I did."

"I'll have to bring them back in, sir. I'm under military orders."

Bill stepped up to the sergeant. "If you bring them back in I'll throw them out and you with them."

"But, sir, what will Captain Murphy say? He's in charge of the logistical support of the school."

"That's right. But I'm in charge of the classrooms. If you're going to work around here, sergeant, it will prevent future difficulties if you understand that."

"Yes, sir. What'll I do now? Where's the work detail?"

"I think they're over in the cafe across the street. If you're responsible for those men I would suggest you go over and have a coffee right now."

"Sir, you're making me disobey a direct order. The captain will give me hell."

"Tell Captain Murphy I gave you a direct order. I'll take the full responsibility, sergeant, so don't worry."

"When he finds out about this the shit's going to fly," he muttered.

"Sergeant, I don't like that kind of language around here when school is in session. I also noticed you smoking out in the hall this morning. You can smoke in the military office or in the supply office but not in the corridor. We have enough trouble enforcing that rule for the students without somebody blowing smoke around under their noses. I insist that we observe some basic rules around here. That's been cleared through military channels."

"Yes, sir."

"I don't see your coffee pot around, Henry." Bill turned to the bus dispatcher.

"As a matter of fact I was just thinking about stoking it up. Drop around for a cup when you can."

"Thanks. Probably be needing some."

The sergeant watched Bill leave and turned to the bus dispatcher.

"He talks like a goddam book. Looks like he couldn't say shit if he had a mouthful of it. Acts like a Sunday school teacher. Captain Murphy ain't going to let no goddam civilian push him around. I can tell you that."

"He's a fighter, that boy." The bus dispatcher looked up from his map. "First school master I ever saw who carries his weight forward on the balls of his feet. He could kick up a bloody shindy, he could. Be interesting to see who does the pushing around here this year."

As an LWR—meaning Local Wage Rate employee—Henry Bennett earned more than Frenchmen and less than Americans doing similar work. But he wasn't upset about it. The money provided a welcome supplement to his Royal Army pension. Keeping a fleet of twentieth century buses moving over medieval roads gave him a feeling of accomplishment. And as a spectator observing the drama of life in the American school he thoroughly enjoyed the show. He smiled as he went back to sticking colored pins in the big map.

Chapter 3

Mademoiselle Colette Bernard stepped off the bus that morning on her first day as French teacher for the Paris High School. She followed a group of American teachers across the grounds toward the main building.

As she came through the double doors some girls in the hallway were chanting:

Je vous aime
Je vous adore
Come on, boys
Let's get that score
Rah, Rah.Rah
Team, Team Team!

On the last line the girls spread their legs and sank to the floor. Mademoiselle Bernard stood rooted to the spot. A soldier standing there smoking his cigarette watched the girls. Coming along the corridor, a man paused and spoke to one of them.

"You'll never be a cheerleader, Marion."

"Why, Mr. Jackson?"

"Because your legs aren't fat enough." The professor chuckled as he walked away.

At this moment a man came out of an office. Mademoiselle Bernard recognized him as *monsieur le directeur*. He stepped forward and clapped his hands. The girls were silent.

"What's going on out here?"

"We're practicing cheerleading, Mr. Helmer."

"Well stop it. You make a terrible racket."

Before Mademoiselle Bernard could say a word *monsieur le directeur* disappeared into his office and closed the door. She went down the hall and peeked into a room marked Teachers' Lounge. It was a smoky little place filled with strange faces and voices all speaking American. Slipping quietly in she found a chair by the window and listened.

"The taxi driver couldn't understand the school address this morning. I was unable to explain it to him. How can you get along here if you don't speak French?"

"You don't need French. The only language they understand is money. Just shove out a few hundred-franc tips and you'll have no trouble."

"That's right. The land of the waving palms."

"I can't wait to see the Louvre with Mona Lisa and the Winged Victory."

"Restaurants? I eat in the Officers Club or the PX snack bar. I haven't gone to a French restaurant."

"But I thought the food was supposed to be great."

"I wouldn't trust any food fixed by a Frenchman. Ever been in one of their toilets? I'd hate to see the kitchen in one of those fancy restaurants."

"Hey, there's a restaurant down by the *Paris Herald Tribune*. You can get a big juicy hamburger and it looks clean."

"I think it will be fun to try out some good French restaurants," a young woman said quietly.

Mademoiselle Bernard knew enough English to be quite uncomfortable. She was relieved to see René Marne, when he came in. René, a veteran at the American school, explained that each French teacher would go around to all the rooms to make a survey of students wanting to sign up for French classes. Then there would be a test in the auditorium for placement of students into advanced classes. She was to get a list of candidates for second and third-year French.

"Do you have it straight? *Vous y êtes?*"

"I think I understand," she said.

A bell rang and teachers started filing out of the lounge.

René turned to her. "Come on. That is for the assembly."

Following him into the auditorium she saw a rainbow of bright colored shirts and sweaters. From her seat in the back row she could see *monsieur le directeur* up in front. His voice seemed to come from a great distance. It was difficult to hear what he was saying so she looked around the room.

Some of the boys were taller than the teachers. Across from her was a group of smartly dressed girls. She stared at their bright lipstick. They could almost be university students. What she saw when some of them met her gaze was a look she interpreted as hostile curiosity. As the assembly finished she wondered in panic if she had missed something important. Anyway, René could explain it to her later.

After the last class had filed out she started down the long corridor. Some boys were gathered around their lockers.

"Hey Tony, what are you doing here? Haven't you been suspended yet? Don't tell me you've reformed or something."

"Cripes, give me time. This is only the first day."

"Hey, fellas, look at that. She can't be a student."

"That's the new French teacher. How'd you like to make out with something like that?"

"With French girls it's a cinch."

"Wow. Do you think that's really true?"

The blood was burning in her face as she approached the classroom at the end of the hall. Some of the boys were almost as tall as the teachers and not bad looking but carelessly dressed, some of them in jeans with shirts or T-shirts hanging loose as they slouched against their lockers.

Colette wrote some simple sentences on the blackboard for the students who were seated and waiting for her. She briefly questioned each candidate.

"*Comment vous-appelez-vous?*" she asked a boy signing up for second year French.

"*Je m'appelle* Joe Dawson."

"*Quelle est votre nationalité?*"

"*Je suis Américain.*"

"*Quel âge avez-vous?*"

"I don't know French for numbers."

"*Quelle est votre couleur favorite?*"

"*Ma couleur favorite...* I don't know French words for all the colors."

"Can you write for me two complete French sentences as short and simple as you want to make them?"

"Wow, that's hard."

"Perhaps you are not prepared for second-year French," she told him.

"I got a credit in first-year French. I got the right to take French 2."

"Your vocabulary in French is limited. You would have difficulty in my class."

"But I got a credit."

"I do not know what that means."

"A credit is what you get for taking a course," the boy answered. "That's the whole point of taking courses, so you can get enough credits to graduate."

"Well I know nothing about credits but you could not come into my class."

"You can't do that. Mr. Helmer will make you let me in. I've got to have two credits to get into college."

In another room a boy surprised her by asking, "Are most French people Communists?"

"No, that is just one political party."

"Are you a Communist?"

"No, I am not."

He looked at her suspiciously.

In a senior homeroom she talked informally about third-year French with a group of students, mostly girls.

"Will third-year French be very difficult, Miss Bernard?" a girl asked.

"Difficult but I hope interesting. It will be mostly literature. We will study some plays and perhaps go to the *Comédie française* to see the dramas we have read."

"Will there be much grammar?"

"Yes. And you will write some original compositions. I would like to give you a good literary background in French. You can then get an idea of French civilization. I am certain you will enjoy that."

"I don't want to load up my schedule with too many tough subjects," said a girl in a cashmere sweater. "Frankly, I'm not much interested in French civilization."

"Then why do you wish to take advanced French?"

"I think a foreign language, especially French, is a definite asset. Quoting foreign phrases peps up one's conversation. My mother's study club in the States had a French name."

"Perhaps you should reflect about signing up. I expect my students to work hard."

"I'm not really keen on it." The girl smiled pleasantly. "But my mother would have kittens if I didn't take French again."

"Your mother would what?"

"She would have—oh, I'm sorry. I mean that mother would be most unhappy."

The girls giggled and Mademoiselle Bernard wondered if they were laughing at her.

To Colette's surprise a girl addressed her in good French.

"Mademoiselle Bernard, est-ce que je pourrais étudier un peu la musique française? Can we learn something about that?"

"What is your name and are you a music student?"

"Je m'appelle Kay Selner. Je joue du violin."

"Welcome to Paris, Kay. The city has a rich history of music. I can give you a bibliography of reading and I recommend that you listen to French radio. Then too there are many concerts and chamber music recitals. We can get you into a student association that will provide concert tickets at reduced prices."

"Merci, mademoiselle." Kay was wondering if her father would let her go out to evening concerts.

The seniors were a diverse lot. At varying levels they had a rudimentary grasp of written French. One boy named Tony Mosca had a fair vocabulary and an excellent ear for pronunciation. But in her opinion his conversation fell far short of a third-year level.

Colette was somewhat mollified when Hal Evans, the assistant principal, stopped her in the hall to say, "Mademoiselle Bernard, I am truly sorry that today has been such a hassle. We just have to hang tough to get started. I think you will find that this won't be such a bad place to work."

She went down the hall trying to figure out an exact meaning of "hang tough".

Later she was sitting in the after-school calm of the Teachers Lounge. She had spent most of the afternoon with her colleague René, both of them correcting the placement examination. The papers were disappointing. Was she expected to teach French to these students? Were they as rude to their American teachers as they had been to her? Would every day be like this in an American school?

She heard the door open and an officer wearing double bars on his shoulders came into the room.

"Good afternoon," she said as pleasantly as she could.

"Hello." He glanced around the room. "This room needs policing. Just look at it."

"I beg your pardon?"

"Helmer should make you teachers keep this place clean, by God." He glared at her.

The little lounge was indeed a mess. Copies of the *Paris Herald Tribune* and *Stars And Stripes* were scattered around on chairs and on the floor. Ashtrays were overflowing and somebody had left a coffee-stained paper cup on the study table.

"I am sorry. I do not understand."

"Why don't you pick up your papers once in a while?"

"I am very sorry."

She gathered up the French papers beside her on the davenport. Then she started picking up some newspapers from the floor bending over awkwardly because her skirt was tight. She looked up to see the officer watching her with interest. She didn't like the expression on his face.

Colette was furious, angrier with herself than with the officer. Why should she pick up papers and clean rooms? Did the Americans think she was a maid, a hired servant who would do extra service after struggling all day with their devilish children?

She sat down again and took up her French examinations staring for a long time at the red corrections on the top paper. Abruptly she stood up and started for the principal's office.

"*Monsieur le directeur.*" She was standing before his desk.

"Yes. Please sit down. I'll be free in a minute." He was adding up a column of figures. He finished quickly and looked up.

"Please sit down. Sorry to keep you waiting."

"*Monsieur le directeur*, I wish to resign."

"Resign? The first day of school? It can't be that bad. Would you prefer to speak French?"

"I prefer to speak English."

"Take a chair. You can resign just as well sitting down. I'm self-conscious with a lady standing. Americans are famous, you know, for their gallantry."

"I am afraid I have forgotten how to laugh."

"What went wrong today? You didn't have a homeroom, did you? I told Evans not to give the French teachers homeroom assignments."

"A homeroom? Oh no. René and I made a survey of students who want to take French."

"Sounds logical. Is it the lack of student interest that discourages you?"

"No. Not that. It is that...well, I did not realize they would be so difficult."

"Look. Do you remember when I interviewed you? I told you it was a rough job. I told you that few students were interested in French culture."

"You were honest with me. But I did not know that it would be like this."

"I would like to know your real reasons for resigning. Cigarette?"

"Thank you." She accepted a light and sat down.

"Let's see. You had experience teaching English-speaking students, didn't you?"

"I taught for one year in England."

"And you find that American children are different?"

"Very different."

"Does their ignorance offend your integrity as a professor?"

"No." There were tears in her eyes. "Their insolence offends my dignity as a human being."

He stood up. "Damn it all, I'm going to buy you a drink at the café. I think we both need one."

It did not occur to her to refuse. Imagine *monsieur le directeur* buying her a drink the first day of school right after she had resigned. She wondered as they walked across to *Chez Maurice* if he had the same ideas as the students about French girls.

Chapter 4

Bill's intentions regarding Mademoiselle Bernard had nothing to do with sex. He was determined at all costs to keep her from resigning. He had probably hired himself a lemon, he told himself, but he simply couldn't face the idea of dealing with security clearances and the *Intendance française* for a replacement. Any other teacher would have a difficult time with the advanced French classes, especially the seniors.

"Now, Mademoiselle Bernard," he said when they were seated Chez Maurice, "tell me what happened today that makes you want to resign."

"It is the first time that I have been treated like a servant."

"The students treated you that way?"

"Yes, *monsieur*. They have no respect in speaking to a professor. And then I heard some boys talking in the hall."

"Well?"

"What does it mean, *monsieur*, to make out with a woman?"

"Aha! It means to have sex. They hear soldiers using that expression."

"I thought it was something like that."

"Nobody went around the homerooms with you—no American teacher, I mean?"

"No, *monsieur*."

"That was a mistake."

"Are your French teachers obliged to go around with a police escort, *monsieur le directeur*?"

"No, but I should have sent Mr. Evans along. He would have taken care of students who made impolite remarks."

"Impolite remarks?"

Bill was trying hard to control his temper. It was almost time for the *rentrée scolaire* in the French schools and he would have a devil of a time finding another qualified teacher. He thought of what Captain Murphy would say if he found out about it. Murphy would love to tell everybody that the principal couldn't keep teachers for more than one day.

"Just what did the students say to you?"

As she recounted the unpleasant experiences of the day her wrath mounted.

Bill leaned forward. "I don't blame you for feeling insulted but it's only fair to get some perspective on what happened today. In a way you represent France to the students. Some of them transfer to you their resentment at bad plumbing, poor heating and uncomfortable living quarters. But if you choose to interpret every remark unfavorable to France as a personal affront that is highly unfair to those who admire your country and feel fortunate to be here."

"Many of the things the students said today were personal." The blood mounted to her face. "Anyway, I do not want to be a representative of France. I just want to be a professor."

"Look, mademoiselle, nor do I wish to be put in the position of defending all Americans. If your experience today has made you anti-American perhaps it is best that you resign. You're judging a whole group of people from the way a few behaved. I detect a certain prejudice."

She shook her head angrily. "I am not prejudiced, *monsieur*, but I am happy that you wish me to resign. Both of us will then be content."

That was the perfect exit line. Now was the time to walk out. She would thank him and....

"Mademoiselle Bernard, I am not happy about your resigning. I hate to see the anti-French sentiment of a few students work so effectively. This is an easy victory for a small number of ill-mannered kids who don't represent the majority. Besides they are capable of changing their ways. Believe it or not we have a pretty decent group of students in our school."

"*Monsieur*, I respect your desire to defend your students. In a French school the director also defends his professors."

"In an American school we try to look out for everybody's interests. We feel a teacher has some obligation toward the children the moment she accepts a position. If every teacher who feels insulted walked out we wouldn't have much of a school."

"After today it is difficult for me to feel that I have an obligation toward your school, *monsieur le directeur.*"

Colette was beginning to feel the strain of a long day in the unfamiliar procedures of a foreign school that seemed to lack any organization. The complacency of the polite man sitting opposite her was maddening. He seemed to accept all of what had happened today as the way a school should function.

She looked at Bill as she reached for her glass, eager to finish her drink and conclude this conversation. Then whatever twinges of conscience she felt about resigning were quickly dispersed by a hot wave of indignation running through her body. She felt the pressure against her knee of a hand starting to explore her leg under the table. Then it was removed. She sucked in her breath sharply and all the resentment of the day was reflected in her face. So that was his game.

"I see that you do take a personal interest in their professors also. Now I know what your American males think of French women, *monsieur.* I do not like your crudeness."

Bill looked at her in surprise. She was sitting there staring at him with contempt in her eyes. She was really an attractive girl. Too bad she was such a bitch.

Colette decided she would throw her glass at him, right in his smirking face if he touched her again. She felt the pressure on her leg for the second time, the hand slowly sliding above the knee under her dress. As she picked up her glass Maurice appeared.

"Sorry," he said, "*je vous demande pardon.* This should not happen but she is pregnant."

Bill sat up straight in astonishment putting both hands on the table.

"I lock her up every night." Maurice gently prodded under the table with his foot as he pushed the dog out, "but she keeps getting pregnant."

Mademoiselle Bernard put down her glass and hastily excused herself. She went into the ladies room where she washed her face in cold water and combed her hair vigorously. The dog had been a close call. She had almost thrown her drink into her director's face.

When she came back to the table she was unable to recapture the intensity of her original resentment.

Bill was laughing. "Another drink, *mademoiselle?*"

She nodded. "*Oui, monsieur le directeur.* Let's drink to our canine friend, *la pauvre.*"

"*Encore deux fines, Maurice.*"

"Cheers, mademoiselle.".

"*A la vôtre, monsieur.*"

She sipped the cognac gratefully trying to keep her sense of resolution. She was certain she was forgetting something. Oh, yes.

"Another thing. I do not like the way your soldier talked to me in the teachers' room."

"What soldier? "

"The man in uniform who came in and scolded me because the room was not orderly."

"WHAT? Let me get this straight. An officer came into the teachers' lounge and bawled you out because it wasn't neat?"

"That is correct."

"Was he a captain?"

"I do not know. He had silver buckles on his shoulders."

"I thought so. Captain Murphy, the son-of-a-bitch."

"How was that?"

"He came in and talked directly to you? Were you alone?"

"I was indeed alone, *monsieur.*"

"And what did he say?"

"I did not understand everything, *monsieur.* He spoke of something about police or policing."

"Why did you let him do that? Why didn't you tell him he had no business talking with you like that?"

She stared blankly at him.

"I guess you had no way of knowing. Look, Mademoiselle Bernard, I promise that will never happen again. You have nothing to do with the military people at school. I am your supervisor. Mr. Evans is my assistant. We are the only people with whom you deal."

"I was confused, *monsieur.*"

"Of course. I'm terribly sorry about that. But if Murphy ever says anything to you again kick him. Hit him with your grade book."

She had to laugh. He was very angry and his concern was obviously genuine.

"Is that how I should defend myself with your students. Hit them with my class book?"

He smiled "Only if necessary."

"Perhaps I could stay, *monsieur*, until you find another teacher."

"That would be damned decent of you."

"Very well, monsieur. But I would only want to stay until..."

"Good heavens." Bill was looking at his watch. "It's almost five o'clock. I have to finish a report and telephone to headquarters." He rose to his feet and called out, *"Maurice, l'addition, s'il vous plaît."*

Back in his office Bill figured the totals of the class sections and called in to the duty officer at headquarters. He was still checking schedules when Hal Evans appeared.

"Hi, Hal. Did you get the duty roster worked out?"

"It's on your desk."

"Thanks. I'll have Maria cut a stencil before I leave. Maria," he called to the outer office.

"She went home hours ago. Do you know it's seven thirty?"

"I had no idea."

"The Army should give us a medal for this."

"God, I'm tired." Bill pushed back a stack of papers on his desk. "You know it's strange. I didn't see Murphy today."

"He was around this afternoon."

"I know. He almost cost me a French teacher."

Bill told Hal about Mademoiselle Bernard's encounter with Murphy in the teachers' lounge.

"The captain came by while you were gone. He asked for you but didn't wait."

"Did he say he'd be back?"

"No."

"That's peculiar. Not at all like Murphy. I wonder what he's got up his sleeve?"

"I don't know. I don't think very well on an empty stomach."

"Why don't we eat dinner together. There's *la Porte Jaune* near here by the river."

"Good idea."

"I better lock the science labs. Murphy always checks them."

"I already locked them."

The M.P. on guard duty snapped to attention as they drove out the gate.

"You know, Bill, this city has really changed since I was here right after the war. The people gave us a great welcome in those days. Why the difference?"

"I've been too busy at school to study current politics but I remember when General Eisenhower came here to be commander of SHAPE a couple of years ago there were street riots. The whole Metro system was closed."

"It was that bad?"

"I almost got caught in a street demonstration in the Latin Quarter."

"But why so much anger?"

"French reporters claimed our troops are waging chemical warfare in Korea. I don't believe that but some people do. This seems to be a critical time for Americans in France. I guess it's worth the effort to live in Paris if the French Government permits us to stay."

"I think so."

Hal Evans had his own private reason for being in Paris but he wasn't ready to tell anyone about it yet.

Part Two: Fall Semester

Chapter 5

With no central military base in Paris the school served as the only common neighborhood for American students. Everyone was looking around for friends and for soft spots in the faculty.

"What do you think of that luscious looking French woman who teaches senior section?" Chuck Mason asked his friend.

"Boy is she tough," his classmate said. "You saw the assignments she handed out the first week. Scary."

"I'm thinking of dropping third-year French. "

"That's an idea. You only need two years for college. Still I'll hang on awhile."

"Tony Mosca is in that class. He says he likes her and he's no book worm."

Bill tried to give special attention to the senior class and to the new teachers. Hal Evans seemed to think things were going well. When Bill asked him how Mademoiselle Bernard was faring, Hal was reassuring.

"She isn't having too much trouble with the seniors although there's some grumbling about her assignments."

Of course she had only agreed to stay until a replacement could be found. Bill, absorbed by orienting the new teachers and facing an excess enrollment, didn't have the heart to look for a new French teacher.

Each year he invited his teachers out to dinner, often in groups of three or four. He invited Colette Bernard individually so he could get a reading on her intentions. His dinner date was for a Friday evening and as luck would have it he was delayed at the office. Just as he was leaving he had received a surprise visit from Murphy convoying some visiting general who wanted to see the school.

It was raining when Bill left the building. He was wondering why he had ever committed himself to a precious Friday evening as he inched his way around the *Place de la Porte de Saint-Cloud* and joined a crawling queue of cars circling the *Place d'Alma*. Arriving home he showered in record time, grabbed his raincoat on his way out.

Near *la Muette* he lost his way hunting the address and when he did find it the street was lined with cars. The lobby of Colette's apartment building was walled with mirrors. It struck him as a bit upper class. Bill looked for a directory of residents but wherever he turned he saw himself in duplicate. A lock of his hair was plastered to his forehead and the V knot of his tie had worked itself under his shirt collar. Studying his image in the mirror he tried to regain some of the composure he felt *monsieur le directeur* should have when escorting a staff member to dinner.

"*Vous cherchez quelqu'un, monsieur?*" A face suspended from bushy white eyebrows peered out at Bill.

"*Je cherche l'appartement de Mademoiselle Bernard, monsieur.*" Bill was exasperated at being caught before the mirror.

The concierge stepped into the lobby and looked him over before he answered.

"*Troisième à gauche.*"

Bill said "*Merci*" in a tone he hoped was sufficiently formal and headed for the elevator.

"*Essuyez vos pieds s'il vous plaît, monsieur.*"

Bill came back to the doormat and wiped his feet furiously. He was opening the elevator door when the old man spoke again.

"*Ça ne marche pas.*"

Without another word Bill slammed the grilled door and bolted up the stairway. Why in the hell couldn't they put an "Out of Order" sign on the elevator? Standing before the double door of the apartment he reached for the bell and paused. He could hear music. It was not a radio he decided, waiting until the music stopped. Then he pressed the button.

"*Bonsoir, monsieur le directeur.*" She looked up from the doorway.

"Sorry to be late." Bill saw the grand piano and he had visions of her sitting there, waiting for the doorbell.

"Oh, are you late? I was just playing the piano." She looked at the mantle clock. "*O là. En effet il est tard.* Please sit down, I am not quite ready. Do you mind waiting for a few minutes?"

"No hurry, mademoiselle." Soaked with rain and perspiration, he stood there trying to figure out why he had ever conceived this misbegotten evening.

He admired the massive solidity of the furniture as he prowled around the room. A broad fireplace was finished in marble with a mirror running from mantle to ceiling. Aware of a pair of intense eyes peering at him from the mirror, he turned quickly. Then he saw the large framed photograph on the piano and walked over to it. The eyes belonged to a young man with a sensitive face. He did not resemble Miss Bernard...

The click of her heels interrupted his thoughts as she entered the room.

"Is this your brother?"

"No. That is Jean Ramuel, a friend. My brother's picture is over there on the wall."

Bill thought it would only be polite to take a look.

"A strong family resemblance."

"My brother was killed during the war."

"Oh, I'm so sorry."

"Would you like an *apéritif* before we go?"

"That would be fine."

She took a bottle from the liquor cabinet and went in search of glasses.

"You are lucky, mademoiselle, to have such a roomy apartment."

"I lived here as a little girl." She started to lift the coffee table. "That is the piano my father bought me before the war."

"Here, let me help you." Bill moved the table over to the davenport. "Your parents live elsewhere now?"

She arranged the glasses. "My mother died a long time ago. Papa was killed fighting on the German front."

"A personal tragedy of war. My sympathy, *mademoiselle*."

Her dress accentuated the curve of her hips as she bent over the tray to pour the drinks. She was attired with an elegant casualness. Bill could see why the senior boys would remark about her figure.

He took her to a little Basque restaurant near by and was disappointed to find it crowded. They stood in line watching the waiters hurrying from one candle-lit table to another. Finally a girl in Basque costume led them along a wall lined with gleaming copper pans to a corner space.

"The last time we talked together," Bill began, "you had just resigned." He decided to put that first in the order of business and see what followed.

"That first day was *un cauchemar*. But I am becoming accustomed to your school."

"Well, I am glad you're satisfied with the school, Mademoiselle Bernard."

"I said I was content, Mr. Helmer?"

"Not exactly." Bill smiled. "I was trying to be optimistic. You aren't really unhappy?"

"It is yet difficult."

"Merci." Bill helped himself to the salad the Basque girl held before him.

"*Qu'est-ce que vous voulez boire, monsieur?*"

"What do you prefer, mademoiselle? We could get red wine or some rosé."

"A rosé would be excellent with Basque food. I like that if it pleases you."

"*Un Rosé de Tavel, s'il vous plaît.*"

Hungry and almost dry by this time, Bill began to feel somewhat expansive.

"The school hasn't affected your looks, Mademoiselle. I hope it hasn't damaged your disposition."

"Do you think it has, *monsieur le directeur?*"

"The way you keep saying 'your school' makes me feel like the owner of a man-eating dog."

"I do not blame you, Mr. Helmer. You have been most patient."

"Some of the boys are still fresh with you?"

"No, the boys who were —fresh as you say—they are better. Now it is the girls I find difficult."

"Are they impolite?"

"No. I could not say that, but the girls in the most advanced class—how do you call them?"

"The seniors."

"Yes, the girl seniors. Some of them have such confidence in themselves. They have almost the grace of French matrons. But I find in their studies, well—they are like little girls in primary school."

"Ah. You think so?"

"I am not sure what to do with them, these young ladies who would be at ease with the President of the Republic, yet cannot analyze a simple character in literature."

"What do you mean?"

She spoke slowly. "They may find a story interesting but they never question why characters behave as they do, why a man can want something so much that he will do whatever it takes to get it—steal, torture or kill."

"You ask them that?"

"Most of my students don't relate the stories they read, to themselves or to understanding everyday lives. I try to show them you can tell the character of the author by how he makes this person behave in his story. Most of them are lost."

"Mademoiselle Bernard, if you can get those senior girls to think philosophically about anything more complicated than dates, you should have a medal."

"That does not disturb you?"

"As a matter of fact it does. This year we are trying to raise standards. And I do think the students are working harder."

"I am sorry, *monsieur le directeur*, to be so critical."

"Go ahead. Fire all your guns."

"Students must learn how to really make good sentences and to choose words."

"We probably don't teach enough of that. What we do gives the kids a lot of feeling all right. Most of them hate grammar."

"They must know something of making language. Otherwise they are only spectators, not experiencing the fear of death, the joy of living."

"How in the world can you test whether or not a student gets this feeling?"

"Testing for the vocabulary is easier," she admitted.

"Is that what we do?"

"That is your way of teaching languages. Students read a lesson and take object tests on what they read."

"Objective tests."

"Yes these tests where they work little puzzles of placing marks in squares to guess which answer is correct."

Bill laughed.

"I said something foolish?"

"That's not a bad definition of objective tests."

"Preparing only for objective tests is not good. How can students profit from reading poetry if they do not feel with their minds and bodies?"

"In our system, "Bill said, "we do not give a lot of time to poetry."

"Why, nothing could be more important!"

Bill was taken aback. "I like poetry. Honest I do. But I don't know much about it and that hasn't blighted my life. I know we have fine poets also."

"One could live without art, perhaps a good life. That is to say if a good life is big automobiles, refrigerators and television sets."

Bill could think of a number of things to say. He only remarked, "I may develop a feeling for art if I live long enough."

"You know," she said opening her handbag, "sometimes I think that you are mocking me and my ideas. Some Americans trouble me."

"You trouble some of the Americans too, especially the males. And you give them ideas that have nothing to do with teaching."

When Bill helped her out of the car after driving her home she held out her hand to say goodnight.

"Thank you, Mr. Helmer. I enjoyed this evening and our talk. You have a good sense of humor."

"It's a handy thing to have sometimes."

"In your American school I think it would be indispensable."

She ran lightly up the steps and disappeared into the building. Bill pulled up the collar of his coat against the rain as he watched the door close after her. He wondered if she would finish the year.

Chapter 6

Bill was uneasy about one of his teachers, Mrs. Wallingford who served as advisor to one of the senior homerooms. She was a faculty member he had inherited when he first came to the school. A toneless southern Belle with an M.A. from a small college in Georgia, Peaches Wallingford lacked almost everything Bill wanted in a teacher.

"I have had twenty years of experience, honey child," she would tell new teachers, "and I understand these children."

"Now children, well begun is half done," she would tell her classes. And as a sort of oral footnote she would chant, "We must have information at our fingertips, right at our fingertips," unaware of the snickering behind her back.

She once told a World Geography class that Austrians came from Australia. And she had informed the amused seniors that the custom of greeting people with a kiss on each cheek was known as the French kiss.

Peaches prided herself on her French, which was puzzling to the Americans and unintelligible to the French. René Marne tried to avoid her in the hall. He had avoided stopping by the teachers lounge for fear of being trapped into conversation with her.

"French is easy, almost like English," she once told him. "Take the word *jambon*. It's just like hambone, which makes it easy to remember."

Bill's worst fears of how she might fare with the seniors were realized even sooner than he expected. Hal rushed into the office one morning.

"I think you better go up to the senior homeroom, Bill. Mrs. Wallingford just had a blow-up and the class isn't covered."

"Where is she?"

"I've got her crying on Mary Serinac's shoulder. I'll go up if you like. But I think it may swing more weight if you take over."

"Thanks." Bill was on his way.

As he walked down the upstairs corridor to the senior room he saw Captain Murphy at the door looking in.

"I know this is not my responsibility, Mr. Helmer, but I thought I better watch the show just to see if they would start tearing the schoolhouse down. That would be my business."

"How kind of you, Captain. I'll take over now."

"I hope you will, Mr. Helmer." Murphy turned and moved down the hall. Bill went into the classroom.

The chairs were pushed around in a disorderly way but the students were all sitting calmly, watching him as he came in and sat down on the front of the teacher's desk. The room became quiet. They could hear the electric wall clock as its wheels moved minute after minute into the past. Bill sat there.

"Well, seniors, where do we go from here?"

Silence.

"My problem is fairly simple. I have to keep order in the classrooms and I know how to do it." He looked around the room. "But your problem may be a little more difficult. No one else can work it out for you. This is your last year of high school. It should be an important one. It could possibly include a good bit of fun. Who has something to say?"

"She just started to cry and then she left."

A low voice came from the back. "We might apologize to Mrs. Wallingford."

"Now," Bill said. "I want each of you to stand up in turn and speak his piece. Give your name and then say anything you want to say as long as it isn't obscene or libelous."

He pointed to a boy in the front row.

"Charles Jensen, sir. I guess we were razzing Mrs. Wallingford a little bit. Maybe we could get a group to go apologize."

Another boy stood up. "Walter Mason. I think we ought to have another homeroom teacher. Mrs. Wallingford is all right but she's kind of old-fashioned and I don't think she's really interested in the class play or the formal dance. If we had another teacher, maybe a younger one, I don't think Mrs. Wallingford would care."

A murmur of agreement greeted this suggestion. They looked at the principal but he obviously intended to hear them all out.

"Kay Selner, sir. I think we should be ashamed of ourselves. We made Mrs. Wallingford have a kind of breakdown. That's a wicked thing to do. We should all of us apologize to her then show her that we might have a class committee to help her with things in the homeroom. Just to let her know we are really sorry."

There was silence in the room as the seniors looked at Kay, some with ill-concealed disgust.

Another boy stood up. "Jack Brewster, sir. Why can't we have senior privileges and run our homeroom without a teacher? In my last school seniors could smoke and had other privileges. I don't see why we need a teacher."

Bill looked at him. "Privileges, in my opinion, are something you must earn. Thus far you people are not deserving of special privileges. You are contributing nothing to the honor of the school and the school owes you nothing in the way of privileges."

It was almost time for the bell when they had all finished. Bill stood up.

"I am going to talk with Mrs. Wallingford and see what she wishes to do. If she wants to come back to this homeroom she has my full support and I will not tolerate a repeat performance of this morning. If she chooses not to return I can certainly understand. In that case I would assign another teacher. Meanwhile all outside senior activities are cancelled until we have worked out a plan for your future homeroom that is satisfactory to everyone."

But Bill knew that he must never let Peaches come back to this class. During a long session with the weeping Peaches it became clear that she wanted to keep her senior homeroom, that it was an important prop for her ego.

"I've had twenty years of experiences, Mr. Helmer, and I have a Masters degree in psychology. I understand these children and I'm sure some of the young teachers couldn't begin to handle those seniors. We must follow through on this."

But he was firm.

"It would be highly unfair to you, Mrs. Wallingford, after your years of service to this school if I left you in charge of that group. Still I know you will be able to give invaluable advice to the teacher who takes over."

When Bill and Hal took stock of the situation they found themselves in an impasse. Everyone on the faculty was overloaded

"How about Jackson?" Hal asked.

"You think Henry's the man for the seniors?"

"Frankly, no. They would raise hell with him." Hal leaned back in his chair. "I know who could do the job."

"Who?"

"Irene Young. She has the other senior homeroom eating out of her hand."

"Well, why not? We can put them all together."

Hal started ticking off on his fingers. "She has only three preps per week and she should have five. She is advisor to the newspaper. She would have to do all the planning for senior activities and graduation."

"Dammit. I can just assign her."

"Nope. Wouldn't be fair."

Hal was right of course.

"We can reshuffle some of her other duties."

"Bill, let me talk to her. That way you don't have to stick your neck out. I'll feel her out. If she's forced into it we haven't gained anything."

"Good. Give her a try."

But Irene wanted no part of that homeroom. A conscientious worker she was already up to her ears and the seniors were rapidly getting a reputation that would make anybody hesitate to take them on.

A week later Bill was still discussing the problem in the office he shared with his assistant principal.

"I have a suggestion." Hal eyed Bill.

"Shoot."

"I have a hunch that Irene is kind of sweet on you. If you did it right I think you could pressure her into wanting the job."

"I wouldn't do that."

"We have to find somebody for that homeroom."

"Let's see…" Bill studied the teacher roster.

"We certainly can't use French teachers."

"No. We are understaffed. That's the trouble."

Bill sat there checking the list of teachers against the class schedule.

"By God, I'll do it."

"You'll do what?"

"Give Irene a try."

When he talked with her after school she was eager to accept a dinner invitation.

Against all the rules of the game, Irene was ready with her coat on, handbag in hand, when Bill rang her doorbell. She walked ahead of him down the stairway and hopped into the car with quick ease before he could offer to open the door for her.

Driving down the *Champs Elysées* he decided on impulse to take her to *La Grenouille* for a fine meal and a little humor. Roger, the patron, had created an ambience that set his place apart from the other restaurants in Paris.

Chez Roger one always stood in a line of people who provided entertainment for those already studying the menu posted on the wall.

"*Eh bien, ma belle blonde.* Sit here with me."

"I see no place at your table."

"On my knee, *ma chérie.*"

"Is that your wife?"

"She is not jealous"

"Does she bite?"

"Bite? *Chérie,* I have fangs and adore young blood."

"No thank you, monsieur. I will wait."

"See that couple? They are foreigners."

"English, no doubt."

"The girl is American. Aren't you, dear?"

"Yes. How did she know, Bill?" Irene asked.

"*Chèrie*," said the woman, "we do not have such nylons."

A dapper young Frenchman noticed Irene as they waited in line and gave her a friendly pinch.

"*Alors, ma jolie petite. J'ai envie de t'embrasser.*"

""He wouldn't mind giving you a kiss," Bill told her.

Irene opened her eyes wide. "Tell him he's cute but I fear his moustache would tickle."

Bill pointed to the menu written in chalk on a blackboard on the far wall. Each table provided a pair of binoculars and it was not considered sporting to leave your place for a closer look.

"I wonder if Mark Twain ever ate here," Irene remarked when they were seated. "He would have found this place amusing."

"He was a little before Roger's time. Anyway, these frogs no longer jump." Bill handed her the binoculars. "Incidentally, you have a choice here. You are not obliged to order *grenouille*."

"Oh, I've eaten frog legs." Irene smiled. "Back in Marble Creek, Idaho, I could pounce on them."

She wanted wine but she also desired some cool water. In her halting French she asked the waiter.

"*Madame, ce n'est pas une pharmacie ici.*"

Puzzled Irene looked over at Bill.

"He said this is not a drug store."

"Well, will he bring the water?"

"Perhaps."

In response to her curiosity Bill found himself telling her some of the things he'd learned about the history of Paris and the places she might like to see. As they were finishing the cheese plate he realized he hadn't mentioned the reason for the entire evening. The senior homeroom was far from her thoughts and he tried to think of a graceful way to introduce the subject.

"What do you say we have coffee and dessert in a sidewalk café?"

She looked surprised. "I'm not really hungry but a coffee would be lovely."

Their table was on the sidewalk and the waiter had to weave his way through the crowd. They sat and watched the life of the Latin Quarter surging along *le boulevard St. Michel*.

"How do you like school by now, Irene?"

"I like it. This is a fascinating place isn't it?"

"You pretty well settled into your teaching schedule?"

"I guess so. I have to pinch myself to realize I'm really here."

After less than three weeks in Paris she was taking French lessons at the *Alliance française* and had explored several neighborhoods.

"Where have you gone at night?"

"Oh—*Montparnasse,, Pigalle.*"

"You walked through *Pigalle* at night by yourself?"

"Certainly."

"You weren't afraid?"

"Of course not. The worst thing that could happen would be being whistled at by an American soldier."

"You're going to like Paris."

"I do already. I love it here."

"You think teaching in that madhouse is worth it to be here?"

"Oh, I like the school, Bill. What happens to these cafés in winter?"

"They enclose the front part in glass and have some kind of space heaters."

"I hate to see winter come."

"Me too. The kids at school get pretty restless."

"The seniors are starting to talk about the winter formal."

"Do you like your senior homeroom?"

"They are a great gang of kids. Lots of pep."

"I wish I shared your enthusiasm for that class."

"You're worried about the seniors, aren't you?"

"Yes, I am. I don't know what to do with Mrs. Wallingford's homeroom."

"I hear that they have some problems. Perhaps the two sections could be put together."

"That would be a big challenge for somebody."

"It certainly would." She hesitated for a long moment. "I could make a try at it. We might all meet together."

"It would take a load off my mind. But it's a heavy workload. I just couldn't force you to take on such a headache."

"That will solve your problems?"

"That would make me feel like jumping for joy."

43

"Tomorrow we can have the sections meet together and start planning. Could you be there?"

"I will be there to give any administrative help I can."

Such a rapid solution caught Bill by surprise. He had a feeling that he had taken unfair advantage of this new teacher.

Walking down the boulevard to the car he offered his arm. When he helped her into the car and drove away he could still feel the pressure of her light grip on his arm. Bill caught glimpses of her cheek in profile against the car window as they drove along. She had the clear skin and fresh scrubbed look of a country kid and he was aware of a faint aroma of her hair. He could imagine her, with barefooted grace and abandonment, catching frogs in an Idaho creek. So engrossed was he in his fancies that he would have driven past her apartment.

"It's right here, Bill."

"Oh, yes." He pulled over to the curb.

"I hate to see this evening end. Would you like to come up for an after dinner drink?."

He hesitated a long moment. "No, thank you. It's pretty late."

"I don't know how to thank you. This has been one of the most marvelous dinners of my life." She took both of his hands and held them for an instant before she walked through the entranceway.

He drove home nursing a sense of guilt at having taken advantage of her good nature, and a feeling of having a narrow escape. Getting messed up with females on the faculty was strictly no good, a sure way to invite trouble. So he had a relatively clear conscience when Hal kidded him about his date with Irene.

"I think she'll do a great job. By God, Hal, we may make something out of this school yet and take some pride in what we are doing."

"Careful, Bill. The Big Lie is a useful gimmick so long as you don't start believing it yourself."

Bill was not familiar with that expression. Feeling vaguely that he had been insulted, he watched Hal disappear down the hall. During the first weeks of school Hal had labored long hours with a single-minded devotion to getting things started. But once the term was under way he departed as soon as his work was done. He had never said anything about his past experience or his present interests. In the office they shared Bill couldn't help overhearing some strange telephone conversations, like something out of a mystery novel.

All Bill knew of his assistant was the information on his transcript. Naturally Hal's private life was his own business.

Chapter 7

During the first weeks of the fall semester Assistant Principal Hal Evans had taken a liking to Bill Helmer. The two of them worked long hours together. But Hal's school day was not the most important part of his existence. It was merely the price he was paying to be in Paris. He was staying in Paris to find Zizi. She was the most extraordinary person he had encountered since his discovery of the Big Lie.

Ever since Hal could remember, the Big Lie had been an important part of his life, eating away at his soul like a malignant growth. It started with little things when he was a first grader.

"Have you been a good boy, Harold?" a lady from the Aid To Foreign Missions would ask when she came to the parsonage.

"Yes, ma'am," he would say. It was a lie, a big black lie. He was mean as hell. His father said so and sure enough he could feel the sin bubbling around in the marrow of his bones.

"Would you like some more ice cream, Harold?" a lady would ask him at the church social.

"No, ma'am. No, thank you." His mother told him that the minister's son must set an example. He must not be a little pig. He loved ice cream; he could eat a whole freezer full of the stuff.

It was the same thing for the afternoon Bible study group. He knew his mother would be upset if he did not go.

What he really wanted to do now that he was starting in junior high school was go play baseball with the town kids. He might have been pitcher if he could get out to Sunday games. But instead he went to Bible study and thought about the kids out on the diamond. Then he'd look around him and wondered about the other kids who sat there reading the Scriptures. He had his own picture of Jesus. He was okay. Jesus was no damned sissy. He'd knocked the piss out of those guys lending money in the temple, hadn't he?

He thought a lot about it. Hal decided grownups were phonies who hid behind the Bible and lived the Big Lie. Take Old Man Harris, for instance. He always weighed his thumb on the scales when he sold meat. Hal used to watch him at eye level from the end of the counter. He'd starve his grandmother for a nickel, that guy, and he was a deacon or something. It was the same thing for the others. And his old man was no better than the rest. He could preach a sermon on love and beat the hell out of his own kid the same day.

Hal's great discovery was connected with the big oak tree over by the church. On summer nights he would duck the Sunday evening sermon sometimes to lie under the old oak, listening to the choir. Sermons and Sunday school lessons were a lot of crap but the music was quite a different thing, something you could *feel*. A good choir belting out a hymn did something to you. You could see it in people's faces. Even Old Man Harris had a kind of soft look when he sang *I Come To The Garden Alone*. If you could have caught the old guy right after a hymn he might have weighed out an honest pound of meat.

Jesus would have liked that music, Hal used to think, lying there comfortably on a Sunday evening when the stars were so bright you could see them through the thin edges of the leaves. Jesus would have sung in the choir for sure. He would feel that music way down deep, the way Hal himself felt it. And he wouldn't preach any long-winded sermons either. After the singing He would have led everybody out under the oak tree and maybe they would all have a beer. Jesus drank wine, didn't he? So why wouldn't He like beer? They would talk, friendly like, about important things— baseball and how the fish were running and the best bait for perch.

Hal had always loved the great oak. It was his favorite place to play. With some other kids he built a tree house in its spreading branches and one night they decided to sleep there. It was one of those summer nights when the wind comes up out of an electric atmosphere and feels and smells of storm. The lights were turned out in the parsonage and everybody was asleep. Unexpectedly the big tree came to life. The creaking branches drowned out the first patter of rain on the leaves and a great hoot owl split the night with a hideous screech.

Then the storm broke. Chain lightning rent the sky. Claps of thunder shook the branches where the boys were huddled. Rain lashed the leaves into a furious mass of spraying water. From the innermost depths of its soul the old oak rumbled in alarm. One by one the boys slipped down from the tree house and ran home—all but Hal. He decided to stay. He crouched there in the tree all night. During the long hours he did a lot of thinking and got his first handhold on the idea of the Big Lie. When finally the storm passed and dawn came to the eastern sky, he was still there wet and exhausted but proud of his courage. He knew he was a man, a man with his own private idea of Jesus and a precious insight into the Big Lie.

Most people in the world, he decided, were like his old man, saying one thing and doing something entirely different. They were all pretending just as he had to pretend when he said he didn't want more ice cream or that he liked Bible reading class. They were trying to be big shots. They would try to punish anybody who threatened to show them up for the jerks they really were, like the story about the Emperor's New Clothes. That's why they liked to have his father tell them that they were made in the image of God, that they were fallen angels, that they would be filled with the divine light of truth as if God had screwed a big light bulb into each one of them and all they had to do was turn it on. That gave the phonies who went to church a chance to pretend that they had turned on the light bulb and nobody else knew where the switch was. These fakers weren't children of God or any such thing. They were just men. That's what they were, just men.

Here was the heart of the thing and the reason the phonies who pretended to be more than just men had invented the worst parts of the Big Lie, like sin and duty and love. These were only gimmicks to keep you with your ass in a sling all your life. Honor thy father and thy mother. That was a laugh. His mother worked hard and she was okay. He kind of liked her but his father, the Reverend Evans. Honor him? Recalling the sting of his father's belt on the flesh of his back, Hal felt little affection for the old hypocrite.

One night that summer, by the light of a full moon, he slipped under the big oak and made his vow, kneeling on the ground with his arms around the trunk of the tree. Then he took his pocketknife and carefully sterilizing the blade with the flame of a match he drew the cutting edge across the tip of his right index finger. Squeezing the blood out he solemnly rubbed a streak along the rough bark of the tree trunk and drew an X on his forehead.

Never, he promised himself, would he live the Big Lie, never would he pretend to be a noble and divine creature who tried to screw everybody else in the name of religion or duty or love or anything else. Never would he care too much for anything or anybody.

His philosophy sustained him through college and two years of teaching. It was amazingly simple, almost like magic. All you had to do was tell the truth. People usually didn't know whether to believe you or not, but it worked almost every time. He knew what he was doing when he started teaching. He liked kids. They were usually more honest than grownups and they could smell a phony a mile off. He found that out the first year, working in a village high school.

"That's an ugly tie you're wearing today," a boy said to him, or "You sure got a funny nose, Mr. Evans." If you could teach just a few of those kids to see the Big Lie, that made your work worthwhile.

Then like other young American men of his generation his life was disrupted by Pearl Harbor. He enlisted in the army and eventually found himself in Paris at the time of the Liberation. He remained on duty there for more than a year. It was then that he met Zizi. Hal never did quite succeed in placing her in his scheme of things.

Zizi was a Yugoslavian refugee. He never found out why she was a refugee or why she had to hide in Paris. In fact he really didn't know much about the unimportant details of her life.

He was sitting alone at the table of a café on the *boulevard St. Germain* when he first saw her. She came directly up to his table and stood there looking him in the eye.

"You like to sleep with me?" she asked.

Here was something completely new. Even waterfront streetwalkers used a more subtle approach. Hal, who had spent much time and energy trying to prove that Freud was right, always welcomed an opportunity to expand his experience. He looked the girl over with interest.

She was so thin that her long hair enveloped her shoulders. Her clear skin and the easy grace of her body suggested a young girl. Faintly prominent cheekbones and large eyes gave her features an ageless quality as if her face had lived a longer time than her body.

"I am open to suggestion," he answered. "You want to sleep with me?"

"No." She met his gaze directly. "But I am hungry."

"Sit down and join me." Hal pushed his bowl of bouillabaisse forward for her to see. "Tell the waiter what you would like."

"The smell of that makes me feel sick." She clutched her handbag close to her chest and leaned against the table.

An eggnog laced with cognac, a bowl of soup and an *infusion* of herb tea suggested by the *garçon* was all she could handle. She seemed almost in a state of shock. Hal could detect no expression in the steady gaze she directed at him while she was eating. Ill at ease he went in search of the waiter for the check. When he returned to their table the wicker breadbasket was empty and Zizi's threadbare handbag was bulging. In an uncomfortable silence he walked home with her.

In the dark stairway leading up to her room an old woman feeling her way down the bottom steps faced them in the narrow entrance.

"Hello, Mother Steiner," said Zizi. "Does your head feel better?"

"Is that your son with you?" The old woman peered without recognition.

"It's Zizi, Mother." She fished into her handbag and handed her some bread. "For your breakfast."

"God will be good to you." The old woman was trembling. "My sister would pay you but she has no money. She can't pay my way. The man came today."

"What did he say, Mother?"

"You have to pay them. God has punished the Jews and He will do it again. We won't even help our own people without money." She shuffled away mumbling to herself.

"She comes from Poland," Zizi said as they went up the stairs. "Everybody is calling her Mother. She is mixed up in the head. Her husband was killed by the Nazis."

"What's that business about money?"

"She found a man who helps Jews into Palestine. He came today. You have to pay and Mother thought it was free. Her sister is there."

On the third floor landing Zizi knocked at a door.

"Hello, Zizi," a voice answered.

"Hello, Elsa. Here." She handed pieces of bread from her bag. "Something for the kids and your breakfast."

"Zizi, you're a real friend. Thanks," Elsa called up the stairs.

Zizi lived in a space that Hal at first considered an under-heated closet. The only outside light entered through a tiny window in the roof. An iron cot was pushed against the mansard wall. On a table near the door an alcohol burner nestled among some pans and dishes. As he squeezed in he saw a pile of canvases stretched on wooden frames at the other end of the room. A sweet smell, like burnt sugar, hung in the air.

"Smells terrible, yes?" Zizi wrinkled her nose.

"What is it?"

"*Eau de Cologne.* I saved a big bottle somebody gave me a long time ago. I had no money for alcohol so I burned this."

"And it works?"

"Yes."

"What did you cook?"

"Potatoes and turnips, mostly turnips."

"You ate them with what?"

"With the skins," she replied.

The room was lighted by one bare bulb. Over the sink hung a pair of freshly washed panties and a brassiere, both almost shapeless. Hal glanced quickly away feeling that he had just peeked through a keyhole.

Looking around he noticed a trophy on a pile of canvases. It was a statuette of an artist holding a palette, mounted on a block of polished hardwood.

"What is this?" Hal tried to read the inscription.

"First prize for design. It was a national contest. A state prize."

"Looks like gold," he said.

"They told me it was gold."

"Do you know what that's worth?" Hal looked at her. "And you never tried to sell it even when you were hungry?"

"It is the only thing I have from…from before the war."

"That should impress your Yugoslavian friends in Paris."

"I have no Yugoslavian friends in Paris."

"Well, it should help when you go back home."

"I am never going back."

Zizi's tone did not invite more questions. She sat beside him on the cot and regarded him with such a direct gaze he was embarrassed. With a little color in her cheeks and a few more pounds of weight she would be pretty.

"You stay tonight?"

"No." He hesitated and added quietly, "but I will be back tomorrow evening."

As he stood to leave he saw her empty handbag on the table.

"You saved no bread for yourself?"

"I forgot Mother Steiner."

He tried to give her a five hundred franc bill but she refused. As he left he slipped the money under her handbag. When he arrived the next day with food from the Post Exchange she gave the money back to him.

He came every day after that and took her to dinner. He didn't sleep with her for a week although she dutifully offered each night.

In an antique shop Hal picked up an old hand-carved wall shelf with a small mirror as the back piece. He put it up on the wall to hold her art trophy and Zizi was delighted. She proudly pointed it out to all her friends in the building.

Every day Mother Steiner came up to Zizi's room and sat on the floor while Zizi rubbed her head. She was often there when Hal came and she would leave hastily, mumbling to herself. The old woman always gave him a vague feeling of guilt.

"It makes her feel better to come up here," Zizi told him. "She has no window in her room."

When he didn't see the old woman for several days Hal asked about her.

"She went to Palestine. The man came to get her. I think they went to Marseille to get a boat."

Sitting on the cot while Zizi prepared dinner on the alcohol burner Hal had the impression that something was missing from the room. He looked around and saw that the trophy was not on its wall shelf.

"Where is your gold statue?"

"I put it away."

Something in the tone of her voice made him regard her curiously. He thought about it watching her back as she worked over the stove. Then he guessed what had happened.

"Could I see it, Zizi? I have an idea for fixing the shelf."

"I don't think I can find it right now."

"Did you sell it?"

Silence.

"Why didn't you ask me, Zizi? You didn't have to sell your prize. I could have helped out."

"She was my friend."

"Zizi," he said after a long silence, "I'll be damned if I can figure you out."

"Do you have to figure me out?"

She had a reserve that kept Hal from asking her any questions about herself and she never once asked him about his past. Hal could only infer that she was some kind of refugee. They were able to behave as if they had both been born the moment they met on the *boulevard St. Germain*. Hal liked that.

They sang a lot and Hal taught her some Baptist hymns. Her idea of a good time was to buy a bottle of *vin ordinaire* and sit by the river watching the boats go by. Sometimes she made sketches of the people along the Seine and he marveled at her skill. She made love with shameless candor and the vitality of a cat.

Hal was a sergeant by this time and he had a soft assignment. He could get away almost every night, so they lived together for seven glorious months during which time Zizi gained a bit of weight. Each evening he would hurry home to Zizi. And he tried to avoid thinking of the future. Yet he knew it had to end sometime. With his pals he sat around counting up points toward a discharge, sharing the general eagerness to get back home. But when his turn came he passed it up, the first time.

Zizi accepted his leaving as naturally as she had accepted his coming. They lied to each other and said that they would write often. Zizi appeared to find their final goodbye more difficult than Hal. They said that certainly they would see each other again. He did send her a Christmas card but received no answer. Then after a while he began to think a lot about Zizi as he earned an M.A. degree under the G.I. Bill.

All the women he met appeared somehow to be uninteresting. He wrote Zizi a long letter saying he would like to come to Paris and look her up. The letter came back stamped *Inconnu*. He wrote her a registered letter and it was returned as undeliverable. Then he signed up with the Army dependent school system and had the incredible luck to be assigned in Paris.

Hal went to the old address on *la rue de Seine* immediately but of course she wasn't there. Elsa no longer lived on the third floor. The old concierge had left and the building had changed hands. The new owner turned out to be a real estate syndicate. The office manager didn't know the former concierge or any of the previous tenants. Just to make sure Hal came back to talk with some of the directors but none of them could give him any information. He met a number of interesting people. He was learning the geography of Paris. His French was improving. But he found not a trace of Zizi.

Chapter 8

Aching with fatigue, Colette Bernard returned home after her day at the American school. Once in her apartment she would never have the energy to go out again so she had shopped for dinner on the way. Arriving at her landing she shifted the bundle of books and groceries for dinner to her left hand while rummaging into her handbag for the key.

She was caught off balance and staggered into the room as the door swung open. Books and shopping bag spilled to the floor.

"Jean!"

He looked amused at her disarray as he stood holding the door.

"How did you get in?"

"With my key."

Restraining an impulse to kick her bag across the floor she swept over to flop on the sofa.

Jean carefully picked up the books, the net shopping bag and the *tournedos* wrapped in its heavy white paper.

"I did not expect you to welcome me with cheers." He placed her things on the table. "But I thought you would at least receive me with courtesy." He walked over to the sofa extending his hand. "*Bonjour, chérie.*"

"*Salaud.*" She turned away.

"So you still love me."

"Leave me alone. *Va t'en.*" Colette sprang to her feet. "And kindly give me my key."

"*Tu m'aimes toujours.*" It was a statement not a question.

She sank back on the sofa and started to cry.

Jean calmly sat down at the piano as if she were not there and started to play.

"Music soothes the soul."

She walked softly up behind him and grabbed the keyboard cover. He withdrew his hands just in time as she slammed the lid shut. He wheeled around on the bench gravely inspecting his fingers.

Colette felt silly. It was a childish thing to do. "Why are you here? What do you want?"

"I would like to talk with you."

"It was kind of you to come," she said. "I am in excellent health and I had a good year in England. Now please give me back my key and go start a revolution somewhere."

"So a whole year of exile didn't help you solve your problem. I am very sorry."

"My problem?" she thought angrily.

She decided it was wiser to keep quiet. He seemed to have a way of winning arguments.

"I brought a bottle of wine thinking you would perhaps invite me to dinner. It is more pleasant to talk on a full stomach."

She kicked off her shoes and settled back on the sofa without looking in his direction.

"Shall I do the honors?"

Without waiting for an answer he went into the kitchen returning in a few minutes with two glasses.

"*A la tienne.*"

She accepted the glass in silence. He wandered out of the room leaving her to finish her drink alone. From the kitchen wafted an aroma of frying steak. She went to change into more comfortable clothes.

Colette was ravenously hungry after the American school cafeteria lunch of warm frankfurter and tomato soup. Despite herself she was relieved that Jean was quietly attending to all her wants at table.

Finally he pushed aside his plate and refilled their wine glasses. Colette accepted a *gauloise*.

"*Merci.*" She gave him a level glance. "How did you know I was back?"

"Pierre told me. He saw you in the street."

"Why did you come?"

"The truth is that I don't know. I found myself wandering over this way probably with the hope of meeting you in the street. I saw the doorway and just naturally came up."

"Still at the clinic with Pierre?"

"Yes, and I am enjoying myself right now. Let me show you my sweetheart." He pulled a photo from his billfold.

"What a beautiful little girl. Who is she?"

"She was brought into the clinic about three months ago. Everybody else was busy so I started working with her."

"Is she Algerian?"

"Moroccan. The father is. I think the mother is French but she abandoned her."

"I didn't know you worked in child psychology."

"I don't, but remember how I liked Piaget ? This girl fascinated me."

"What is wrong with her?"

"Everything happened to her. Welfare picked her up in the slums. She couldn't talk, no toilet training, fits of screaming, classified as mentally deficient."

"She does not look it." Colette studied the photo.

"She is as bright as a new twenty-franc piece. Now she can talk and knows colors. Imagine that, a three-year old."

"You sound like a proud papa."

"I started making up stories about each color for her." His face glowed. "I took her to a marionette show. She kept shouting to the puppets." Jean put the photo back in his billfold. " And you, *chérie*? What are you doing?"

"I have work."

"Are you really working for the *Amerloques*?"

"I teach at the American school."

"Good God."

Flushing with guilt she was furious with herself. There was nothing to feel guilty about and what business was it of Jean, anyway.

"It is challenging work."

"How can you do it? How can you, of all people, do such a thing?"

"You act as if I were a traitor."

"Listen, would you have worked for the Nazi occupation troops?"

"Don't be ridiculous. That was different."

"I know. I was teasing. But is it so different? We are occupied by American troops and corrupted by American dollars. They are arriving by the thousands. We need to be careful. Do you think Roger would approve of your new job?"

"Leave my brother out of this."

"Do you think he would be pleased with the American occupation if he were alive?"

She was crying furiously and furious to be crying.

"Sometimes I could kill you. I wish to God I had never ever seen you."

"I am not happy about what you are doing to yourself."

"Let me worry about that. I can take care of myself."

"Then why are you so angry to talk of this?"

"Why don't you run along and work on your world revolution. There is much to be done and I am certain that is more important than my problems. Besides what I do is no concern of yours."

"Colette, I love you. You told me once that the happiest time in your whole life was when we were together. Sure, I care what happens to you."

They were both standing now.

"I must live my own life."

"Tell me you do not love me and I will leave."

"I detest you."

"That may be true but you didn't answer my question."

"Would you believe anything I say?"

"Chérie." He looked at her. "Even with your bourgeois conscience you cannot look me in the eye and tell me something you don't believe."

"So you are now a Marxist analyst. I thought Freud was on the party index."

"Very amusing. Answer my question."

She sat down and put her head on the table.

"I hate you. I hated England. I hate teaching. I hate that terrible American school. I hate myself. I wish I could die."

He led her over to the sofa and sat with his arm around her while she wept.

"What can I do, Jean?"

He went into the kitchen and came back with half a bottle of cognac. They drank sitting close together holding hands on the sofa.

"I only want you to be happy, *Chérie*. Do you really want me to go?"

"Yes. In a little while."

Colette thought she had never been so tired. As she relaxed against Jean's shoulder she could feel herself breathing against the side of his face. The firm pressure of his arm around her felt solid and reassuring.

She awoke with Jean's arm resting lightly across her, his hair pressing against her cheek as he lay on his stomach, bare and crosswise of the bed his feet sticking over the edge. Slipping out of bed she headed for the bath, luxuriating in the hot water.

She was eating breakfast when Jean stumbled into the kitchen wearing only his underwear shorts and lazily rubbing his chest.

"Cold in here."

"The heat is not yet turned on. Put on some clothes, you silly goose."

"What are you doing up so early?"

"I am going to work."

"You do not plan to stay at that American school?"

"Of course."

"I thought we settled that last night. You said you hated the school."

"I didn't know we made any decisions about me last night."

Colette resented being brought back into contact with her problems before she felt ready to face the day. She was at the point of telling him she planned to resign anyway, but something stopped her.

"I am sorry to see you serving the Ricains."

"I must make my own decisions."

"I hope you will reflect about this one, *mon chou*."

"*Mon ami*, let me live my life. I have no wish to tell you what to do or how to think." She looked up at him. "Why do politics make you hate people?"

"I hate nobody. I do not hate Americans. Many of them died in France fighting the Nazis."

"Then how…"

"*Chérie, je t'en prie*. I hate capitalism. I detest a system where money and property are more important than people. The Americans are hiring us as servants; they are buying up our industries; they are financing the French government. Do you think we could have a Popular Front government now? They would never allow it. They are paying most of our bills. We must force them out of France."

"They claim they are here to protect us."

"Protect us, hell. We need no protection. They are here to protect French capitalists from the French workers. Companies with American military contracts are obliged to investigate their workers. Many of the very people who fought in the *Résistance* cannot get jobs because the Americans won't let them work at NATO military bases right here on French soil. They are using us to fight their dirty cold war. And you are helping them."

"I am not making bombs. I am teaching children and God knows they need teaching. Perhaps what I do will make a difference in the way they feel about France. They have some terrible ideas right now. The director was honest enough about that."

"Ah, I suppose the director is a handsome young officer."

"The director is a civilian. But that is not your concern."

"You ought to know what the Americans think of French women. He may want you to sleep with him to keep your job."

"So now I am a whore. Associating with me may hurt your precious standing in the Party. You are so damned righteous. Karl Marx and John Calvin. Oh God." The anger squeezed up exploding in her head.

"You bastard. I'll…I'll kill you."

She snatched the nearest thing at hand, a boning knife from the kitchen table and flung it at him. He ducked as the weapon flew above his head. They both turned to look at the knife, its point embedded in the doorframe, the molded handle quivering.

She sank into a chair covering her face with her hands, "Oh God!"

Jean pulled the knife from the doorframe. He tossed it on the kitchen table and went into the bedroom. When finally she got up from her chair he had dressed and gone.

Out in the street Colette hailed a taxi and tipped the driver generously to arrive at school as the nine-o'clock bell was ringing.

Chapter 9

Maria Stepanovic was something of a mystery. She worked at the American school for three years, but nobody had ever visited her in the student hotel where she lived. Every night at five o'clock she disappeared into the throng of Parisian commuters and every morning at eight she appeared in the school office impeccably groomed and cheerful.

Bill noted, however, with increasing irritation as the year wore on that she had a weakness for students who got into trouble. When sent to the office for discipline they were always received sympathetically. She would present a culprit at the office door.

"Mr. Helmer, this is Donald. He was sent to the office by his homeroom teacher. While he was waiting he did several errands and he has been a great help to me." She would smile sweetly. Somehow it took the punch out of anything Bill might say. After one particularly trying day he exploded. "Damn it all, Maria. You coddle these kids too much. When they come to the office for punishment they should sit right there and not budge."

"They need understanding, Mr. Helmer. You have said that yourself. They are really wonderful children."

"There is a difference, Maria, between showing understanding and being too soft. These kids know how to work you because you are too damned understanding."

"Is it possible to be too understanding? We can be hurt if we are too trusting. But sympathy and kindness can work wonders. I have seen it done."

"Where was that?"

"I worked in a refugee camp in Poland after the war with people who had seen their families tortured and killed, their homes burned and their possessions seized. I witnessed many of them respond immediately to somebody who would talk with them, look them in the eye and smile."

Bill didn't have the heart to reprimand her again but he asked Hal and the counselor to keep discipline cases from waiting too long in the outer office.

For her part Maria tried to remain neutral. But it wasn't easy. One afternoon she paused in her typing to watch Tony Mosca slumped in an office chair. She hoped he would look up so she could give him a smile. But he just sat there staring at the floor. Mr. Helmer had been firm when he brought Tony out of his office a half hour ago.

"Maria," he said, "I want Tony to sit right in this chair and not move until I call him. He is not to run errands nor to leave this chair under any pretext whatsoever."

Tony had been dragged into the office by Mr. Jackson at the end of the noon period, both of them flushed with anger. They were shouting at each other, so Maria couldn't help hearing everything they said, though she tried to concentrate on the report she was typing.

"Take your hands off of me. Don't you touch me."

"You are lucky I didn't put my fist in your face. If you ever threaten to punch me again, school rules or no rules, I'll knock your teeth down your throat."

Maria winced.

"What's all this about, Mr. Jackson?" Pitched at a lower level Mr. Helmer's voice came into the argument.

Jackson replied, "I was on noon duty and keeping everybody out of the auditorium because it's decorated for a dance tonight and it's off limits to all students. This character tried to push past me when..."

"I had a right to go in there. I'm on the..."

"I told him he couldn't go into the auditorium, so he tried to push past me. When I grabbed him he threatened to 'pop me one'. Anyway he's been giving me a bad time all year, always shooting off his face in English class. I've had enough."

"Well, Tony?" Helmer's voice was calm.

"He grabbed me by the shoulder, put his hands on me and started jerking me around."

"Quit stalling. Did you or did you not threaten to hit me?"

"Yeah. I guess I said something like that but…"

"No buts about it. There you have it, Mr. Helmer."

Maria concentrated on her time and attendance report crediting herself with 100 hours of work for the first week of the pay period. When she tried to erase the figures the paper tore. She jerked the form out of the machine and removed the carbons to set up four new copies.

"I have a class waiting for me upstairs so I must leave but I wanted to get this straight before I left."

"Thank you, Mr. Jackson. I'll take over from here."

Maria closed the office door. She felt better now that Tony was alone with Mr. Helmer.

In the principal's office Tony stood in front of the desk with his jacket pulled back over one shoulder and his hair mussed up from the tussle with Jackson.

"Tony." Bill tried to keep his tone conversational. "How many times were you suspended last year?"

"Four times, I guess."

"That's right. Three times for fighting and once for impertinence to a teacher. Doesn't that record suggest anything to you?"

"Yeah. I guess I get in a lot of trouble."

"That's putting it mildly. And this business is even more serious. A school can't operate without some authority and the teachers have responsibility for maintaining discipline. We simply can't tolerate your complete disregard for authority."

Tony said nothing as he looked out of the window.

"Why did you talk to Mr. Jackson that way?"

"I was on the decorating committee and had a right to go in. He called me names and almost jerked my head off in front of the other kids. After he yelled at me I said, 'O.K. so I'll come out. Just give me time.'"

"Your going into the auditorium is not the point in question right now. It's the fact that you talked…"

"He's got no right to cuff me around that way. Nobody can push me around. I won't stand for…"

"Don't interrupt me, Tony, when I'm talking to you. I'm trying to tell you…"

"He can't push me around like that. He's just got it in for me. He's been riding me all year in English class, always making sarcastic remarks…"

"Hold on."

"I had a right to…"

"Just a minute, Tony, I…"

"Cripes, nobody can talk to me like that…"

"You just listen to me. When I tell you to keep still I mean it." Bill pounded his fist so hard on the desk that the telephone bells jingled.

There was a long silence. Then Bill said, "Tony, anger is a terrible waste of energy. It makes a lot of noise and flames but accomplishes nothing. You lost your temper and got yourself into trouble. I regret to say that I lost my temper. Now you go out and sit in the outer office until we both cool off. Don't for any reason leave that room."

"Cripes, nobody can push me around." Tony marched into the secretary's office.

Some time later Maria reminded Bill that Tony was still waiting.

"Cripes, Mr. Helmer. I lost my temper," Tony said as he came in. "I'm sorry."

"Now I think we are both in a better frame of mind to talk about this."

"I'm sorry I sounded off to Mr. Jackson, too. I'll apologize if you want me to."

"Do you really want to, Tony?"

"No. But I'll do it if you say so."

"I don't think Mr. Jackson would be satisfied with an apology and I don't blame him. I want to impress upon you, Tony, how serious it is for a student to threaten a teacher. In my opinion this is your worst offense and it calls for a stiff penalty."

"Cripes, Mr. Helmer, I really been studying this year. I got mostly "B" grades so far and yesterday I got an "A" from Mr. Corson. If you suspend me now I'll lose out on everything."

Bill took the grade sheet from Tony's file.

"You are doing better now and that's to your credit. But you should have thought about that before losing your temper and insulting Mr. Jackson."

"But, cripes, he yelled at me and jerked me around. You think the teacher is always right?"

"Any student who feels he has been seriously wronged by a teacher can always come and talk it over. This school has always granted students the right to protest but they can't go around threatening to 'pop' teachers."

"Gee, this is going to be rough on my folks."

"I'm going to call your father right away."

"Dad is away on an assignment."

"Well, I'll have to talk with your Mother."

"Ma won't like this. She's going to be mad."

"Tony, your mother and I are both on your side, but it won't help much unless you do your part. I think you owe your mother a lot of consideration. She's one of the most understanding people I know."

"Yeah. Ma's a good egg."

'Mrs. Stepanovic will get you transportation. You know by now that you are to go directly home."

"Say." Tony asked as he turned to leave, "can I play in the soccer game next week? Mr. Corson is counting on me."

"You can't play while you are suspended."

"Mr. Corson will be disappointed."

"It seems that several people will be disappointed in you, Tony."

"Cripes, suspended indefinitely. That's not fair," he said as he left.

Maria had almost finished her report when she saw that she had placed Mr. Helmer in the substitute teacher column.

"Mr. Helmer, I would like to go out for a cup of coffee," she said.

"Get transportation for Tony first. Then go get your coffee. I will answer the phone."

Bill was sorting some papers when he heard a knock on the door. It was Tony.

"Excuse me, Mr. Helmer. Mrs. Stepanovic isn't here so I just knocked."

"I thought you went home. What is it?"

"I've been thinking about the Math and Physics I'll miss. Can I go see Mr. Corson before I leave and get my assignments?"

"That's up to Mr. Corson, but I don't want you to disturb his class." Bill looked at the clock. "If he wants to give you the assignments between classes it's all right with me. You can take your books home with you."

A little later Tony stuck his head through the door and said, "I'm going home now."

"Did you get your assignments?"

"Sure. Mr. Corson said I could phone him at his house if I got stuck on a problem. He's a swell guy."

"Tony, I admire your determination. I hope you'll think over what I said a while ago."

"Yes, sir. Goodbye."

Bill watched Tony cross the parking lot and climb into the staff car before he turned back to his work.

Henry Jackson dropped in right after school. Bill told him he was considering a two-week suspension. He felt that was a severe penalty coming at the mid-semester marking period.

Jackson went straight to the Teachers Lounge. He was disappointed to find only Irene Young.

"Can you beat that? Know what that Tony Mosca did to me?"

She listened to his story.

"If he'd punched me in the nose," Jackson said, "I suppose Helmer might have given him three weeks. How can he expect us to have any discipline when he doesn't support us? Doesn't Tony give you a hard time, Irene?"

"He has been a help to me in the Senior play," she answered. "Tony is a problem, all right, but he's not really mean."

"Mean? Look, the kid threatened to hit me. What do you think of that?"

"Why, I suppose it's natural that students want to punch us sometimes." She picked up her red pencil. "But of course they shouldn't say it out loud."

Jackson stared at her in surprise.

"Well," he said, "If Helmer won't do anything about it I will. Before the end of the year I'll make that brat sorry he ever shot off his big mouth to me."

Maria was thinking about Tony, too. When she came back from her coffee break she went into the principal's office.

"Mr. Helmer, do you have to suspend Tony? He is really not a bad boy, you know."

"You keep your nose out of this, Maria, or so help me I'll suspend you, too. I'll send you home for a week."

"You have a bad conscience."

"Sure, I've got a bad conscience. Let me take care of my conscience and you go take care of your typewriter."

"My typewriter is shiny clean and in good working order." She closed the door behind her.

Chapter 10

Bill was to look back often on his first conversation with Kay Selner and wonder if he could have said or done something to change the course of events.

One morning Mrs. Stepanovic ushered a girl into his office.

"Mr. Helmer, this is Kay Selner. She would like to talk with you."

"Hello, Kay. Come in and sit down."

"The secretary said I ought to talk with you." She was perched on the edge of her chair.

"Are you having trouble with Mrs. Stepanovic?"

"Oh, no, sir. She's a nice lady. I came in and told her about something and she thought I should see you."

"I enjoyed your violin solo at the assembly the other day."

"Thank you, sir."

"You have amazing talent."

"I had a wonderful teacher."

"You're a senior aren't you, Kay?"

"Yes, sir."

"I especially like to get acquainted with all the seniors. Is your father with SHAPE?"

"No, sir. My father is with the local command. He's the chaplain."

"I see. Well, what was the reason Mrs. Stepanovic thought you should see me?"

"I don't know exactly how to tell you."

Bill occupied himself with stacking the papers on his desk into a neat pile.

"It has something to do with cheating and Mrs. Stepanovic thought maybe I could tell you about it without…" She hesitated, "without you asking me questions."

Damn Maria, Bill thought.

"I take it you don't want me to ask you who cheated. You don't want to be an informer."

"Why—no sir."

"I try not to force students to be informers," Bill told her, "so you don't have to worry about that. But I certainly can't promise not to ask any questions."

The girl hesitated a moment. Then she opened her bag and took out three mimeographed sheets of paper stapled together."

"Here." She handed him the papers. "I wanted to tell you about this. It's a copy of the chemistry test Mr. Krell is going to give next week."

"And you wanted to—a test he is going to give?"

"Yes, sir. A review of the basic elements."

"And how did you get this?"

"Somebody gave it to me but I don't want to say who."

"It wouldn't help much if you did tell me, Kay. There's a classic answer to that one. Whoever gave you this found it in the wastepaper basket, or on the floor. Do you know how many of these are in circulation?"

"No, sir. I have no idea, but I saw other copies."

"Do you know if any of the copies were traded or sold?"

"I don't think so. I believe they were just sort of passed around."

Bill glanced through the papers and noted the dateline. Somebody had stolen Krell's test, no doubt about it.

"Somebody gave you this copy and you came directly to me?" he asked.

"No, sir. It was given to me yesterday. I took it home with me last night and studied it, but afterward it didn't seem right. I thought a lot about it so I came in during my study period and talked with Mrs. Stepanovic."

"Did you mention this to your father?"

"Oh no, sir."

"Kay, I think you have done an honorable and courageous thing by coming to tell me about this. There's some dishonesty in every school, of course, but I don't think we've ever had any organized cheating here. We don't want it to start."

"Thank you." She rose to leave. "Sir, there's one more thing."

"Yes?"

"Please don't tell anybody, not even Mr. Krell, that I gave you the test. None of the kids like me anyway, and if they found out I was the one who told, that would be the end, simply the end."

"Nobody will know who told me, but what makes you think your classmates don't like you, Kay?"

"I don't know. But it's been that way everywhere."

"Why don't you talk about it with Miss Serinac, our counselor? She's easy to talk with and she usually has good ideas."

"I've been counseled before," Kay said, "and it doesn't do any good. This is something I have to work out by myself."

Seldom had Bill seen such a curious mixture of common sense and social timidity. He wondered what her folks were like.

Kay's father made himself known to the school sooner than Bill expected. A few days after his talk with Kay, Mrs. Stepanovic announced Chaplain Selner and showed him into the principal's office. Hal, who shared the space with Bill, was working at his desk in the corner.

"I'm Chaplain Selner. Are you the principal?"

"Yes, I'm Bill Helmer. Glad you dropped in, Chaplain Selner. This is my assistant, Hal Evans."

"Glad to know you, Chaplain. I hope you will excuse me if I keep working. I have some reports to get out."

"Certainly, my boy, go ahead. Whatever your task, work heartily, as serving the Lord and not man."

Hal turned and busied himself with the papers on his desk.

"Sit down, Chaplain." Bill pulled up a chair. "I've been anxious to meet you. I have already met your daughter."

"She has been in no trouble, I trust."

"Not at all." Fortunately he knew nothing about the chemistry test. "I had the occasion to talk with her briefly and I was impressed with her qualities of character."

"Well, we have tried to give her a good Christian upbringing." The chaplain looked pleased. "But I really came to discuss something else with you."

"Fine. Go ahead."

"I have a plan for bringing some Christian training to the children in your school. I've outlined some of my ideas in terms of a year's program but I wanted to talk with you about it first."

"We will be happy to cooperate with you in any way, Chaplain, in organizing catechism classes after school."

"I do want to organize catechism classes as soon as possible," he said, "but that isn't what I have in mind now. I'm thinking about basic moral training that would be a part of the school program, inspirational lectures, life problems and perhaps a bit of Bible history."

"I should think, Chaplain, that those things would be included in catechism classes. We couldn't offer religious instruction during the day. That would be contrary to Army policy. Some families would certainly object to such a plan. The Army makes the school building available after school to all religious groups, provided it does not interfere with regular school activities. They even will provide bus transportation for your classes. Father Reilly has already started meeting with Catholic students."

"Is that so?"

"Yes," Bill said. "We ran a survey asking students to fill out a form on a voluntary basis. They were asked to indicate religious preferences and interests in church activities. I'd be happy to give you the forms for Protestant children."

"Thank you. I'll take them with me today if I may. But I have in mind something that will reach all children. I can't believe that Army policy discriminates against Christianity. What could be the objection to a little moral training as a part of the school program?"

"For one thing, we have classes scheduled for each period of the day. I'm not opposed to a discussion group on moral problems as a voluntary activity. You might organize something with the Catholic and Jewish Chaplains and it could be set up for our activity period."

"That isn't at all what I had in mind. I thought of the homeroom period you have which would not interfere with regular classes. Two or three homeroom periods each week would suffice for such a program. That would reach every child."

He had obviously done a great deal of thinking about this, Bill realized. He probably knew the daily schedule by heart.

"I'm afraid," Bill said, "that other religious groups might object to a completely Protestant program, even as an elective activity."

"The majority of your students are Protestant, are they not?"

"Yes, I believe so."

"A non-denominational program shouldn't offend anybody. Paris is a wicked place, Mr. Helmer. These American children need strong moral guidance and it isn't always provided by the parents. I am disappointed that you are opposed to including such an effort in your school homeroom program."

"I agree with you, Chaplain, that these children may need moral guidance," Bill said, "but I can't see why an afternoon program won't answer that need."

"Mr. Helmer, I don't like to see Christianity put on the same level as activities like basketball or stamp collecting. There are few churches available to our children here. If the Christian way of life is to be safeguarded it must have a place in the school as important as any other subject."

"I'm afraid we can't agree there. I believe in the separation of church and state."

"I approached some members of the P.T.A. and they seemed quite pleased with the idea."

"Well, my friend, the P.T.A. cannot change Army policy. If we imposed religious instruction in our high school we would be inviting trouble."

"Yet you impose other kinds of instruction. You require a course in science for graduation from high school, do you not?"

"Of course."

"Every student must take at least one course in science whether he wants to or not, yet you ignore the spiritual basis of our civilization. Our Savior said, 'Let the children come to me, and do not hinder them, for to such belongs the kingdom of heaven.'"

Chaplain Selner rose to leave.

"Thank you, Mr. Helmer, for your time. I must tell you that it disturbs me greatly to have my daughter in a Godless school. Good day, gentlemen." He closed the door behind him.

Hal arose behind his desk.

"Why did you let that Baptist Blaster talk to you like that? I would have punched him in the nose."

"I believe it's against regulations to punch a Chaplain," Bill said gravely. "Anyway, I found that intellectual exchange most stimulating."

"Intellectual, my ass. You sat there like an angel of patience and let that hypocritical hallelujah howler insult you. I know his kind. He's cut from the same cloth as my old man."

"Hal, I hereby appoint you official representative of the high school to deal with spiritual problems."

"I'd waste a hell of a lot less government time than you do."

"I have an uneasy notion that we have not seen the last of Chaplain Selner."

Chapter 11

Captain Michael Murphy's military career started off with a great disappointment. When he stood in line for hours to enlist the day after Pearl Harbor, he would have chosen to be a Leatherneck in the Marines. But the United States government made him a Dogface in the Infantry so he applied himself to being a good soldier. As sergeant of a platoon he had displayed such courage and skill in battle that he was awarded a field commission. Since then he had risen to the rank of Captain and had revised his original opinion of the Army. He decided to be a thirty-year man.

His first assignment in Paris was with Transportation. This was an office job and he didn't like it. He was happy when the C.O. called him in for a different assignment.

"Captain Murphy," the Old Man told him, "I am pleased with the way you've tackled the duties I've given you. This one, however, may challenge you. When you get several hundred Army brats cooped up in a building all day you got trouble. Plus you have to get along with a bunch of schoolteachers. Anyway, we got these dependents on our hands and we have to take care of them."

"Sir, you can count on me. I'll do my best."

It was not long before he got the picture. He found the school in one hell of a mess. If this was what the schools were preparing for the Army of the future he hoped to Christ the United States never had another war.

Once after the last war he had made a pilgrimage to his ancestral domain. The conditions he saw in rural Ireland were his first real contact with poverty. Those people could make a living off the stuff the high school kids threw away. His mother in the States was trying to live on a pension of one hundred dollars a month. Murphy would have reneged on his officer's club dues sooner than miss sending a monthly check to his mother. He hated to think of her paying taxes out of her pitiful pension to support schools that allowed such senseless waste of government property.

If Murphy could only command the outfit for two days (Forty-eight hours, O Lord, is all I ask) he could show those civilians a thing or two.

Candy bar wrappers gave him an opening. He was inspecting the fire extinguishers in the school corridors when he discovered the first one. Some student had lifted the lid and simply tossed in the crumpled paper. In five out of twenty-one extinguishers he found other bits of wastepaper. Clutching the sticky wrappers in his hand he charged into the high school office. The principal was talking on the telephone so his assistant looked up to greet him.

"Do you see these?" Murphy shook the fistful of wet paper.

"Looks like candy bar wrappers."

"Know where I found them?"

"I have no idea."

"In the fire extinguishers, that's where. If this joint caught on fire—and I expect some kid to try that any day now—these extinguishers wouldn't work. Mr. Evans I won't tolerate dangerous practices like that in an institution under my command. What are you going to do about it?"

"How many did you find, Captain?"

"Five."

"Only five? That's not bad, especially since the Army hasn't got around to putting wastepaper baskets in the halls."

"Only five." Murphy took a deep breath. "All right, I'm asking you. What are you going to do about it?"

"Well…" The assistant principal scratched his head. "We can run a notice in the daily bulletin warning students about touching the fire extinguishers. We can notify student hall monitors to keep an eye on them. We could also try to find out who put them there, out of hundreds of students—well, it's important to prevent it in the future."

"So you don't intend to do anything about these?"

"Certainly. I agree that it's a dangerous practice, but finding the five students who put those wrappers in the extinguishers may not be feasible."

"Godammit, you can call them all together and make them stay here until we know who did it. Keep them all night, if you have to. That'll learn them something."

"We can't do that, Captain," Helmer said, hanging up the phone. "We have a class schedule to follow and we can't lose half a day of school to find out who put five candy bar wrappers in the fire extinguisher."

"O.K.," Murphy replied. "Now we know where we stand. But by God, if you don't intend to do anything about it, I do."

He slammed the door behind him.

The second skirmish in Murphy's campaign was touched off by a locker incident. One morning on his daily inspection Murphy found a locker door with its hinges removed. This time he knew what to do. He stood by the locker until classes changed and captured the culprit, a freshman girl, when she came to get books for her next class. He took her by the arm and pulled her to the office.

"Here she is, Mr. Evans. This time I did your damned police work for you." He stalked out.

The girl stood there for a moment. To Hal's surprise she threw herself into a chair and started to cry.

"Will the Military Police come right away?"

"What Military Police?"

"It's the first time I've been arrested. I've never been in a jail before."

"Nobody is going to arrest you. What gave you that Idea?"

"He did." She pointed toward the door. "He said it was a crime to damage government property and I could be arrested. He said my daddy could be court-martialed." She started to cry again. "Daddy will have to find a new job."

"Nothing like that will happen to you. Now tell me what you did."

"I forgot my key at home today and I had to get my Algebra book, so I took off the hinges."

"How?"

"With my finger nail file. I just unscrewed the hinges."

"You better sign up for shop next year."

"You aren't going to arrest me?" She stared at Hal like a frightened deer looking into headlights.

"We aren't going to do anything to you. I'll send a note home to your father telling him that if the locker is scratched and needs repainting he'll have to pay for it."

"Oh, thank you, sir. I'll never do that again."

Captain Murphy came back the next morning to check on the disposition of the case.

"You didn't suspend her?"

"No. We warned her and sent a note home to her father."

"Captain," Bill cut in. "May I suggest that you report things like this to the school office and let us handle them in the future. That girl was frightened out of her wits."

"That's what I intended. Is that all the thanks I get when I do your police work for you? I've been waiting a long time to catch one of those kids."

"I appreciate your interest, Captain, but suppose you let us handle the students and we won't interfere with the way you handle your enlisted men."

Captain Murphy was not an inarticulate man but Mrs. Stepanovic was present. He was not only an officer; he was also a gentleman. He turned on his heel and walked out.

The third skirmish took place when Colette Bernard and the vocal teacher were planning a concert to which all the French people in the surrounding area would be invited.

Bill presented the plan to the School Officer with whom he shared responsibility for the building.

Murphy shook his head. "Can't do it," he said. "This is an American military installation. There's a lot of Communists in France. Can't open the joint to have foreign nationals crawling around in every corner. That's poor security."

Bill called the Old Man and the Post Security Officer. Neither had any objections to the concert plans. The Old Man even said he thought it was a good idea. When Murphy found out about that he went straight to the military office. With the aid of a Webster's Student Dictionary and a corporal-clerk who had been to college he composed an Internal Route Slip.

Bill found the green form on his desk next morning with a buck slip attached to it.

I.R.S. # 1

SUBJECT: Improper Care of Government Property and Lack of Discipline in The American School.

Recently numerous instances of improper use of government property have come to my attention during daily inspections. The following measures will be enforced immediately:

1. All students changing classes will be supervised by their instructors.

2. No classes will proceed to the next class until all papers have been picked up from the floor, under desks, etc. All chairs in classrooms will be evenly aligned in straight rows. If necessary Post Engineers will be requested to bolt them to the floor.

3. Reply requested by endorsement.

"What do you think of that?" Bill's hands were shaking when he handed the letter to Hal.

"Wow. I wonder who wrote this for the captain?" Hal studied the I.R.S. "What are you going to do about it?"

"I'll make the bastard eat those words."

"Got any ideas?"

"Yes." Bill folded the paper and slipped it into his shirt pocket. "But first I want to go over to FOUSA and talk with Colonel Callahan in the Finance Office. Tom Callahan is a friend of mine."

Tom Callahan looked up from the papers on his desk when Bill walked in and handed him the I.R.S. He whistled softly to himself as he read it.

"Strong stuff," he said. "The Captain is out of line on this."

"It's worse than that." Bill was disappointed that Callahan was not more excited. "That's military interference with the civilian function of the school."

"What do you have in mind?"

"I'll have copies made of this and send one to my civilian headquarters with a complaint of military interference. I'll make the bastard prove that I'm incompetent. That's why I want your advice."

"Hup. Hup. To the rear—March!" Callahan barked. "If you want my advice, Bill, you should go directly to the Old Man with this. It's proper protocol, it's good strategy and it's the most intelligent thing to do."

"All right, Tom. I'll give it a try."

Callahan insisted on telephoning immediately for an appointment. Upon his arrival the secretary showed Bill into the office.

"Hello, Mr. Helmer." Colonel Carpenter said getting up to shake hands. "Pull up a chair."

"Colonel." Bill handed him the I.R.S. "Have you ever read this?"

"No, I've never seen it before," he said after he read the letter. "Captain Murphy obviously lost his temper." He smiled. "A man who falls in love or loses his temper should never put anything in writing."

"Well, that's part of the written record now and I'm not going to take it."

"This does not represent the opinion of the command. The School Officer has overstepped his bounds of authority. It is an insulting letter. What do you want me to do about it?"

That was a dirty trick. The Old Man had cut the ground from under Bill's feet.

"Well," Bill hesitated. "I intend to take this up with my civilian headquarters and file a complaint against military interference, but I wanted you to know about it."

"I appreciate your coming to me. You are quite free of course to work through your own civilian chain of command. I would prefer, however, to keep this quarrel in the family. I would like to feel that you have confidence in my ability to handle the situation."

"Good enough," Bill said, "but running the school is a full-time job. I can't spend half my time fighting the School Officer."

"I take it that you and Captain Murphy are not on the best of terms."

"We haven't been sending flowers to each other."

"Mr. Helmer, the U.S. Army wasn't organized to run a school system. I'd be only too happy to ship all dependents home, except my wife of course. But we are stuck with support of the schools and have to do our best. I could take Murphy off the job but I don't operate that way. Let's give him a chance."

"All right but I still don't like to have people push me around."

"I hope you will make a real effort to understand Murphy's job. It isn't an easy one, you know. I'll see that the file copy of this letter is destroyed. I'll also see to it that Murphy apologizes. Is that satisfactory?"

"Colonel Carpenter, I will try. I'll shake hands with Murphy and forget this whole deal."

Driving back to school Bill had an uneasy feeling that he should have handled the situation differently.

When Murphy came back to school next day from his interview with the C.O. he headed for the principal's office.

"Why did you jump channels and go over my head to the Old Man? Why didn't you come to me and settle it man to man?"

"I might ask you the same question, Captain." Bill looked him in the eye. "I'm always here and I never refuse to see anyone. That was a nasty letter for the record."

"I lost my temper, dammit. The Old Man ate my ass up to the shoulder blades if that gives you any satisfaction. He ordered me to apologize to you. That was a military order so I'm apologizing, see."

"I'll give you a certified statement that you executed the order, Captain."

"Right now it looks like I just can't win. But I ain't licked yet. I don't like this assignment but I'm going to do a good job running my part of the school."

"Splendid, Captain. If we both stick to our jobs there shouldn't be any trouble."

"Yeah, we'll see. Keep your eyes open, Mr. Helmer. I'm sure as hell gonna protect myself."

"I'll be on the lookout from now on, Captain."

"There's more than one way to skin a cat," Murphy told the supply sergeant that afternoon. "If that bastard, Helmer, is gonna jump channels I ain't gonna work in the chain of command either. I will find a way to open the Old Man's eyes to what's really going on in this school. We have to work out some strategy to get Colonel Carpenter on Helmer's ass. Strategy, that's the stuff. That's the difference," he added confidently, "between a captain and a fat-assed sergeant."

"Yes, sir," the sergeant said, gingerly feeling his buttocks.

Chapter 12

Bill's second conflict with Chaplain Selner occurred in a curiously indirect way. Jim Parsons, the regular coach, was sulking because he couldn't have varsity football and refused to have anything to do with soccer. John Corson, who had played in prep school, volunteered to coach the team. He lined up a full schedule of games with French schools.

The French lycée in Villeneuve challenged the American soccer team to *un match de football*, the featured event of their town festival. After Corson had arranged the game, which was scheduled for a Saturday, the mayor's secretary phoned the school inviting *monsieur le directeur* to be a guest of honor.

"I hadn't planned to go," Bill confided to Maria, "but if it's that important I had better make an appearance."

"Oh, you must attend. When *monsieur le maire* has *la gentillesse* to invite you as a guest of honor it would be an offense not to go."

Without prodding, Captain Murphy provided a special bus for the team and supplied some small American flags for the players to present as gifts. Surprised, Bill thanked the Captain warmly.

"I saw your last game," Murphy said. "Your man Corson has taught those boys some discipline. That's what your school needs."

"I'm glad you approve, Captain."

When Bill arrived for the game the mayor offered his hand with a certain formality. He then presented him to members of the city council and other dignitaries before seating him in a special section of the bleachers. After the match Bill's French host led him to the city hall to *porter un toast de champagne en honneur de l'amitié francaise-américaine.*

The American guests followed their hosts into a large reception room, one wall of which had been decorated with crossed American and French flags. Rows of crystal goblets had been arranged at the banquet table that occupied the center of the room. Bill found himself at one end of the table to the right of *monsieur le maire* while the *directeur* of the French Lycée and John Corson were on the left. The soccer teams lined up along each side of the table as waiters arrived with bottles of champagne. *Monsieur le maire* served the boys at his end of the table. When all glasses had been filled he reached into his pocket for a slip of paper.

"We have great pleasure to receive your American team as guests at our annual festival. For us it is a special honor. We shall forget never the arrival of American soldiers to help liberate us in 1945. Perhaps some of your fathers were among them. Myself, I remember fighting by the side of Americans in 1918."

Bill realized that the preparation of this speech had probably cost the mayor a tremendous effort, and he was grateful.

"We are also honored by the privilege of playing a match with such good sportsmen as you. I congratulate your director and your trainer. I hope this will be the first of many meetings between our teams. We would be proud to receive you in our homes to meet our French boys and girls. We shall have a team for basketball and would be honored to arrange between our teams *un match de basket.*"

The mayor paused a moment and then raised his glass. The boys took their glasses and stood there awkwardly watching their host.

'Now," he said, "*un toast dans l'honneur des grands Etas Unis de l'Amérique* and to the fine spirit of your American team I offer this as a small gesture of appreciation for your kindness in coming to make a success of our festival." Raising his glass he took a sip and the boys followed.

"*Monsieur le maire*, may I offer a toast." Bill said in French, "to the hospitality of our French hosts and to Franco-American friendship. We hope you will be able to accept an invitation to our next concert at the American school."

They all finished their glasses and the boys stood there, waiting to see what would happen.

"When you leave," the mayor told them, "*monsieur le directeur du lycée* will be at the door with free tickets for the carnival in the public square. He will give you some if this tempts you."

Corson suggested that his team thank their host. They filed by in a line, shaking hands with the mayor. They were unusually quiet as each waited his turn to say a word of thanks.

The following Tuesday morning Bill found Corson waiting in his office when he arrived at school.

"Bill," he said, "it looks like I'm in trouble or rather both of us. I came early to tell you about it."

"What happened?"

"I met the Zimmermans in the P.X. last night. They told me that several parents of boys on the soccer team are pretty upset. Know why?"

"No."

"Because we encouraged the boys to drink champagne."

Bill whistled softly. "You know, I never thought of that. Who is upset about it, do you know?"

"Well, they said the local chaplain was whipping up a big fuss about it. A Chaplain Simmons or something like that."

"Oho, it's Chaplain Selner."

"Yes, that's the name."

"Don't worry about it, John. But drop in tonight after school and I'll bring you up to date."

Bill was going to take the initiative by calling the chaplain, but before he had a chance the telephone began to ring. Two mothers called in quick succession to protest the school encouraging students to drink alcohol. They expressed themselves in such similar terms that he was suspicious. The next call was from the Old Man.

"Good morning, Mr. Helmer," he said. "I called to ask about the soccer game on Saturday."

"Morning, Colonel. We lost by one point but our boys played well." Dammit, this was a civilian affair. The Old Man had no business interfering and he would tell him so.

"I consider this a purely educational matter," the Old Man said, neatly disarming Bill in advance. "I don't want to stick my nose in it but I thought you should know about it if you don't already."

"Thanks, Colonel Carpenter. I found out this morning."

"I'd like to be briefed on what happened just for my own information."

Bill told him about *la coupe d'honneur.*

"What would you have done, Colonel?"

"The same thing you did." The Old Man chuckled. "Was it good champagne?"

"Excellent."

"That's the main thing. I don't want you introducing our children to second-rate stuff," he said. "I understand my chaplain is the one who started this. Was his kid on the team?"

"No. He has a daughter in school but she isn't on the team."

The Old Man laughed. "I suppose the chaplain will be coming to see me. In any event I want to talk with him. What do you think about all this?"

"Frankly, Colonel, it burns me that he has taken such an indirect way of criticizing the school. I don't like to have somebody whip up excitement among the parents. If the chaplain had called me directly I would have more respect for his objections."

"Right. He's definitely out of line. He should know enough about military channels to go directly to the responsible people. I'll tell him about that. But what do you think about the drinking aspect of this thing."

"Personally, I think it's a petty reason for attacking the school but I suppose parents who feel strongly against drinking have a legitimate complaint. I can't defend encouraging high school kids to drink if the parents interpret it that way. What I propose to do is to call the parents of all the boys on the team. I'll feel them out, and if they object I'll take full responsibility and apologize to them."

"That sounds reasonable to me. I'll try to calm the chaplain. That's a good one—a C.O. trying to soothe the chaplain."

"Thanks for your help, Colonel. That ought to satisfy him."

Bill kept thinking of Kay and he mentioned her to Mary Serinac, the counselor.

"I wish you would talk with that girl, Mary. She's a pretty unhappy kid."

"Maybe she needs a different outlook," the counselor said. "I think we can help her."

"Frankly, I think she needs a different father. But we can't do much about that."

Chapter 13

Colette Bernard rose from the piano to answer the doorbell.

"Good evening, *monsieur le directeur*. Please come in."

"Hi, Colette." He shook her hand. "You know, when you say that it makes me feel fifty years old. Can't you call me Bill?"

"I noticed some of the professors do that at school. But it is difficult for me to use the first name of ...of my director."

"I wish the United States Army took me that seriously."

"Very well—Bill." Colette went over to the liquor cabinet. "I believe you prefer *Amer Picon?*"

Bill took his glass and seated himself on the floor beside the fireplace. Colette carried her drink over to the sofa.

"Why not be comfortable? It's great to relax out here by the fire."

"You may fit the floor better with one of these cushions."

"Had a nice day?" He stretched out his legs.

"I washed my hair. It does not behave."

"Looks beautiful to me. Then what else did you do?"

"I corrected French papers."

"That's no way to spend a Saturday."

"And you? You passed an amusing day?"

"Terrific. Slept late and spent the rest of the day playing records. I started with Mozart and ended with Louis Armstrong."

Colette smiled.

"Incidentally, I listened at the door for a minute," Bill said. "You have a fine touch."

"I studied at the *conservatoire*."

"Were you a child genius?"

"No but my father thought I might be one. He was disappointed when I turned out an ordinary child. Perhaps you play also?"

"No. I have to settle for listening. What were you playing when I came?"

"A Bach fugue."

"Oh."

"Did you like it?"

"You played it well."

"But you do not really care for his music?"

"I have some records of the Brandenburg concertos. I like those trumpets." Bill poked at the burning log with the tongs. "I did go to a Bach concert and got pretty tired before the end of it. Perhaps you have to be a musician to appreciate him."

"That may help."

"He doesn't give me that feeling you were mentioning. Bach must have been a cold potato."

"Oh, no. You must listen to this." Going over to the piano she ran her fingers over the keys then turned to look at Bill. "This has real feeling. It is like…well, the pouring out of a man's soul."

"Perhaps so."

"To be truly creative, feeling must be disciplined. To appreciate it the listener must also work."

"Some blues music moves me. A hot trumpet makes my skin crawl. Is that too sentimental?"

"But one tires quickly of such music. It is so easy. Real feeling takes effort. The students at school might find Bach difficult at first. But he is never sentimental."

"That's funny. Sam Weinberger, our music teacher, was complaining to me over the kids' musical taste. Why don't they like serious music?"

"Perhaps their studies do not give them the discipline to understand great music or even literature." Colette paused. "One might say that many Americans are rich in sentiment but poor in feeling. That is why your musical comedies have such great success. The melodies and stories are so simple, like the comic books students read."

"I guess that just about takes care of American musical taste."

"But now you are angry. I love your Gershwin." Colette stood up. "Perhaps I should serve dinner."

Bill walked over to the phonograph and started sifting through the discs.

"Do you find anything interesting?" Colette stood in the door putting on an apron.

"N-o-o. You don't—oh, yes I do." Bill pulled out a record. "Hey, what are you doing with this? Edith Piaf singing *La vie en rose*. That's sentimental as hell."

"I like it."

"Want me to play it for atmosphere?"

"*Non merci.*"

As she went into the kitchen he continued to browse through her record collection. It was more eclectic than he expected with a large Gershwin collection along with other American composers with whom he was not familiar, names like Howard Hanson, Aaron Copland and Carson Cooman.

Colette came in with a loaded tray which she placed on a coffee table before the davenport.

"Speaking of sentiment," she said as she picked up her fork, "I was reminded of your cheerleaders. They frightened me the first day of school. I want to know what they do."

"Why, they cheer."

"Oh." She waited for him to continue.

"Well, it's not easy to explain what cheerleaders do. They're supposed to be guardians of school spirit, whatever that is. In theory they get other students interested enough in sports to come to the games and cheer."

"But the things they say seem quite foolish."

"French people don't yell at games?"

"Certainly. Whenever we feel like it. But we do not organize such a thing. Does this happen in all your schools?"

Bill laughed. "On a given Friday afternoon in the United States thousands of cheerleaders dressed in their school colors stand in front of thousands of students dressed in bobbysocks, Sloppy Joes or what have you, and go through the same gyrations, shouting the same yells, from Maine to Oregon."

"How horrible."

"Well." Bill poured Colette some wine and served himself. "It's a pretty good way to let off steam. It gives the boys and girls a socially approved excuse for a little exhibitionism. The girls can show off their legs in a way that everybody accepts as good behavior. The boys are of an age to enjoy the spectacle."

"You make everything sound so reasonable. Yet I cannot believe that one considers this a serious part of education. What are you really trying to do at school, Bill?"

"Hmm. I guess you are asking what are the teachers trying to do to educate the students?"

"Exactly."

"Well, most of these parents expect us to get the kids prepared for college. I agree we should do something about that. Then I want to challenge them in their thinking, to be critical so they can contribute to the political intelligence we need, to be unafraid to ask questions and disagree."

Colette continued to look at him expectantly.

"And I would hope that we manage to help them lead a good life."

"What does that mean? These rich children have fine cameras that contribute nothing to art, to seeing the world in a different way or searching for beauty. Some have tape recorders. What do they do with them? They play with them. Only one student has used his machine to help him learn French. Now that's pretty clever."

"And you think our school is like that, playing with toys?"

"No but instructors are often satisfied with minimum effort. Sometimes I feel sad. My students seem intelligent. Only a few like Kay Selner will have a rich life because of her studies. I want to shake them and say, "You value comfort and entertainment more than knowledge. One day you will realize this.""

Colette paused to watch him as she sipped her wine. With a gesture he encouraged her to continue.

"Sometimes in classes when we talk about France there will be students who say they do not like my country. If I ask, 'Why are you here then?' somebody may say, 'We are here to protect you against Communism.'"

"Well, I suppose that's why they think we are here."

"Then should not your students know something about that subject? They know nothing. Students ask me, 'Do you know a Communist?' And when I say yes I do, then they sit up and say, 'What is he like?' as if I were talking of some rare animal."

Bill nodded. "You're dead right about that. But if any of us started teaching the kids about Communism we wouldn't have any place to teach. And that would really shake up the military."

"You accept that?"

"To be honest about it I guess we all do. Otherwise we would have no jobs." He flushed, feeling guilty and resenting her for making him feel that way.

"I am sorry, Bill. I just try to understand Americans."

"Colette, I'm willing to admit most of your arguments about our weak points but you seem to attach no importance to our strong points. We do have a strong government; we do have technical skills; to help other people we have material goods that we share mostly for self-interest but all the same with a certain generosity. This is probably our strongest defense against Communism right now."

"The Romans were a lot richer and had better engineering than anybody once but they rested on their laurels and neglected their life of the mind. They lived by their military power and for their creature comfort."

"Do you believe that?"

"Yes. Do I make you angry?"

"You bet. You like to probe our weak spots. Colette."

"I think French students are encouraged to argue, to question, to seek deeper meaning of their lives. My English students wanted to be socially correct, to do the proper things. Your American students want to be successful, to be able to buy the best things."

"I am happy that you are so interested in the school. We may never do what you think a school should but we are making progress and teachers like you are terribly important."

"Perhaps I am not a good professor for your students."

"On the contrary you are an exciting teacher for our young people."

"Would you join in a cheer for after-dinner coffee?"

To Bill's astonishment she sprang to her feet waving her arms like a cheerleader. Twirling an imaginary baton she marched into the kitchen.

She entered balancing on one hand a coffee service tray with two small cups.

"I will prepare this while we have dessert."

"Allow me." Bill took the coffee grinder from her and turned the handle energetically as she returned to the kitchen. "Okay, coffee's on," he called.

"*J'arrive.* Oh, but you put it on the fire logs."

"Sure. Makes the best coffee, like a campfire."

"But the *cafetière* will be black."

"I'll wash it."

Colette, laughed. "Imagine *monsieur le directeur* cleaning a coffee pot."

"*Mademoiselle*, my honor is at stake."

After dinner Bill took off his coat, rolled up his sleeves and tackled the blackened pot. He could find no steel wool so started rubbing with a rough cloth until bright spots began to appear. "

"Let me finish that," she said.

"No, by God."

She stood watching. A bubble of soap splashed on his white shirt.

"You see? Bright as a new dollar."

She pushed him gently out of the kitchen.

"Well, thanks for everything." Bill stood by the door pulling his scarf round his neck. "Wonderful evening."

"I enjoyed it also."

"You know, I still favor sentimental ways of saying goodnight." He put his arm around her shoulders. "Shaking hands seems too rational for me."

"If you really feel sentimental"— Colette adjusted his scarf and stepped back, "You could cheer." She held out her hand, "Good night Bill."

Colette went back to the davenport and sat down. The thought of Bill accepting a handshake made her smile. How different he was. Jean would have swept her into his arms. She kicked off her shoes and curled up against the cushions, watching the dying embers of the fire.

Chapter 14

On a warm October afternoon Hal Evans swung his little Fiat into the long line of cars waiting to get into the PX parking lot on *le Quai Bleriot* overlooking the Seine. The U.S. Army Post Exchange was the first place most government employees visited when they arrived to get Kleenex, cigarettes, toilet paper and other necessities. And it was the last place they visited to purchase tax-free perfume, liquor and French souvenirs for the folks back home. Thanks to the PX one could have the best goods of America and with good fortune a French maid into the bargain.

The queue of American cars almost blocked the narrow street in front of the store. If he took longer, Hal decided, he would be too late. He eased his car out of the waiting line and drove along the quay trying to find a place. He turned off on a side street, finally parking several blocks away. Cursing his luck he ran back to the rear entrance of the building where the military offices were located.

The guard at the door directed him to the Provost Marshal's office and he arrived just as the big wall clock pointed to five. The clerk at the reception desk had covered his typewriter and was ready to leave.

"Sorry, sir, we're closed. Did you want to register an automobile?"

"Nothing like that," Hal said. "I just want some information. I really wanted to see the French liaison officer."

"Well, he goes home at five, too. Wait a minute. There he is now. That's your boy going out the door. If you hurry you can catch him. He can't fix parking tickets though," the clerk called after him.

"Sorry to bother you after working hours," Hal said, "but I can't get away from my office much before five. I think you can help me."

"I am willing to try," the officer replied. "But I can do nothing about parking tickets. Curious, almost everybody else in Paris can dispose of parking tickets for you but I cannot because of my job."

"That is not my problem. I'm trying to locate a certain person in Paris and I want to know the best way to go about it."

"That sounds interesting."

"It interests me a great deal. You live in Paris?"

"Yes, I take the five–fifteen bus."

"I can give you a lift if you like. I have my car here."

"That would be kind of you. We can talk on the way."

"Would you like an *apéritif*?" Hal asked.

"Of course one is always more lucid over an *apéritif.* There is a little bistro across the street."

When they had settled themselves Hal briefly recounted his search for Zizi. The French officer listened carefully.

"It is possible of course that she has left Paris. Some time has passed since you were here."

"Yes, that's quite possible," Hal said, "but I feel certain she's still here. She loved Paris and I can't imagine her anywhere else. Perhaps that sounds foolish to you."

"Not at all. There are some people who belong in Paris, who would not think of living anywhere else. Some students and artists come here to study a few months and never leave. I hope your friend is one of those."

"I didn't expect that you could help me directly," Hal said, "but I thought you might be able to recommend a private investigator or detective agency that finds missing persons."

"I do some liaison work with the police but mostly on traffic regulations. I know very little of police work. There are some agencies in Paris."

"That's what I would like to know about."

"I have an idea. I know someone who works at the *Préfecture de Police.* He would certainly know about this sort of thing." The officer looked at his watch. "Perhaps I can get him on the telephone. He works until six o'clock. Excuse me a moment, please."

He went to the telephone booth in the back and lifted the receiver.

"*Bonne idée,*" he said when he returned. "Here are the addresses of two agencies. Both of them are honest my friend says. You can go up and talk with them. You speak some French so you should have no difficulty."

Hal drove the officer home and thanked him.

"Good luck," said the officer as he stepped out of the car. "I hope you find your friend."

"You are very kind. Anyway, I'm going to give it a good try."

"*Histoire d'amour?*"

Hal paused then nodded, "*Oui, histoire d'amour.*"

Hal thought about it as he was driving home. *Histoire d'amour.* He was surprised and pleased at the idea. Well, Evans, what else would it be? You're not hiring a detective agency to find the girl just so you can say "Hello." But if you really loved her why did you wait to come back...and where does love fit in with the Big Lie? Was that why you were afraid to do anything about it?

That evening he called Bill to say that he would be late to school on the morrow. After more than a month of blind alleys in his search, Hal began to feel time slipping away from him. Now he intended to make an all-out effort.

The man did not fit Hal's idea of what a detective should be. Slender and dressed in a neat blue single-breasted suit, he might have been a junior executive in an insurance company.

Hal recounted what he knew about Zizi, her former address and the dates he had known her.

"Have you looked in the *l'annuaire de téléphone?*" the detective asked.

"*Bien sûr.*"

"That may sound like a foolish question," the man said, "but occasionally we have clients searching a missing person who is listed right here." He picked up the Paris directory and checked.

"Now are you absolutely certain that you know her correct name? Did you ever see a birth certificate, for example, or a passport with that name on it?"

Hal admitted that he had not but he was reasonably certain of her name.

"You knew," the detective continued, "that evidence obtained by a private investigator in France has no value in court?"

"No, monsieur. I did not."

"So, if you seek evidence for court testimony, a report from us has no value. If for example you need to locate this person for evidence in a divorce case, our report is not acceptable evidence."

"This is not a divorce case and I am not interested in evidence. I just want to find this girl."

"*Bien*. I wanted you to understand."

The man questioned Hal at length about Zizi and Hal found himself unable in most cases to give answers. He had been interested in the real Zizi, not her height, weight and mannerisms. How in the hell could you describe for a detective the things that made her different from all other women?

"I guess I never paid much attention to little details like that," Hal said apologetically.

"Most people don't. That is why detectives need special training. Do you have a picture of her?"

"*Oui*." Hal took a faded photo from his billfold.

The man studied the picture for a moment. He was frankly pessimistic.

"If your friend is registered as an alien it should be easy to find her. If not, it may be almost impossible. We have very little precise information, Monsieur Evans. The picture is the most valuable clue. We will copy and enlarge it."

"I thought I gave you quite a bit of information."

"First, if she is not registered, the name is practically worthless," the detective said, counting off items on his fingers, "even if it is her real name. Secondly, the former address may give us a lead but it is doubtful. She was there during the war and immediately after the *Liberation*. Many Parisians would prefer to forget that period of time, so it is difficult to get this kind of information. Even the picture has limited value. She may have gained weight. She has undoubtedly changed her hairstyle. Women can change everything but the color of their eyes."

"That's not very encouraging."

"Monsieur, we are an honest agency. If we think you are wasting your money we will say so. Of course we have ways of getting information not available to the private citizen."

"Good. Let me know if I can give you any more clues."

"I have one suggestion that you might work on," the detective said. "It would be sheer chance but perhaps worth trying."

"What is that?"

"Your friend was an art student. Visit all the art exhibits, especially private showings of young or new artists. Talk with some of the art students who follow that sort of thing and perhaps try to find other Yugoslavian artists."

"*Merci, monsieur*," Hal said. "That sounds like a good idea."

He was discouraged but certainly not ready to give up. Leaving the agency he reached into his pocket for a cigarette. *Histoire d'amour* the liaison officer had said. If that was true why had he waited so long? It was just that—well, how in the hell could he have known that Zizi would stick in his memory? He had forgotten lots of other girls, hadn't he?

In the excitement of returning home after the war and entering graduate school he had in fact forgotten Zizi for a while. It was in his last semester that she returned to his memory. He was steadily dating an attractive classmate and beginning to think about his future after graduation. As he returned home after an evening with his date, Zizi would unexpectedly invade his memory. Sometimes he could almost envision her in that *petite chambre de bonne* about the size of his dormitory room. He had tried unsuccessfully to contact her by mail.

Hal flicked his lighter and inhaled deeply. All right, so it is *une histoire d'amour*. And when you find her? What do you want to do about it, marry the girl?

These reflections led directly to the question he had been avoiding. What if Zizi had found happiness with some other man? Perhaps his male egotism ruled out the idea of Zizi loving anybody else. Zizi, he told himself, was much too honest a woman to make such a commitment.

The thought never once occurred to Hal that Zizi might not want to marry him.

Chapter 15

"The bell has rung. Take your seats, *s'il vous plaît*."

"Mademoiselle Bernard?"

"Yes. Gordon."

"I spoke some French last night to our landlord and he understood what I was saying."

"Tell me about it."

"He came up when the fuse blew out. Dad can't speak French so I talked to him. And he could understand me. Imagine that."

"Of course. And did you understand him?"

"*Oui*. He talked slow. He asked if Mom was using *un fer à repasser*. That's an electric iron. I looked it up."

"*Bravo*, Gordon. I am proud of you for using the dictionary."

"We talked about bicycle races and I used some sentences we've studied in class. It was just like speaking French."

"You were speaking French, Gordon."

"Hey, Mademoiselle. You going to read us a story?"

"Perhaps but you must speak French in class, Grace. How would you say 'hey' and what does it mean?"

"Gee, I don't know. That's slang I guess. You have slang in France, don't you?"

"*Mais oui*. It is called *argot*."

"Can you say some words for us?"

"If you work hard today we will take a few minutes at the end of our class to talk about some English and French slang."

"That will be fun."

"Now please take a sheet of paper for dictation."

"Do we have to write with ink?"

"You may write with pencil, Sharon. Are you ready? Here is the first sentence. *Paris a quatre million cinq cents habitants.*"

"What was that last word?"

"A-bee-tan."

"I'm sorry I still didn't get that."

"A-bee-tan. You should know that, Sharon. It was on your vocabulary list."

"I didn't understand it the way you pronounced it."

"Les rues de la capitale sont pittoresques."

"Mademoiselle, would you please repeat the last word?"

"Pee-tor-esk, Sharon. Did you not read your lesson?"

"It isn't the same thing on the list as it is when you say them. Don't you want us to ask questions?"

"Certainly. But when you ask several times about one word it takes the time of the entire class."

Sharon sat with feet firmly planted on the floor. With her back straight she gripped each side of her desk until her knuckles were white. Her sharp tone and rising inflection made everything she said sound like a challenge.

"Well, I would like to know whether we can ask questions or not?"

'Please do not ask unless you miss something completely. Let us agree not to ask more than once about a word."

"Now I understand. Thank you, mademoiselle."

"Le quartier Latin est très ancien."

Sharon raised her hand. "What was the second word in the sentence, please?'

"Kar-tee-ay."

"And the third word?"

"Sharon, ask no more questions until we finish the list."

"I was only asking once about each word like you said."

"No more questions until I complete dictation. Then anybody in the class can ask about these words."

"I will have forgotten them by the time you finish, mademoiselle."

"Oh, come now, Sharon. You can check on your vocabulary list. All the words are there."

"I don't see how I can ever learn French if I can't ask questions."

"After the dictation we will discuss your errors. Here is the next sentence, *Les ponts de...*"

"But we can't ask questions until you finish, even if we miss the whole sentence?"

"No. And it is very rude to interrupt constantly, Sharon. I will not allow it in my class."

"Yes, mademoiselle." Sharon looked directly at her and smiled.

An oppressive silence prevailed as classmates witnessed the brusque questioning.

"Cripes, lay off, Sharon," a voice growled. "You're a bore."

'Next sentence, please. *Les ponts de la...*"

"Mademoiselle," Sharon said, "I just can't..."

"Sharon, go to the office and tell Mr. Helmer I sent you out of class."

"Right now?"

"Immediately."

"Yes, ma'am. Shall I take my books?"

"Take all of your things and go to the director's office."

Sharon took her time gathering up her books and papers before she went out into the hall. Then she slammed the door.

"Mr. Helmer, I'm Sharon Breen," she said as she entered the office. "Mademoiselle Bernard sent me down to see you."

"Hello, Sharon. Why did she want you to see me?"

"I don't know, sir."

"Does she need something for her classroom?"

"Oh, no, sir. I think she was angry with me."

"I see. And why was that?"

"I have no idea, sir. I was just asking questions in class. She jumped all over me."

"What kind of questions, Sharon?"

"About our French lesson."

"You don't know why she wanted you to talk with me?"

"No, sir."

"In that case we don't have much to discuss, Sharon. Do you have a study period this afternoon?"

"Yes, sir. Right after lunch."

"Well, you go to study hall for the rest of this hour. Then come in during your afternoon free period. Perhaps we'll know more about this after I talk with Mademoiselle Bernard."

"Yes, sir."

Before he had a chance to go up to her room Colette came into his office.

"What's the story about Sharon Breen?" he asked.

"I am sorry to disturb you with this."

"It's not that serious. Sit down and relax."

Colette sat on the edge of her chair, her clenched fists in her lap.

"This is the first time I have sent a student to you."

"Look, Colette. It's perfectly normal to ask the help of the principal. That's why I'm here. All the teachers send kids to the office."

"Yes, but I should be able to direct my classes. I do not wish to have special help because...because we are friends."

"That has nothing to do with it. Just tell me about Sharon."

"She keeps asking me questions. I encourage my students to ask about things they do not understand but she does this many times, even when I am talking. She is trying to...to...there is an English word for that."

"She's heckling you."

"That is it. She does not like me. I cannot understand why."

"Other teachers have the same problem sometimes."

"This is a friendly class. They are interested. Why should she do this?"

"Have you ever tangled with Sharon over something serious or punished her?"

"Never. She has been this way from the beginning but now it is worse."

"I'm glad you came to see me. No teacher in my school has to put up with this sort of behavior. Just leave it to me."

"What can I do? What would you do?"

"Listen, Colette, I'll..."

"Her face is angry, as if she hated me. Every day before this class I am almost sick. Why does she feel this way about me?"

"It cannot be that bad, Colette Please let me do the worrying."

"I am sorry. I will leave now."

"You're going to sit right there." Bill rose and placed his hands on her shoulders. He looked down at her.

"I must go."

"You're going to the concert with me Friday night?"

She nodded.

"We might as well have dinner together, too."

He walked to the door with her.

"I'll talk with Sharon. I'll also take her out of your class for a few days so you can relax for a while. We'll straighten this out."

"Thank you very much, Mr. Helmer." Colette tried to smile at Maria as she left the office.

When Sharon came back to see Bill that afternoon she talked readily.

"One time Mademoiselle Bernard wants us to ask questions and the next time she tells us not to. I just don't know what to do."

"Sharon, there's a time to ask questions in class and a proper way to do it. Students cannot harass teachers in this school. That's one thing we won't tolerate."

She stared straight ahead.

"You've never had trouble like this in your other classes. Do you have any special reason to dislike Mademoiselle Bernard?"

"No, sir."

Bill removed her from the class for three days and sent her mother a note requesting a conference. He received no answer.

A week later Colette appeared in his office leading Sharon by the arm.

"Mr. Helmer," she said, "Sharon openly disobeyed me this time."

"Yes?"

"When I gave her a note to you she refused to leave. She opened my note and started to read it before the class."

"That is extremely rude."

"I don't understand Mademoiselle Bernard very well. I wanted to...."

"Sit down, Sharon. Thank you Miss Bernard. I'll take over now."

"Thank you, Mr. Helmer." Colette departed.

"Sharon, you seem to have no trouble with your other teachers. What is your problem in Miss Bernard's class?"

"My other teachers are American and I understand them. Mademoiselle Bernard is always lording it over us in class. I talked to my mother about this."

"What do you mean by 'Lording it over you'?"

"Well, she's always saying things about French civilization just like it was better than American. She even claims we got a lot of ideas for our constitution from the French. Our French maid speaks English but she knows a lot of French. Sometimes she helps me with my homework. But she doesn't put on airs like Mademoiselle Bernard."

"Sharon, the French teachers in our school have exactly the same status as American teachers. They don't work for us like servants; they are a great addition to our language program. We're lucky to have them. If you review your American history you will find we borrowed ideas from France and from many other countries."

"If the French are such hot stuff why do we have to give them money and come over to France when we hate it just to pull them out of a hole? Mother says they're still living in the middle ages. It makes me mad to have somebody like that trying to push us American kids around."

Bill removed Sharon from French class for the rest of the year and notified her mother. Mrs. Breen came into his office the next morning. She greeted Maria with a curt "Good Morning. Is Mr. Helmer in?"

"Good morning, I will…"

Before Maria could finish the visitor strode over and opened the door to the principal's office.

"I'm Sharon Breen's mother and I'm very upset about her French class," she announced.

Startled, Bill rose to his feet.

"Kindly be seated, Mrs. Breen. I'm glad you came in. Did you get my note last week?"

"Yes. Sharon has been terribly unhappy about leaving her school in the States to come over here. Of course she wants to get into a good college and she needs a foreign language."

"She has time to finish her language requirements. I am much more concerned about her attitude right now."

"What attitude would you expect her to have? This French woman obviously doesn't know how to handle American children."

"Miss Bernard is an excellent teacher. This is the first time she has had any serious discipline problems with a student."

"That's not what Sharon tells me. And what about her language requirements for college, Mr. Helmer?"

"She can complete second year French next year. Perhaps she will be mature enough to behave in class and profit from studying with a native teacher."

"Mature." Mrs. Breen pulled her chair forward and faced Bill across the desk. "Mature. What about the attitude of that teacher? Maybe she needs to develop a more mature attitude. And I question your authority to take Sharon out of a required subject."

"French is an elective subject. It's a special privilege we offer our students, to study with a native teacher in the country where the language is spoken. But it is not a one-way affair. Students must cooperate or they lose all the benefits."

"Just because that woman can't handle American children Sharon has to be a victim. What qualifications does Miss Bernard have to teach our children? Has she taught Americans before?"

"No. She has a *licence* in French and English from the *Sorbonne,* which is like our M.A. degree. She has taught in England. She is well qualified."

"I'd like to see her qualifications. Can I look at her teaching certificates?"

"No, Mrs. Breen. The teachers' files contain recommendations, ratings from supervisors and other confidential information. They are not available to the public or even to other teachers."

"Who can authorize me to see them? I am not convinced that this woman is qualified to teach my child. As a parent I have a right to know."

"Headquarters of dependents' schools would have to authorize it."

"Where is that? Who is your superior officer?"

"You'll have to see Mr. Carlson, school inspector. My secretary will give you the telephone number and address if you wish."

"Well, I'll tell you frankly, Mr. Helmer, that I'm hopping mad. I can understand your wish to support your teachers but you're carrying it too far in allowing this French woman to make my daughter unhappy."

"I'm sorry you feel that way. We try to encourage a better attitude toward France on the part of our students."

"What do you expect the children to think when everybody can see how backward these people are."

"Just a minute, Mrs..."

"You should see the toilets in our apartment building. They don't know how to build a decent bathroom nor do they know how to keep it clean. Smart American children can see what a mess this country is."

"Mrs. Breen, we try to help our students open their minds to understanding people who have different ways. I don't encourage that kind of criticism in our school."

"With all the help we are giving the French I would expect them to show a little more gratitude for our efforts. They might be able to learn something from us."

"Mrs. Breen." Bill leaned across his desk. "I would urge you to think a bit more about the opportunities your daughter has here to study another culture."

"I still want to see if that woman is really qualified to teach American children. I'll do whatever is necessary. I have friends in Washington. No French woman is going to push my child around."

"I am sorry you feel that way. Mrs. Stepanovic will give you the information you need to contact Dependents School Headquarters in Germany."

"I think the P.T.A. will be interested in this, too. I believe all of us parents have an interest in school policy."

"I will be happy to discuss this with the P.T.A. Any time you have further concerns about Sharon's studies I am at your service."

She stormed out of the office stopping only to get the address of Dependents School Headquarters from the secretary.

Chapter 16

Classroom doors swung open and the long corridors came to life as students streamed out that Friday, freedom bound for the weekend.

"Hey, Joe, I'm hungry. Let's go down to the PX."

"Why not join us at the Embassy Snack Bar? Their milk shakes aren't bad."

"Have you heard of *la Cave Noire*? They have a terrific strip tease there tonight."

"Any age limit?"

"You kidding? If you're tall enough to reach your money up to the window you can get a ticket. You coming, Walt?"

"Say, Max, where do you sell your cigarettes?"

"I haven't got a ration card."

"You sixteen?"

"Yeah."

"Well then, if you get your old man to sign a paper, you gotta a card. They're giving five hundred francs a carton in the black market down on *la rue des Rosiers*."

"You coming, Tony? We're going to Pigalle."

"I already said I'd come. But I gotta be careful about money. Dad's counting the francs lately."

"It won't cost that much. We can all chip in on a couple bottles of wine. Got a date?"

"Not yet. Hey, Kay," Tony called down the hall. "You got a date tonight?"

"No." She was taking a violin case from her locker.

Tony came up and leaned his arm against the locker.

"Want to come with me tonight? Jack's got his dad's car. The gang is going to this night club in *Pigalle*. A real cool place, floor show, dancing and everything."

"Oh, I'd like to go but my folks would never let me. They're away this weekend and I'm going to stay with Martha."

"For cripes sake. Don't you ever go out anyplace?"

'Not on dates. My folks let me stay at Martha's house sometimes."

"You got a key to your place?"

"Of course."

"Well, you could just stay there and let them think you were at Martha's place."

"That would be a lie. My father would call it a sin."

"Cripes. Are you kidding? Don't you ever tell lies?"

"I never have." she said. "I'd be afraid to."

"Are you on the level?"

"Cripes," he said searching for words to express his feelings. "Look, Kay, I would really like to have you go with me. Why can't you just go over to Martha's place first and then come with me. You can honestly say later that you were at Martha's. That would be true and do no harm to nobody."

"Wait a minute. I'll go over and check with Martha."

Tony tossed his books into his locker, slammed the door and snapped the padlock.

"It's O.K.," she said when she came back. Martha will be home tonight so I'll go over there after dinner."

"Why bother going over there at all? We can pick you up around the corner from your house."

"Oh, but that would be such a big lie. I couldn't do that."

"You're just too goody good."

"Tony, if you talk like that I won't go with you. That's not nice."

"Look, Kay, I'm sorry. I do want you to go with me or I wouldn't have asked. Will you be there?"

"It doesn't seem like the right thing to do." She put the violin case under her arm. "But I've never been to a night club."

"You'll really get a bang out of it but don't be late. Jack gets sore if he has to wait for anybody."

Tony would have cut out his tongue sooner than admit that he'd never been to a night club either.

The club wasn't exactly at *Pigalle*. It was upon the *Butte de Montmartre* but Jack parked the car at *Place Blanche* and they walked around a little before climbing the narrow street to the club. Kay had never seen such crowded streets and such a strange assortment of people. She stared at a girl standing in a doorway. She had the tightest skirt Kay had ever seen and it was split up one side almost to the waist. She was wearing too much lipstick and her blouse was half open, the edges pulled tight across her breasts.

"Look at that girl," Kay poked Tony. "I wonder what she's doing?"

"That's a street walker," Jack broke in, "a hustling broad. In French they call them *filles de joie.*"

"Oh." Kay looked puzzled.

"Lay off, Jack. This kid's really innocent." Tony said. He turned to Kay, "She is a prostitute," he told her.

"It's a little early for the club. Look at that broken down bistro over there." Jack pointed. "Let's go have a drink just for kicks."

An unwashed front window did not admit much light into the little café. Bare electric bulbs lighted four or five men in blue work clothes standing at the bar. Against the opposite wall the tables were empty .

The men stopped talking to stare at the young Americans as they came in. There were no other women customers in the place and the strange atmosphere made Kay nervous. When she saw a cardboard sign on the wall near their table with the inscription *"Américains en Amérique"* she was scared.

"Let's get out of here."

"Why?"

'See that sign."

"Listen, these Commies don't scare me." Jack pulled out chairs for the girls. "This is a public place, isn't it? Patron," he called out.

The man came to their table. Jack did the talking. Kay was surprised that he spoke such fluent French.

"May we see your wine list?"

"I have no wine list. I can give you a good Beaujolais, vin ordinaire or an apéritif."

"What kind of bistro is this? You have no good French wine?"

"I have good wine but no wine list."

"What about some good vintage wine?"

"Monsieur, I have no vintage wine."

"Right here in France, the country of great wines, and you have no vintage wine."

Kay was frightened. She saw the old man straighten his shoulders and a strange expression come into his eyes.

"You have made a mistake. There is vintage wine and champagne in the clubs near here. That is where you should go."

As he turned to walk away Jack called out to him, "Hey, aren't you going to serve us?"

"*Non, monsieur.* You are perhaps too young to drink in a bistro. If you want something go to *une boîte de nuit.* They will take your money."

"This is a public establishment. You can't refuse to serve us."

"I prefer not to serve you. Now go or I will call the police."

Jack jumped up but before he could say anything Kay tugged at Tony, "Please, let's go before there's trouble."

"Yeah. Come on, Jack. We don't want to stay in this joint anyway."

"*Patron*, your bistro does not please me," Jack answered in a loud voice as he walked over to the sign that said *"Américains en Amérique"*. He reached up and ripped it from the wall.

Before the others realized what had happened two young Frenchmen at the bar had seized Jack by an arm and escorted him to the door. He spread his legs wide apart and resisted their efforts to put him out but the two husky workmen spun him half around and shoved him onto the sidewalk. They stood there blocking the entrance.

"I'm an American citizen. You got no right to lay your hands on me." Jack started toward them.

One of the men whistled and waved at a passing M.P. Jeep. The driver swung sharply to the curb directly in front of the bistro. A colored private walked up. The Frenchmen repeated *"Américain"*, gesturing toward Jack.

"Is your father with the military?" the M.P. asked.

"None of your business. I'm a civilian. Now buzz off."

"Are these kids with you?"

The two Frenchmen moved out of the door so the others could come out.

"You kids are from the Army?"

"Yes," Kay replied.

"Let's see your I.D. cards."

A curious crowd had gathered around them.

"Go peddle your papers."

Another M.P. walked up swinging his club.

"You can show us your I.D. cards or we'll take you down to headquarters and call your parents. Which will it be?"

Jack jerked his wallet from his pocket and held out his card.

"Look, Mac, my old man's a General and if you get tough with me he'll bust your ass back to buck private and ship you home to Alabama."

The two soldiers studied the card and looked at each other. Then one of them took it over to the sergeant sitting in the Jeep.

Kay overheard some of their conversation.

"Must be General Brewster with the Special Mission group. Better let them go."

"I suggest you all get out of this part of town or you may get a lot more trouble." He handed the card back to Jack.

Kay had already started walking away and Tony followed her. She was sick with shame remembering the face of the old Frenchman in the bistro. She wanted to go back and tell him she was sorry but she was afraid.

"No need to panic," Jack said when he caught up with them. "I knew they wouldn't do anything."

The nightclub was so jammed that you couldn't lean back without touching the person behind you. The smoke made Kay's eyes smart and the orchestra was too loud. She watched a couple at the next table. The girl was young, not much older than Kay, and the man looked about the same age as her father. His bald head gleamed as he bent over resting his chin on the girl's bare shoulder, staring down at the top of her evening dress.

"This sure isn't the Lido. I was there last week. Do they have a cool floorshow!"

"This is a real rat's nest. We got better clubs in Spokane, Washington."

Kay was thinking about the lies she had told. She started counting and was dismayed. She had told three, one to her folks and two at Martha's house. She could remember her father's words, "Deliver me, O Lord, from lying lips, from a deceitful tongue."

"Have you heard the story about the old maid and the cat?" Jack was asking.

Kay had always abhorred dirty jokes partly because she believed that they were sinful and partly because she felt so stupid. She tried not to listen.

"Well," Jack began, "this old maid was very old. She had always been good to people and everybody liked her. One day when she was sitting on her front porch a good fairy came…"

"Since when have fairies liked old ladies?"

"Shut up," Jack said. "This is my story. As I was saying before I was so rudely interrupted, a good fairy came to her and told the little old lady that since she had always been so good she could have any three wishes she could think of and they would be granted. But she could have only three, no more. Well, the old lady thought for a long time and then she said, 'I wish I could be young and beautiful'…Presto! She was once again a young and beautiful girl."

"Then the good fairy asked for her next wish, reminding her that she had only two left. The little old lady who was now young and beautiful thought a long time and finally said, 'I would like to have a lot of money'…Presto! There was a pile of gold coins beside her. Then the good fairy told her to think hard about the next wish because it would be her last one. She could never have another wish granted or change it if she made a mistake. She had to be…"

"Come on, Tony," Kay was watching the musicians getting ready to play again. "Let's dance."

"Just wait a jiff. I want to hear the story."

"…And the little old lady who was now young and beautiful and rich thought for a long time. Then she noticed her old tomcat on the front porch. She said to the good fairy, 'That old tomcat has been a good faithful friend for many years. I wish he could be changed into a tall, handsome young man,'...Presto! There he was...a tall, handsome young man standing there smiling at her." Jack paused for a drink of wine.

"Come on, Tony. Let's dance."

"Wait a sec."

"The handsome young man gazed at her for a long time, then came over, put his arm around her and kissed her. He looked deep into her eyes and said, 'Now aren't you sorry you had me castrated?'"

"This is a neat joint." Tony held Kay tight as they danced. "You having fun?"

"Not really," she said.

"For cripes sake, what's eating you?"

"I don't care for dirty stories," she said. "This place gives me the creeps. It's so...so sordid."

"Oh, don't be a goopy square. Drink some wine and you'll feel better."

"Oh, I couldn't do that. I've already lied and now if I drink wine that would be...well, just awful."

But she did drink some wine. It was quite good, she decided, like fruit juice really, but not sweet. The first glass she had ever drunk made her feel better, Jack stopped telling stories and they listened to the orchestra which made her feel more at ease. The floorshow was extraordinary, especially the acrobatic dancer. She couldn't always understand the master of ceremonies who told some stories that made everybody laugh. None of them could follow his French but they laughed heartily and applauded with the crowd. They didn't want to be taken for dumb tourists.

When they left about midnight Kay decided she had never had such a fine time. They piled into Jack's car and he gunned the motor out into a stream of traffic headed for la *Place Clichy*.

"Careful, Jack, or you'll get a ticket."

"I have C.D. plates, man."

"What does that mean?" Kay asked.

"It means Corps Diplomatic. Most foreign government people have them."

Tony and Kay were in the back seat with the other couple. Tony felt a pleasant warmth in his stomach. Anne and her date were wrapped together in their corner. Tony put his arm around Kay and pulled her close. She turned her head away but let him hold her cheek to cheek.

"Here we are at your place, Kay." Jack pulled in to the curb.

"It's only two streets away. Let's get out here." Tony held the door for Kay, who looked at him in confusion.

"Why don't we go into your place for a little while."

"Gee, that doesn't seem right." Kay fumbled in her handbag for the key.

As they sat close together on the sofa Kay was feeling the two full glasses of wine she had drunk, a pleasant sort of dizziness.

When Tony kissed her she awkwardly held her mouth partly open and pulled away a little.

"What's wrong?"

"I never kissed a boy before."

"Cripes."

"You must think I'm stupid."

"I think you are great, Kay. When you play the violin you are really beautiful."

Nobody had ever told Kay that she was beautiful.

She gave Tony a full, wet kiss and held him tight. He pulled her gently over on the davenport.

"We shouldn't be doing this, Tony."

"Cripes, it's okay, not like I didn't love you. I really do, Kay."

Contact with Tony as he unbuttoned her blouse and the touch of his hand on her breast evoked in Kay a lightness of being, a sensation even more exhilarating than her first reaction to wine.

In the grip of an unprecedented excitement Tony embraced Kay, kissing her while gently stroking her body.

She pulled him onto her in a firm embrace.

"This is like a dream." Kay closed her eyes.

Chapter 17

Kenneth Clarence Wilson, pianist, director of Ken Wilson's Rhythm Trio, was whistling a calypso tune as he strode along *le Boulevard Saint-Michel*. He had just ended three months of unemployment by signing a contract for his Trio at a nightclub in *Montmartre*. Turning into *la rue des Ecoles* he was hurrying to his hotel where he could telephone the boys.

He went up to the desk and called out a *Salut* to the clerk.

"*Bon soir, Monsieur Wilson*." The young man continued to leaf through a stack of papers.

Ken watched him for a moment. "My key, please."

"Sorry, Monsieur Wilson, the patron told me not to give you your key."

"What? When did he say that?"

"This afternoon. He said you do not pay your rent."

"*Zut*. Where is he? *Patron*."

A man came out of the back office.

"*Je suis désolé*, Monsieur Wilson. Since two months you are not paying for your room. I took away your things. To have them you must pay your rent."

"I've lived in this hotel for three years. THREE YEARS, *monsieur*. And I always paid my rent. Today I found work. I can pay you next week."

"You tell me this before. You are here a long time but you are paying no rent for two months, Monsieur Wilson. EIGHT WEEKS with no rent. My clients must pay me. I am not *l'Armée du Salut*."

Ken lowered his voice. "I need my key to get into my room. I cannot work without my clothes and my music."

"They are no longer in the room. I must keep them until you pay me."

Ken had a vision of his sheets of music for the Trio, his clothes and most important of all, his concerto being tossed into a clothes closet.

"You have no right to touch my things. Some of them are valuable. I want an inventory. I'll call the police."

"Telephone the police from here if you wish."

"Look," Ken said softly, "I cannot work without my suit and my music. I do have a job for next week *l'Oiseau Bleu* in *Montmartre* and then I will be happy to settle my bill. If, however, you keep my music and my evening clothes I can never pay you."

The patron hesitated a moment. "*Monsieur Wilson*, you may take your music and one suit. Nothing more."

"Kindly give me the key then."

"I will go with you, my wife also."

His wife shuffled out into the lobby avoiding Ken's eyes. She is not so hard-hearted as her husband, Ken thought, cursing his luck. If he had come when she was alone maybe she would have let him take everything.

The three of them mounted the stairway to the third floor where the *patron* unlocked the door of a small closet and turned on the light. There on two shelves were Ken's belongings. The patron allowed him to retrieve his toilet kit, a pile of sheet music and his tux. Ken started rummaging around for some letters but the man stepped in front of him.

"The other things when you pay me."

"I need my personal letters. There's one from my mother who will be worried."

"She must remain worried, Monsieur Wilson."

Thankful at least that it was not raining, Ken walked along the street with his tux over one arm and his music under the other. He slipped into Dupont's on the corner of *le boulevard Saint-Michel*. He was bundling up the music, securing it with the suspenders from his tux when the waiter approached with his cognac. This he tipped into his coffee and sipped slowly the warmth invading his being. He lighted a cigarette.

He sat with closed eyes trying to organize his thoughts. It would be at least a week before the new job paid off. He hesitated to put the other boys on the spot by trying to move in with them. They hadn't paid their rent either. He looked out into the dusk of a gray November afternoon, watching people hurrying by. They all seemed to have someplace to go.

Ken paid his check and stepped out onto the sidewalk. The Latin Quarter was in the throes of its six o'clock effort to disgorge the particles of humanity flowing through it toward the precious cubic meters of space they called home. But Ken was in no hurry. He stopped to look at the man huddled against the grill of the park *Cluny. Clochards* sleeping on sidewalks were a common part of the Paris scene, but for the first time Ken watched with a special interest as the man mumbled in his sleep and arched his back away from the iron grill. Maybe a retired musician, Ken thought, as he wandered along the street looking into shop windows. Ken halted before a restaurant and studied the menu: *Prix fixe: 450 francs, vin, service, non-compris.* He pulled out his wallet and placed the coins in his open palm. Four-hundred and six francs. Slipping the money into his pocket he continued down the street humming. "If I never had a dime, I'd be rich as Rockefeller. Just direct your feet..." He resolved to spend his last *sou* for dinner. He could decide on a full stomach what he was going to do for the night. He turned into *la rue de la Harpe* and went directly to *Les Balkans.*

Ken hung the tux on a hook under his topcoat and squeezed past the people to a place in the corner. He slipped his package of music under the chair and picked up a menu. The room was warm and smelled of frying onions. Watching the crowd, he made no attempt to get the waiter's attention. Finally the man came to take his order.

"*Et vous, monsieur?*"

"*Oeuf dur mayonnaise.*"

"*Ensuite?*"

"*Biftec, à point,*" Ken said, "*et un quart de rouge.*"

As he ate he tried to get some perspective on his present problem. Three years is a long time and he had grown rather fond of his shabby hotel room. It was the hub of a new universe he discovered in Paris when he had come as a G.I. student. Back in the United States he was just another colored boy who played piano. Here he was a man free to dream of a future as a composer. He was sure his concerto would…

"Hello, Ken. What are you doing here?"

Startled, Ken looked up. It took an instant to recognize the face leaning over the table across from him.

"Bill," he said, "Bill Helmer."

"I thought artists hung out at *Saint Germain des Près*."

"Not the poor ones. Tourists have pushed the prices up and the artists out. What are you doing, Bill, slumming? I thought rich Americans never came into this section."

"I like this restaurant so I brought Colette—oh, excuse me. Mademoiselle Bernard, may I present Kenneth Wilson."

"We already have something in common." Colette shook his hand. "We both dislike *Saint Germain des Prés*."

"Maybe we aren't the type. I could never learn to smoke a pipe. Do you smoke one?"

Colette laughed. "No but I have a black roll-neck sweater."

"Let's sit down." Bill pulled out a chair for Colette. "Ken and I came to Paris about the same time. We both had some G.I. Bill left and decided to study here."

"You also studied at the Sorbonne, Ken?"

"No. Bill was the scholar. I studied music."

"At the *conservatoire*?"

"Yes. I learned a lot but didn't win any prizes."

'I studied there, too. And I also won no prizes."

"We'll compare notes sometime."

"Blue notes of course." Bill waited for an appropriate groan.

"I haven't seen you for months, Bill. Still at the school?"

"Yes. I'm afraid so. Still at the same hotel, Ken?"

"That's a sad story. To tell it properly I'll need a musical background, a violin, say, playing Rubenstein's Melody in F."

"What happened?"

"The patron of my hotel and I just couldn't get along. He insisted I pay my rent when I have been out of work and find myself *sans sous*. As of two hours ago I am homeless."

"I have an extra bedroom in my apartment, "Bill said. "Stay with me for a while."

"Give me a decent interval of time, say one second, to consider before I accept."

After dinner Bill and Colette were going to a café to see some Flamenco. Ken declined their invitation to go along, preferring to occupy his new living quarters immediately.

"There's cold beer in the refrigerator." Bill handed him the key.

Ken walked along the quay toward the *Ile Saint-Louis,* watching the lights of *Châtelet* reflected in the river and whistling a few bars from his concerto. First thing he'd phone the boys in the Trio about their new job.

Chapter 18

One December day a lady hurried along *la rue Gabriel* toward the United States Embassy. Inside the entrance gate a Marine guard examined her passport and waved her toward to the main lobby. From her handbag she fished out her restaurant card and flashed it at the guard. He nodded her in.

For a moment she stood looking around the dining room. Only a few tables were occupied and she chose a place in the far corner. The waitress appeared almost immediately.

"I'll order later. I am waiting for someone."

The waitress appeared not to understand and she stood hesitantly by the table.

"For heaven's sake." Mrs. Breen looked up and stopped short as the blood drained from her face. There was a familiarity about that face—the wide-set eyes, strong chin and snub nose. The waitress bore a striking resemblance to Paulette.

The unexpected confrontation destroyed her poise and she stared at the girl with hostility.

"I told you I will order later."

Mrs. Breen watched as the girl walked slowly toward the kitchen. She did not seem to have Paulette's walk, a kind of gliding movement with plenty of swing. Paulette's manner, Mrs. Breen reflected, was as phony as everything else about her.

From the very first Charlotte Breen had been dead set against a tour of duty in France, deserting the best stateside assignment they had ever had. Daughter Sharon was a member of the Golden Circle Club in her freshman year and she liked her teachers. But Edwin unexpectedly made the decision to go overseas. Starting as a West Point graduate, Colonel Edwin Breen at age fifty-seven saw overseas service as his last chance to retire with the rank of General.

When Paulette appeared out of their new Paris neighborhood in Neuilly offering her services as a French tutor to Sharon it had seemed a sensible idea. And Mrs. Breen even encouraged Edwin to take private lessons supplementing his French classes at SHAPE. She trembled at the thought.

With relentless compulsion Mrs. Breen's memory led her back through well-worn paths of mortification.

Sharon had become sick to her stomach the minute they were seated at the Opera. They left immediately and arrived home to find Edwin and Paulette—in the living room of all places—no chance to protect Sharon from seeing the unbuttoned confusion of her father and the disarray of the tousled French whore whom she had looked upon as a teacher…

A voice interrupted her thoughts.

"Good afternoon, Ma'am."

She looked up with a start.

"Captain Murphy." She reached out to shake his hand. "How nice of you to come. Please sit down."

"Thank you, Mrs. Breen."

She beckoned the waitress and ordered ice cream and coffee. Murphy asked for a beer.

"I have been wanting to tell you, Captain, how much I appreciate your work at school."

"Thank you, Ma'am." Colonel Breen was on the Promotion Board. If he played his cards right, Murphy figured, this could be a real break.

"Captain, I know you have a heavy schedule. So we might as well get down to business. Did you get the information we were discussing when I suggested this meeting?"

"Yes, Ma'am."

"By the way, Chaplain Selner just might drop by for a minute this afternoon. He was interested."

"Fine. I have written down some things and Sergeant Wicker—he's the supply sergeant at school—gave me several things he knows about." Murphy pulled a file of papers from his pocket.

"There he is now. Yoo hoo, Chaplain Selner. Here we are."

"Ah, Mrs. Breen. How are you, Captain Murphy?"

"I think I told you, Chaplain, that Captain Murphy has been doing a fine job at the high school. He is concerned about improving things and he is anxious to cooperate with the P.T.A. in helping us to plan."

"Good for you, Captain. We all have a responsibility for our American children overseas."

Mrs. Breen was studying the papers Murphy had given her.

"This is interesting. Would you be kind enough to go over these for Chaplain Selner and me?"

The two of them pulled their chairs around the table on each side of Murphy.

"This is an I.R.S. I sent the Principal last month. He went to the Old Man and cried on his shoulder so nothing happened. No action has been taken to correct these things. If anything they are worse now."

"Shocking."

"Wicker and I poked through a few lockers last week and looked at the textbooks. Some of them are marked up, pages torn out and pencil marks on them. Most of these books cost seven or eight dollars."

"And nothing is being done about it?"

"I don't see Helmer doing anything about discipline. He runs around having teachers' meetings and setting up special classes. But he sure as hell—excuse me, Ma'am—he never gets on to the teachers."

"The children are wild?"

"The whole building is a mess. The toilets aren't policed..." Murphy looked at another piece of paper. "There are no American flags in some of the classrooms. There's a regulation about that. School assemblies never start with a flag salute. I don't know if there's a regulation about that but we always did it when I was in school. We're all Americans, by God, and Helmer acts like he wasn't proud of it."

"You may have something there, Captain. And Mr. Helmer doesn't seem to think American girls are good enough for him."

"I've heard he squires Miss Bernard around a lot."

"That woman's a disgrace. Mr. Helmer backed her up when she mistreated Sharon. He hasn't heard the last of that yet. I'll fight like a tiger when it comes to protecting my daughter. Is there anything wrong with that, Chaplain?"

"I wish more of our mothers had such a desire to give their children love and protection, Mrs. Breen."

"Well, I propose to do something about this."

They sat silently a few moments before Mrs. Breen spoke again.

"Captain Murphy, as an officer assigned to the school you should not be asked to take an active part in our plans. But you can help us with information like this. I really don't know about your position, Chaplain."

"I agree with you that Captain Murphy must be careful. I feel no such restriction in my case. I am free to do the work of Christ as I see fit."

"Good. I have talked with several people in the P.T.A. and I know we have support. If we can elect our own officers for next year I have some ideas."

"You can count on me to help," the chaplain said.

"Incidentally, who is really Mr. Helmer's commanding officer? How did he get assigned and by whom?"

Murphy answered. "By Dependents School Group in Germany. The school part has a civilian director but the real boss is a full colonel commanding the military group and responsible to the Commanding General."

"I happen to have some information on that." Chaplain Selner leaned forward and lowered his voice. "The Chief Chaplain for the European Command has his office in the same building as the school people. He tells me that Mr. Helmer is not too popular with the civilian directors up on the Rhine River at Wiesbaden. He hasn't returned some survey questions about religious studies that they sent him."

"We can start working on the P.T.A. election right away."

"How about a mail ballot?"

"Why, Chaplain?"

"Mr. Helmer will be at the meeting and probably Colonel Carpenter. That might influence some people. We can certainly get more votes for our side by mail."

"Maybe we have to vote at the meeting."

"No. I checked the constitution."

"Well then, how do we get rid of him?"

"I know it is difficult to get people fired from a civil service position."

"How about replacing him with Mr. Evans? He does not appear to be a trouble maker."

Murphy shook his head. "I don't know. He seems to go along with Helmer on most things."

"He has always been polite with me. He probably doesn't run around with a French woman anyway," Mrs. Breen remarked.

Chaplain Selner spoke up. "Somebody said his father was a Baptist minister."

"What would happen if we, the P.T.A. Executive Council that is, recommend that school headquarters transfer Mr. Helmer from Paris?"

"Yes, it may be wise to suggest a transfer. Would we do that directly or through a commanding officer?" Chaplain Selner wanted to be careful about channels.

"Look," Murphy said, "if this gets into military channels I could really get burned. In fact, I better not even know about it."

"It is important that you be protected, Captain." Chaplain Selner looked at Mrs. Breen and she nodded.

"I don't really like this business but I don't know what else to do," Murphy said. "I have a military inspection every month and I always get chewed. Nobody ever inspects Helmer. It's not fair."

"You have legitimate reason to complain, Captain."

"This may be out-of-school tales but I know some of the teachers aren't too happy with Mr. Helmer." Mrs. Breen looked from one to the other.

"Is that so, Captain?" Mrs. Breen made a mental note. "I don't think he has many friends on the council except Mrs. Callahan. Mr. Helmer is thick as thieves with the Callahans."

Colonel Callahan swung a lot of weight in the command. Mike Murphy made a mental note of that.

"Captain Murphy, what you said about the flag salute interests me. Mr. Helmer is so impressed with the French that he might not be a very loyal American. Have you thought of that?"

"Yes, I have." Murphy stared thoughtfully at the papers on the table. "He has invited these kids from a French school coming every week for some kind of a club meeting. How do we know they aren't communists?"

"How about the woman?"

"What do you mean, Ma'am?"

"Do French teachers have a security check?"

"They're supposed to…Sa-a-a-y, that's an idea. I might look into that. I got a friend in security."

"Now," said Mrs. Breen. "I think we are getting somewhere. Captain, we should look into this unAmerican angle."

"If we can get the Old Man on Helmer's back he might…." Murphy hesitated. "Say, look at that."

They turned to watch Bill Helmer and Mademoiselle Bernard walk through the door and sit down at a table across the room. Bill had brought Colette for the express purpose of introducing her to a great American institution, the banana split. She had heard her students speak about it and was curious. When their order came she stared at the three great scoops of ice cream hidden by strawberry and pineapple sauce then covered with a dollop of whipped cream. She took a deep breath and picked up the small spoon.

Her observers watched her push back the dish after a few nibbles.

"I'll bet he doesn't bring all of his teachers down here to the Embassy."

Mrs. Breen rose to leave. "Let's keep in close touch then."

Chapter 19

December rain alternating with freezing temperatures turned the streets of Paris into skidways and deposited fringes of ice along the river's edge. Even the sparkle of Christmas scenes in *les grands magasins* could scarcely dispel the gloom.

"This is a terrible time at school," Bill remarked to Ken one night in the kitchen.

"With Christmas coming up how can that be?"

"We have no basketball games during the holidays. That worries Coach Parsons. Murphy has managed to date Irene Young, my best homeroom teacher. That worries me. Morale is low enough as it is."

"You could have a Noël celebration for the teachers."

"Have them dance around a tree in the auditorium?"

Ken laughed in his deep bass voice. "I was thinking of something here in the apartment."

"Oh ho."

"A party might cheer up the school marms. I can invite some of the gang from the club to bring their instruments. We could have a real ball."

"Pregnant idea, Ken. Let's see." Bill scanned the calendar. "We could set it for a week from Friday. Would some of them be free?"

Ken clapped his hands. "I think so. I will take care of refreshments. Better buy the liquor at the PX. After all, we want to work up a bit of Christmas spirit."

The night of the party Bill answered the doorbell about seven thirty, before he and Ken were prepared for guests. A tall black man and a slender blonde woman in the doorway looked surprised to see him.

"Hello. Is Ken here?"

Ken appeared and ushered them inside.

"Bill, this is Mr. and Mrs. Cooper, Marguerite and Larry."

"Hi." Bill shook hands. "Welcome."

"Larry plays the hottest trumpet this side of the Atlantic."

"You with the band here?"

"No. The only thing I get paid for blowing is an automobile horn. I'm a corporal in the Army Motor Pool."

"Well, come on into the kitchen and we can start the evening."

While sipping, Marguerite was studying Bill.

"Marguerite is a bit nervous with Americans." Ken put his arm around her. "Bill is okay, Marguerite. He's especially scared of pugnacious women."

"What is that?"

"That's what you are, honey." Larry laughed.

She smiled and clinked glasses with him.

Colette arrived early. Bill steered her into the kitchen where they were setting up the bar.

"Colette, I want you…"

"Marguerite!"

"Colette Bernard."

The girls embraced warmly talking at the same time.

"The last time I saw you was when?"

"Almost two years ago. I thought you were in England. Sorry I didn't send you a birth announcement "

Colette turned to Bill. "Marguerite and I were friends at the university. What's this about a birth announcement?"

"Colette, this is my husband Larry."

She started to shake hands then gave him a hug.

"You are a lucky man, Larry, and a new father already."

"I appointed myself hostess for the evening," Marguerite told Colette. "Come on and help me. We'll move the gentlemen out."

As the guests came through the door and spread out in the double living rooms overlooking the Seine, the apartment appeared smaller and smaller. Madame François and her husband had agreed to help until midnight. They chased the girls out of the kitchen.

The party was well under way when Bill answered the bell to find Irene Young at the door accompanied by Captain Michael Murphy, resplendent in his dress uniform.

Bill saluted smartly. "Enter, Captain, with your fine lady."

"Good evening, sir."

Murphy glanced over at Larry. "Well, hello there, Corporal."

By eleven thirty they had settled into small clusters laughing, drinking and talking.

'You an artist?"

"I paint."

"Do you know a Yugoslavian artist named Zizi?"

"Zizi? Is he abstract?"

"She's a girl."

"Sorry. Never heard of her."

"Who is this Monsieur Helmer? He must be wealthy".

"Ken said he was director of an American School."

"You are joking. Look at his furniture and his collection of discs. He must have a wealthy wife."

"Zizi? Sorry. Don't know her."

A woman sitting on a hassock smiled at Ken as he passed. He stopped to greet her.

"I'm afraid I have forgotten your name, Madame."

"I'm Irene Young."

"Are you having a good time?"

"Oh, yes."

"Can I get you something?"

"Yes, please. Would you mind passing me some of those... those...

"Brazil nuts?"

"Thanks. Is that what you call them?"

Ken laughed. "We called them Nigger Toes,"

"So do I." They both laughed.

"I'm looking for an artist, a painter called Zizi."

"Sounds like a foreigner. Afraid not."

In a corner Hal and Henry Jackson were holding glasses and leaning against each other.

"Listen, Evans, I read Veblen in college. That's old stuff."

"I don't care if you read him in your mother's womb. Just listen and stick to the argument."

Ken came up beside Bill. "We better keep an eye on those two."

A few minutes later Ken led the pair over to the piano and Bill heard them swing into action.

Hal clapped Jackson on the back. "Let's sing some good old Baptist hymns."

Stone sober, Hal was an indifferent piano player and now his enthusiasm outpaced his talent creating a gap he closed by sheer volume. He and Jackson belted out "The Old Rugged Cross" and windows vibrated.

"Well, I guess that's better than a fist fight."

Bill moved over to Colette.

"Good God, we're making a lot of noise. The neighbors will probably be calling the cops."

"You did not tell your concierge about the party?"

"Why should I?"

"Everybody in Paris has the right to one all-night party each year in addition to some other holidays."

"What a great idea."

"But your concierge must know so he can inform the *commissariat de police* in your district."

"What wonderfully practical people the French are. But will I go to the guillotine?"

Colette laughed. "The police would not say much anyway. Americans are privileged people."

"I thought you were less suspicious of Americans by now."

"I try," she said. "You are very American tonight, you know. It is amusing to see you at this party with your fellow citizens."

"What do you mean by that?"

"Well, you are all just like teenage boys."

"I suppose you find us less sophisticated than the mature European male."

"Don't be angry." She smiled at him. "I like you that way, with enthusiasm and eager to have a good time."

"How are we like boys?"

"The way you drink and sing. You do not drink to enjoy the taste. You do it to keep up with one another. Did you see Mr. Evans and Mr. Jackson? I never saw anybody drink so rapidly. And it is whiskey."

"Look, I don't like…oh, oh, there's the doorbell."

He went to the door half expecting to see his second floor neighbor who had complained once before about the noise. But the slender Frenchman standing there was a stranger, although he looked vaguely familiar.

"Bon soir, monsieur. Is Mademoiselle Bernard here?"

"You must be a friend of Colette. Come on in."

As Bill led him in and pointed out Colette, he saw Ken signaling to him from afar. After helping him sweep up broken glass from an unsuccessful juggling trick with a tray of wine glasses he went in search of Colette.

Somehow Bill had an uneasy feeling. By this time in the morning his thoughts did not focus readily, but finally he realized. The last arrival was Jean, that fellow in the picture on Colette's piano. By the time he found them Jean was in action.

The end of the room became quiet where people clustered around Jean and Jackson engaged in loud argument. Murphy, standing close by, frowned.

Jackson's face was red. "Where in the hell would France be if we hadn't bailed you out of two World Wars?"

"You were fighting for us, monsieur?"

"You're damned right we were. We got no territory or colonies out of either war. We were fighting for democracy and for your freedom, not ours."

"It was my understanding that you fought because Japan attacked you in the Pacific, just as Russia fought when she was attacked."

"Where would your economy be if we weren't spending money here?"

"Knock it off, Henry." Bill stepped up. "This is a Christmas party, remember?"

"Come on, Jean. Let's go." Colette pulled at his arm.

"Bill, are you letting him get away with this? I'm leaving anyway." Jackson slammed his glass down on the piano and walked unevenly out of the room..

"Jean, please. Let us go."

'Will you come with me?"

"Yes."

She pulled him to the door, pausing for a quick word with Bill.

"I am sorry. I did not ask him here. I hardly know what to say. See you tomorrow. Goodnight, Bill."

A moment later Jean reappeared in the hallway and walked over to Bill.

"I apologize about your friend." Smiling he extended his hand, "Thank you, monsieur."

"You're welcome." The reply was automatic. "Jackson was out of line."

After Colette left Bill found the party less exciting. He tried to calm the tension of Jackson's exit by talking briefly with each guest. He thanked Murphy and Irene Young for coming and wished them a happy holiday as they departed. Later in the evening as people were leaving Ken wished them well for the season. Bill was alone in the kitchen.

He piled empty bottles in a trash bin and started to tidy up the place. But the effort was too much. He picked up a bottle of bourbon and started thinking about his conversation with Colette. What had she called him, a boy? By God, this boy could hold his whiskey. He tipped the bottle to his lips. When he took his drink back into the living room he found it deserted.

How had everybody gone home without his being aware? Ken must be asleep already. Strange that Hal Evans would leave without saying goodbye. Bill switched off the light and stumbled through the bedroom door in darkness. He tried to pull down the blankets but there was something on the bed, a pile of clothing. Some people must have forgotten their coats. Maybe they had too much liquor. A strange sound filled the bedroom.

Removing his shoes Bill plunged into the pile of clothing and was asleep. In his dreams the rumbling grew louder. Was that the sound of marching feet?

The squad of soldiers led by Captain Michael Murphy in dress uniform was approaching Bill across the athletic field. Murphy drew his sword.

"Come on, Helmer, and show us that you are a good American. Let's hear you sing all the verses of the national anthem." He leveled his weapon. "Up against the fence, Helmer."

Bill took a deep breath as he pressed against the wire fence and tried to sing out the opening words, "Oh say can you see"…but his throat was paralyzed. He tried to call out to Colette for help but no sound came.

"We haven't got all day, Helmer. Show a little discipline and sing."

Bill felt the tip of a sword touching his back and pushed with all his might against the fence. The rumbling stopped as the fence moved aside on the bed and mumbled, "Zizi…Zizi…"

Chapter 20

Bill reached over to stir the embers.

"Should I put on more wood?"

"I think not. We must leave soon." Perched on a leather hassock Colette finished buffing her nails.

"This has been a busy time at school. We haven't been together very much since the Christmas party."

"That reminds me, Bill, that I must talk with you about something."

"Go ahead."

"Well I'm not certain how to say it. I am beginning to feel troubled about being with you so much. Some of the other teachers don't like it."

"Colette, what we do after school is our business. I don't have to get a faculty vote of approval for my social life." He flicked his ashes toward the fireplace. "Anyway, I doubt that they even notice."

"But they do. Teachers are curious about such things."

"Has any of the faculty said something to you?"

"No."

"Aren't they friendly with you?"

"I just feel that some of them resent your going places with me."

"What the faculty thinks of my personal life doesn't bother me."

"Perhaps they believe that you favor me."

"But I hardly ever see you at school."

"No." She searched for words. "But they would be right if we were too...*trop intime.* We must not be like that. How do you say it?"

"Personal, I guess."

"I like to go places with you and receive you here. If we can do things together in this way, we could feel right and it will not bother us at school."

"Look, Colette, I haven't made any passes at you. Everything we've done together could be posted on the student bulletin board."

"I am speaking about what we feel and think about."

"Now that's something different. If you knew what I'm thinking you'd probably be wearing a chastity belt."

Colette laughed. "Please be serious, Bill."

"I see why you feel on the spot, Colette. I agree to go along with that for the moment."

"*Très bien.* We will shake hands. An impersonal relationship."

"A done deal. I'll make like you are my aunt Daisy." Bill pulled her up from the hassock.

"How much time do we have?" She picked up her handbag and stopped in front of the mirror.

"It is almost seven."

"And we must be there at eight-thirty."

"Better skip the apéritif. A friend told me about a fine restaurant in that neighborhood. Shall we try it?"

The restaurant had Doric columns and a uniformed attendant at the entrance. As they walked in the headwaiter approached with a huge menu card under his arm. Bill looked over at the tables near the stringed ensemble in the corner. A few were unoccupied.

"It would be fun to sit there by the music. Would you like that, Colette?"

"Sorry, sir, those tables are reserved."

"They are reserved for distinguished people," Colette said softly. "Those who give thousand franc tips."

"That burns me." Bill reached into his pocket.

"Frankly," she took his arm, "I think it is not worth that much to eat among American tourists."

"Let's go then."

They left the headwaiter standing erect with his menu card.

"What makes you so sure they were Americans?"

"Oh, Bill. It is simple. They were eating dinner early and the man spoke English. Did you see the pitchers of ice water on the tables? We never drink ice water with our meals. Our wine suffices."

"I love France. I love the French language; I love the French people but by God I hate your damned chauvinism about *la cuisine française.*"

"It is not really good food?"

"It is the best in the world but you need not be so damned smug about it."

Bill was striding and Colette skipped along to keep up with him.

"There is a little restaurant across the street."

"O.K. We can't be choosy now."

After dinner they hurried down the boulevard to the Opera, arriving just as the warning buzzer was sounding. Colette had purchased tickets in advance so they mounted the great curved stairway leading from the foyer to the orchestra. Bill started for the entrance..

"No. We go up these stairs."

"What seats do we have?"

"Cinquième loge de face."

"Why didn't you get orchestra?"

"I am not paid in dollars."

"Does *cinquième loge* mean five flights up?"

"Yes and you still have a good view."

"I can imagine," Bill said following her upward. "We probably can't see the stage with a telescope. Your damned architects love to build seats directly behind big round columns."

"It must be sad to be exiled into such an uncivilized country."

They were alone in the tiny loge, side by side with a full view of the stage. No sooner were they seated than the orchestra stopped tuning their instruments. The lights dimmed. Colette's perfume was delicate, vaguely disturbing, as he glanced at her profile during the overture,

In a great burst of flame Mephistopheles appeared. Bill gasped and leaned forward with his elbows on the railing. Colette looked at him, her eyes sparkling, as he gave his full attention to the opera. At the end of the second act a cabaret full of waltzing, drinking students left them in a gay mood and thirsty. At intermission they wound their way down to the bar.

"You know, this is the first time I ever really enjoyed opera. The stage is *magnifique*." He handed Colette a glass of champagne. "Is this the serious music you were talking about?"

"Well, hardly. There is much sentimental music in Faust."

"Oh, hell."

"But I do like it."

"Good."

"I like many kinds of music."

"If you stick around school long enough you may learn to appreciate jazz. You'll have to…hey, there's the bell."

Bill joined in the enthusiastic applause after the final curtain and shouted "Bravo" with the crowd.

Descending the front steps of the brilliantly lighted Opera House he felt a part of a mob scene as they moved into the street. Patrons were hurrying off in all directions. He turned up his collar and took Colette by the arm.

"That was wonderful. Wow."

She looked up at him. "Happy?"

"I feel great, and you?"

She nodded.

"Let's go someplace and celebrate. Just think, this is the beginning of Christmas vacation."

"C'est vrai."

"Where shall we go…*Pigalle, Casino de Paris,* the *Lido*?"

"Oh no."

"Well, suggest something."

"We might go to *Les Halles,*" she said as they headed down *l'Avenue de l'Opéra.* " Have you ever been there late at night?"

"Once a long time ago. I didn't speak much French then and I was afraid somebody would try to sell me something."

Colette laughed. "You speak much French now. You can defend yourself with the merchants. And I will protect you from the girls on the sidewalk."

There was little traffic along the quay. Parking their car on *le Boulevard Sébastopol* they followed a narrow street to the sprawling night market then threaded their way past trucks and carts, sidestepping porters bent under the weight of wooden racks loaded with vegetables or trays of iced fish. A *marchand de quatre saisons* leaned against his cart and waved his arms at a man over the price of Brussels sprouts.

In a doorway a truck driver, his hands jammed into the pockets of his leather jacket, was arguing with a girl in fur coat and high heels. The cafes and restaurants were brightly lighted. The mixture of potatoes and sausages frying in deep fat blended agreeably with the fragrance of oranges and fresh vegetables.

"And they say our stockyards in Kansas City smell bad. Jesus, did you get a whiff of that garlic?"

"Yeah. Do you suppose these people eat the stuff all..."

The gabardine topcoats trailed off down the street.

Colette pinched Bill's arm. "I love the sophistication of American men."

They were now near the center of *les Halles*, approaching the huge covered sheds that sheltered the milling crowds.

"*Regardez*. Must weigh a couple hundred kilos."

A man was rolling a great circle of cheese out to the curb. A boy helped him load it onto a cart.

"Shall we walk down this way?" Colette asked. "I would like to buy some flowers."

She purchased long-stemmed gladiolas, sprigs of fir boughs and holly.

"So what will you do with all that?"

"Decorate my apartment of course. Since I never come here in an automobile. I want to profit from this occasion. "*Combien, monsieur? Merci.*"

"Ah, so I'm just your chauffeur? *Attention!*" They dodged an oncoming hand-truck.

They passed a steaming window where a leg of lamb was revolving slowly over a bed of glowing charcoal.

"Would you like to try *la spécialité des Halles*?"

"What are we waiting for?"

They were soon leaning over bowls of onion soup filled with chunks of bread and melted cheese. Bill yawned as they sat in the warm restaurant.

"We must go," said Colette. "You are sleepy."

"I yawn all the time, especially late at night."

Bill drove in silence through the empty streets. When he parked in front of Colette's place he took the gladiolas from the back and placed them in her arms. Then he gathered the load of fir boughs and followed her up the stairway.

"Your place is damned near as bad as the Opera."

"One day the elevator will be repaired."

"Here. I'll help you."

She was fumbling in her handbag. As she turned the key Bill pushed the door open with his foot. They put the flowers on a coffee table.

"Wow." He sank onto the davenport. "I must be getting old."

"*Oui, monsieur le director.*" Colette was getting out vases.

"Dammit all, aren't you tired?" Bill rose to his feet.

"Me? I feel fine."

When they finished arranging the flowers he sat down.

"I'll get moving in a minute."

"You can rest tomorrow."

"Thank God. I'd never make it to school. A-a-ah." Bill stood up and stretched. "I'll leave and let you go to bed. Unless of course you invite me to spend the night."

"I could make a bed for you on the davenport."

"Oh I wouldn't put you to the trouble of fixing an extra bed."

"It would be no trouble."

"Colette, have you ever seen Lautrec's painting of a couple in bed?"

"They say it is two men."

"I can't believe Lautrec would do that. A man and a woman in a big double bed with just their heads showing above the covers."

"Perhaps their feet were cold."

"I have warm feet, just like a hot water bottle."

"My down comforter works very well. And it would be difficult to be impersonal in a double bed."

"Have you ever tried?"

Bill moved over to the door in a good mood and suddenly less tired. Colette was right that they should be careful. He had an uneasy feeling that he was already more involved than he should be with a member of his teaching staff. But he could see no reason why he shouldn't kiss her goodnight. No use carrying the impersonal angle to ridiculous extremes. He placed a hand on each of her shoulders and pulled her toward him.

She was no longer there. Stepping deftly aside Colette kissed him lightly on each cheek and pushed him out the door.

A nimble witch with good footwork, Bill thought as he descended the stairs.

Part Three: Spring Semester

Chapter 21

Bill's supervisor from headquarters in Germany had just dropped into the Paris High School office.

"Everett," Bill began, "don't you think we should do more to give our students an understanding of why the Americans are here in Europe?"

"Maybe we don't do enough of that, Bill. I don't think most kids even know much about NATO or SHAPE. "

"And that should include studying other systems of government, don't you think?"

Everett paused for a moment. "Maybe in social science classes."

"They should study and really know something about democracy, fascism, socialism and communism."

Everett Carlson, a former county superintendent of schools in Wyoming, had been hired as an administrator when the Army Dependents School System was first organized for a handful of American children.

"Wait a minute now, Bill," he said. "Especially they should know what's wrong with communism."

"I think they should learn as much as they can about each method of governing people, what's wrong, what's right and how it works."

"You're asking for trouble there, Mister. No siree. We better leave that one alone. Our job is to teach them why democracy is the best system of government in the world."

Maria came into the office to remind Bill of a meeting.

"I'll be tied up for the next hour or so with the P.T.A. Executive Council," Bill told Carlson. "Meanwhile take a good look at our school in session. If you're free tonight we might have dinner together."

"Fine. You should know the good restaurants here by now."

There was a quiet elegance about the place Bill chose, tapestry-covered walls, crisp white cloth on tables marked by slender silver vases of fresh flowers.

"Well," Bill said when they were comfortably seated, "how did you like our school?"

Carlson cut a generous slice of *pâté de fois gras* that he spread on his morsel of bread. He chewed and took a sip of wine before he answered.

"Frankly, I'm not too happy about what I saw. Headquarters has been a little worried about you lately. They asked me to take a good look around when I came to Paris."

"Oh, really. And your observations?"

"I'll make a written report and you'll get a copy of course, but I always like to lay my cards on the table. I'll give you the gist of my criticism now if you wish."

"Good. I am always interested in your ideas."

"First of all, you got a special faculty in Paris. It's a little bit different from any of our other schools. You got some Harvard men, for instance, who were hired locally."

"That's right. Corson and Krell. I hired them and they are both good men."

"You know, sometimes these Harvard guys are eggheads, think they're better than everybody else. They know literature but not much about life." Carlson flicked crumbs from his coat sleeve. "Certain of your teachers are up in the clouds with fancy plans for organizing their subject. We teach children in our schools, not subjects."

"I wouldn't give a damn for teachers who aren't enthusiastic about their subjects. Otherwise how can they interest the students?"

Bill had a familiar electric feeling in the back of his neck.

"Now don't get up on your high horse," Carlson replied. "You wanted the straight goods. Well, even some of your teachers think you're running a little college down here, and you encourage that, Bill. You don't know who your good teachers are."

"Unfortunately I have some who teach children as you put it, because they are incapable of doing anything else. They're just expensive baby-sitters."

"That's where you are wrong, Bill. Take Corson, for example, and his ideas about teaching mathematics."

"Let's take Corson." Bill leaned forward. "Good math teachers are rare and he is tops. Last year he worked up a course in calculus for our students and it was highly successful. We had a letter from a college student this year telling us how much it helped him in pre-engineering."

"We can put our finger on something there." Carlson put down a forkful of *coq au vin*. Corson is tied up an hour every day teaching calculus to about ten kids. He ought to be teaching second year algebra to thirty or more. And something else. Corson told me he discouraged some students from taking advanced algebra."

"That's right. Kids who couldn't make the grade."

"That smacks of ability grouping."

"We take ability into consideration in counseling students and assigning them to class sections. The bright youngsters get more out of their studies that way, especially in math and science—and in French."

"That's where you're off base. Don't worry about the bright students. Your job as a public school administrator is to look out for the slow ones. That's democracy in American education and you better be finding it out."

"We simply don't agree on what the public school should do. I can't believe that setting up standards is undemocratic. And we do care about slow learners."

"The only way to hold the slow ones is to keep them interested. Otherwise they'll be out in the streets and in trouble. More bread please."

Bill handed him the basket. "We set out this year to raise standards in the school. I know some of the teachers aren't happy about it but the skilled ones appreciate an emphasis on scholarship."

"You're right about that. You have some unhappy teachers on your staff. The team morale isn't good I'd say. I was talking to Parsons today."

"He is one of my weaker teachers."

"I can see that but he's a fine coach and he has a real complaint. Eligibility for varsity sports is higher in Paris than any other school. Here you require a "C" average."

"I think requirements are too low in Army schools. Know what they are?"

"You bet. Passing in three subjects."

"A student flunking one subject and three D-minus grades in others is eligible."

"Why not? They are the ones we want to keep in school. Why do you want to keep kids from playing ball?"

"I want all students to profit from playing ball. I simply don't want the weakest ones taking time from studies to be hauled all over Europe to play other American teams. In addition it seems a waste of taxpayer's money when we could play nearby French and German teams."

"Let headquarters worry about taxpayer's money. That's their job."

"We didn't have the equipment nor the time for proper physical conditioning to have varsity football this year. We had a soccer team and played a full schedule with French teams."

"I'm all in favor of international understanding but it can be carried too far." Carlson fluttered his napkin. "Our American kids need to get together with other American students. The trouble with you, Bill, is that you've gone native."

"I suppose that any American who speaks a foreign language and doesn't read comic books has gone native."

"Keep a hold on your blood pressure, boy. It seems to us that you're more interested in French culture than you are in the American school. You've picked up a lot of French attitudes, you know." Carlson winked. "First thing you know you'll be marrying yourself a French wife."

"Look, we publish an expensive yearbook for Army high schools in Europe but make no mention of the culture of the country hosting them. Germany and France have been around for a long time."

"*Pâtisserie, messieurs?*" A girl was standing by the table with a colorful tray of desserts.

"I'll have some of that." Carlson pointed. With silver tongs the girl placed *un éclair au chocolat* on his plate..

Bill shook his head. "*Merci, mademoiselle.*"

"Look at the lines on that filly." Carlson watched as she walked away. "If she's a stray I wouldn't mind throwing a halter on that."

"You know, Everett, our instruction in music and art is the weakest part of our program and those happen to be the most valuable points of contact with European culture. We have an opportunity unique in modern history to have a school system that promotes real cultural cooperation and understanding."

"Whoa, now, whoa. Get the blinders off that horse." Carlson hunched forward. "Now look here, Helmer. Lots of our kids go to college back in the States when they finish high school here. And they must have a good American education to cut the mustard in college. So what if you do turn out a kid who speaks French like a professor at the Sorbonne? What will he do with that back in the States? A boy who gets a fine job with a corporation or with the government can always hire somebody to translate for him. Europe is lousy with people who speak four or five languages and they're willing to work for us uncultured Americans for coffee and doughnuts ..."

"You don't really think, Carlson..."

"You said your piece. Now just listen. This blind worship of everything European is a high-toned twist on the old saw that the grass is always greener on the other side of the fence. If the grass in our pasture makes better horses why not just keep eating it? You got a good education, Bill, and you're a smart boy. You don't have to cling to dead traditions with a bunch of skinny short horns. You're just in the wrong corral and you're too damned stubborn to jump the gate."

"Your simile is most apt," Bill said. "If I don't run with the herd I'm wrong. That's exactly the idea a lot of our kids and teachers have."

They finished their dessert in silence. Carlson offered to pay the check but Bill insisted on paying his half.

"I can take you to your hotel." Bill rose to his feet.

"I don't think I'll go directly back. Thought I might go up to Pig Alley, the Red Mill maybe, and see some nightlife in gay Paree. I'll take a taxi."

"That's on my way home. Come on, I'll drop you off at the Red Mill."

"Better let me buy you a drink."

"No, thank you. Ordinarily I'd like to make a night of it with you. But I've had a long day."

They drove in silence along the outer boulevard. At the *Place Blanche* Bill stopped in front of the *Moulin Rouge*. Carlson turned the handle of the door and hesitated before getting out.

"Bill," he said, "you're an ornery halter-shy maverick if ever there was one, but despite that I like you. I hate to see you get yourself into trouble with headquarters. I gave you the straight dope because I'd like to help you."

"Everett, I appreciate your frankness more than I can tell you. I think I have a fairly good idea of where I stand now. Since we are being honest, I'll tell you what I've been wondering about. When the chips are down, just what can headquarters do to me?"

"They can't fire you," Carlson agreed, "but they can transfer you out of Paris. You wouldn't like that, Bill."

Chapter 22

"Mr. Helmer, it is almost time for the P.T.A. Council to meet."
Maria was standing in the office door. "You asked me to remind you."

"Oh, yes, thanks. It's for five o'clock, isn't it?"

Bill stretched wearily, wishing that Easter vacation had already
arrived.

"Is the library set up, Maria?"

"The chairs weren't arranged yet but Captain Murphy is down
there. I think he'll get things ready."

"Thanks. I better go now." He was already at the door.

"Don't forget this." She said handing him the typed agenda.

He found Murphy alone in the library looking out the window.

"Hi. Guess I better get this ready for the meeting." Bill pulled two
tables together.

"I'll give you a hand."

"I thought everything would be ready."

"My boys usually set up for the meetings." Murphy slid a chair over
to Bill. "But I'm being careful lately not to muscle in on civilian jobs
around here."

"I might as well take care of it. Just so we know who's
responsible."

"Oh, no," Murphy said. "From now on I'll have the boys do it. I'm
ready to cooperate any time."

"That's a commendable attitude, Captain. Let's see..." Bill paused
to count the chairs, eight, nine, ten. That should be enough."

"Congratulations, Mr. Helmer."

"How's that?"

"I'd have bet there weren't ten unbroken chairs in the whole place."

"Come now, Captain. It's not that bad."

"Do you ever look around this installation, Mr. Helmer?"

"As a matter of fact I do. Coming down the hall I noticed that the lockers aren't very neat."

"Neat? Mr. Helmer, I've seen brothels that looked better the morning after Army pay day than this school looks now."

Before Bill could reply other members of the P.T.A. Council started coming in. Peg Callahan was among the first arrivals.

"Bill," she said, pulling him aside. "I'm on the spot. I'm recording secretary and I'm supposed to read the minutes of the last meeting. I can't do it today."

"You read them beautifully, Peg. You haven't suddenly become shy?"

"It's not that. I don't have them. Tojo put them in the fire."

"He did?"

"Yes."

"Say, that could be serious."

"You think the council will be upset, Bill?"

"I don't know. I was thinking of Tojo."

"Oh, he's all right. He used the fire tongs."

Major Banks, the treasurer, Mrs. Breen, and two other members came in. They gathered around the table awaiting the president.

"It looks as if she won't be here," Bill said finally. "I suggest we start the meeting."

"Who will preside?" Major Banks asked. "The vicepresident, isn't here either."

"Why don't you preside, Major Banks?"

'No. I defer to Mr. Helmer."

"I'm an ex-officio member of the council so I think it would be better if a parent took over."

"Then I suggest Mrs. Callahan," Major Banks paused. "I don't have a copy of the constitution with me but it seems logical that the recording secretary would be next in line."

"Go ahead, Mrs. Callahan," Bill said. "It's five thirty now. We may be here all night."

"All right. The meeting will please come to order."

Just then a young Air Force lieutenant walked in.

"I'm Lieutenant Borne," he said. "Colonel Conley couldn't get here today so he asked me to sit in for him. I work in his section."

"Glad to have you with us, Lieutenant," Bill introduced the other members of the council.

"I'm afraid I won't be of any help but I'll take notes for Col. Conley."

"The meeting is now called to order." Peg rapped on the table. "I don't remember whether we had any unfinished business from the last meeting. Does anybody know?"

"A point of order, Mrs. Callahan." Major Banks cleared his throat. "I believe it is customary to start by reading the minutes of the last meeting."

"I find myself in an embarrassing position," she said. "You see, the minutes have been lost."

"I move," Bill said, "that we dispense with the reading of the previous minutes."

"Hold on," said the major. "Are you certain, Mrs. Callahan, that they aren't just misplaced?"

"I'm afraid so."

"We might defer the reading until the next meeting in the hope that you will recover them."

"Oh, they won't be recovered. My son burned them."

"Burned them? Are you sure?"

"I'm certain. He was standing by the fireplace watching the last corner go up in smoke when I found him."

"That must be the way so many unattended children have fatal accidents," said Mrs. Breen.

She and Peg Callahan exchanged glances.

"I don't think it's worth making a fuss over an accident. Let's just skip the minutes." Bill was becoming impatient.

"How many minutes did the boy burn?" quipped the young Lieutenant.

"I can't agree with you, Mr. Helmer," said Major Banks. "This council votes the expenditures of P.T.A. funds. As treasurer, the minutes are my only official authority for drawing money. What will the auditor say? They are very precise on accounting for funds."

"The P.T.A. money is an unofficial fund, Major. I don't think it comes under Army regulations."

"That is correct, Mr. Helmer. But we ask for an audit every year just to show that everything is in order. We can't ignore a set of missing minutes."

"I can make a statement of what happened if you like," Peg offered.

"All right. If you make a certified statement and have it notarized by the adjutant I suppose that's better than nothing." The Major settled back in his chair.

One of the notes on Bill's agenda was a request that the P.T. A. Executive Council provide a petty cash fund of twenty-five dollars for purchasing items not supplied by the Army.

"That sounds reasonable," Peg said. "Will somebody put that in the form of a motion?"

"I thought the Army provided complete logistical support for the school," Major Banks said quickly.

"In theory, yes." Bill looked at him. "But it's a question of urgency. We needed distilled water, for example, in the chemistry lab. I ordered it through supply channels with a 'Rush' notation. The School Officer sent the request to Supply Center. They kicked it to Quartermaster Section. They bucked it to the General Dispensary. The Dispensary has no pharmacy section so they sent it to the Army Hospital. It took three months. We could have bought it very reasonably from a French laboratory in one hour."

"Can you trust chemical products bought on the French market?"

"I have heard that their distilled water works beautifully, Mrs. Breen."

"We're wide open to criticism if we buy things already provided by the Army."

"Major," Bill replied, "we've been waiting four months to get a projector lamp through supply channels. We aren't allowed to stock them and the last one burned out eons ago. The projector is gathering dust in the storeroom."

"If the high school kids and teachers took proper care of government property," Murphy observed, "we wouldn't need as many replacements."

"Is that so, Captain?" Major Banks looked interested

"I didn't realize things were so bad, Captain Murphy."

"I've been telling you for a long time, Mr. Helmer."

"Maybe we should appoint a committee to look into that," the major suggested.

"Good idea," Bill said promptly. "Since Captain Murphy has the military responsibility for supplies I suggest that he be appointed as a one-man committee."

"I can't do it."

"Excellent idea." Major Banks turned toward Bill. "We will then know where we stand. There should be a report on broken and damaged equipment needing repair or replacement."

"Oh, no," said Murphy.

"Right," Bill agreed. I'd further suggest a written report for the record. When you talk about a lot of small items of equipment it's hard to keep everything in your head."

"By all means."

"It might be helpful while we're about it," Bill added, "to see what supplies are short. There is a table of distribution for each school in the supply catalog. Some of the things authorized for the Paris High School have never been issued."

"By God I won't..."

"Good idea. Captain, you will see that we have a full written report at the next meeting."

"Yes, sir."

"What was the name of that report? Colonel Conley will want to know." The young lieutenant sat with his pencil poised.

""Let's see." The major rubbed his chin. "That would be a report on broken, damaged and unserviceable equipment and items short of authorized supply strength. You got that, Captain? "

"No, sir. Can I get it from you later, Mrs. Callahan?"

"Certainly, Captain Murphy." She was trying to write the minutes at the same time.

"Mrs. Callahan?"

"Yes, Mrs. Breen."

"I think the P.T.A. should investigate the high school activity program. I've talked with several parents about it and some of us think the children need more and different activities."

"Perhaps we should name a committee to study that. What do you think, Mr. Helmer?" the major asked.

"I also think," Mrs. Breen added, 'that we need more American activities. My daughter says they spend a lot of time going on local trips and having French people come in to talk."

"I don't think that is within the province of the P.T.A.," Bill said. "I agree that our activity program could be improved but the classroom instruction is the responsibility of teachers and administrators."

"I thought the P.T.A. had the authority to review any school policy."

"I'm always happy to explain our policies to parents and to discuss suggestions or criticisms. But the planning of classroom instruction is handled by the faculty and the principal."

"I'm sure you know more about it than I do, Mr. Helmer. From what my daughter Sharon says I just had the impression that they do an awful lot of running around on school time."

"Do you use unscheduled transportation during the school day?"

"Yes, Major Banks, quite frequently. For field trips and other activities."

"Perhaps we should have a committee study that?"

"Fine with me."

"I don't have the time." Murphy sat up straight in his chair.

"I would be interested to see a full report on what transportation we have used," Bill continued. "If there's any way we can economize on buses I'd be the first to cooperate."

"That's a fine attitude, Mr. Helmer. Who is the military liaison with Transportation?"

"The school officer."

"I already got too much to do."

"Captain, could you give us a written report on transportation needs during school hours?"

"Sir, I already got a report to write. I got a lot of things to do."

"Perhaps Captain Murphy can get a report from the transportation officer."

"All right, I'll get some dope from Lt. Grady."

"It might be better to see Colonel Larson. He is in command of the section." Bill knew that Larson would make Murphy as a junior officer do the work.

"Right," the major agreed. "Go right up the chain of command to the responsible officer. You'll get a report then, Captain?"

"Yes, sir."

"I'm afraid we got away from the subject," Peg reminded them. "I think we should provide a petty cash fund for the school right away. How many in favor?"

The motion was approved 4 to 3.

After the meeting Mrs. Breen stayed to talk with Captain Murphy who took her on a tour of the building. Two enlisted men were watching them because it was beyond quitting time and they weren't too happy unloading books from crates.

"The captain left yet?" one asked.

"Naw, he's still convoying some dame around."

"You would think these books were atom bombs the way he acted."

"Here they come now."

Captain Murphy showed the lady into his office and closed the door.

"Christ, they have been in there for an hour. You suppose they'll be there all night?"

"Can it. They're coming out."

"Captain Murphy, this had been a real eye-opener for me. I certainly thank you for your time. I think we may be getting somewhere now."

"I'm always happy to cooperate, ma'am. "

"Well if we work together I'm sure…" Their voices died away as they walked toward the entrance.

"You still here? Why don't you knock off?" Murphy called to the men.

"Sir, you told us to finish these books tonight."

"That will keep. You can finish tomorrow. Go get some chow and a good night's sleep."

Murphy gave the supply sergeant a clap on the shoulder.

Chapter 23

Surveying the rain-swept *Champs Elysées,* Hal Evans wondered if the composer who wrote *April in Paris* had ever been there in March. Chestnut blossoms and tree-shaded café tables seemed far in the future as he walked along pulling tight the collar of his raincoat. There was little Sunday afternoon traffic. The expanse of avenue leading to the obelisk at *Place de la Concorde* gleamed in the rain, reflecting the unique light that illuminates Paris on gray days.

Seeking shelter from an abrupt downpour he ducked into the doorway of the T.W.A. building to consider his next move. Hal was cursing the whole race of French mechanics for taking forever to repair his car, forcing him afoot in such weather. He dashed across the street down into the George V metro. A blue and white plaque listed the stations—LOUVRE, seven more stops.

Art exhibitions had become a habit with Hal since he lost faith in the detective agency. They continued to report regularly to him but he was beginning to think they were taking his money for nothing. He had placed ads in the "personal" columns of newspapers and art reviews. He had started following special exhibits and *vernissages* in private galleries.

He decided he rather liked some of the abstract painters, Hans Hartung, for example. The first time he saw a Hartung it reminded him of the school kids back home with their crayon drawings, bold and strong and honest. It struck him that this man knew all about the

Big Lie. By God he might be thumbing his nose at the world with a paintbrush.

Some of those artists aren't satisfied to paint plump, rich women or wild-eyed politicians, Hal thought as the train rumbled along. They aren't about to make Christians look angelic, the rich virtuous and the poor romantic. They're out to cut right through the Big Lie.

The car rolled to a stop and Hal looked out the window. CHATELET read the sign in the station. Damn! He'd gone past his stop. Jumping to his feet he squeezed through the slot in the sliding doors and stood there for a moment. He stared vaguely at a girl in a light blue raincoat sitting in the next car. She glanced out the window and returned to the book she was reading. There was something familiar in the shape of her head and the way she moved, he thought. He stared as the train started out of the station. Unexpectedly Hal stiffened.

The car had rolled past by the time he could wheel around and start running alongside the train .

"ZIZI, ZIZI, ZIZI! Get off at the next station. *Descends à la prochaine.*"

Then the red lights of the train were winking at him from the tunnel. He pivoted and ran the length of the platform, brushing past the *controleur* who tried to keep him from running up the down stairway.

"If you can catch the metro train that just left in the direction of Vincennes," Hal told a taxi driver, "I'll give you a tip you will never forget."

The man touched his cap and shifted quickly into second gear, gunning the motor as he swung the car around the corner into the quay.

Hal leaned forward to explain briefly, "And she's wearing a light blue raincoat."

"You will never be able to get on the train. The *rue de Rivoli* is one way against us," he said, "but with luck we might keep up with it."

Swinging into *Place de l'Hôtel de Ville* he stopped by a subway sign.

"There is an exit over by the corner of the *Bazaar de l'Hôtel de Ville*," he pointed. "Look at that first and then check this one coming back. I will turn around."

Hal was starting back across the street when the driver motioned him to hurry. He jerked the cab into motion before Hal had closed the door.

"I talked to a man coming off the train," he explained, as they hurtled across *Place St. Gervais* into *rue François-Miron*. "Just three people got off the train. All men."

There was but one entrance at St. Paul. The first passengers were appearing in the street as the taxi approached. As they pulled away slowly, Hal watched through the steaming rear window for a patch of blue.

"This will be difficult," said the driver. "Exits all around *la Place de la Bastille*. I will swing to the right. You can cross the *Place* to the left of the monument. If I see any lady in a blue raincoat I will try to keep her until you get there. Pick you up *rue de Lyon* across to the right."

In the beating rain the big *Place* was almost deserted. Hal darted across, scanning the exits. Several people came out into the street. Nobody in a blue raincoat.

Following *la rue de Lyon* they came up behind an old woman pushing a vegetable cart. They eased over to the inside lane and were starting to pass when she turned her cart across the street directly in front of them. Hal threw his arms up before his face. The cab swerved sharply to the left and the old woman jerked her cart back just in time. They heard her scream after them.

"Espèce de con."

The driver gripped the wheel. And sucked in his breath as a pedestrian dodged across the street in front of them.

"Watch out!" Hal braced himself as the cab closed in on the back of a truck, then turned just in time to avoid a crash.

Hal's head was aching as he tried to compose his thoughts. How could he have missed her like that? If he'd only got into the other car.

The driver snapped his fingers. *"Merde.* I just thought of something."

"What?"

"She could have changed trains. There are several transfer points. At the *Bastille*, for example."

"You are right. I didn't consider connecting lines."

"Want to keep going?"

Hal leaned forward. "Might as well run it out to the end of the line."

Zizi's raincoat had been unbuttoned as she sat reading on the train. Hal had a hunch she was going all the way to the terminal.

At the *Gare de Lyon* there was no way of watching the gates inside the station, so they checked the street exits and went on along *le Boulevard Diderot*. They were slow getting across *Place de la Nation* but were able to make good time down to the terminus. There were no people out of the stairway and the neighborhood was almost deserted when they arrived.

Hal ran down the steps and talked with the *controleur* on the platform.

"Did you notice a girl in a light blue raincoat on the last train?"

"I don't think so. I check each train to be sure everybody gets off at the end of the line. Is she pretty?"

"Very."

"I am sure she was not on this train."

Hal climbed up to the street where the driver was waiting in his cab.

"Want me to take you back to *Châtelet*?"

"No. I think I will walk around for a while by myself. But first, can I buy you a drink?"

"Well, my shift is finished today. I might accept a *coup de rouge*."

They went over to a café and sat down at a table.

"You have no luck." The driver sipped his wine and put down his glass. "Perhaps it's for the best. Me, I have a wife who is all right I guess. Yet if she left me I think I wouldn't go chasing *métro* trains to find her."

But Hal wasn't really listening as he looked out the window, watching thin sheets of water dripping from the awning of the café.

Chapter 24

"I can't wait," Bill told Colette, "to get out under the open sky after all these months in Paris."

On a Good Friday they were speeding along *l'autoroute de l'ouest*.

"*Moi aussi*. I think I would rather be a peasant than a professor."

The early morning traffic was light. Bill felt relaxed and cheerful. Talking Colette into coming on this trip had not been easy but now it seemed worth the effort.

That April morning sun bathed the western horizon in golden splendor. As they topped the crest of a hill the spire of *Chartres* cathedral appeared, pinpointed in the early light. They gazed in silence for a few moments.

Bill reached for her hand and they drove along watching the towers of the cathedral push higher, its eastern windows gleaming.

"*Que c'est beau*." Colette squeezed his hand.

Bill nodded as he eased up on the accelerator. "I read the story of that cathedral in a biography of Peter Abelard."

"He was from Brittany, you know. Perhaps after our holidays you will be inspired by his revolutionary manner of teaching."

"At the moment I'm more interested in the romantic tradition of Abelard. Would you like to be my Heloise?"

Colette laughed.

"You're the lady who talks about getting lost in a story. Here's your chance."

"You know how the story ends?"

"Well, yes. I would want to rewrite certain episodes."

"A desecration of history."

"Well, if something has to be desecrated let it be history."

"How American of you to choose a happy ending."

"I dare say Heloise would have preferred that."

Arriving in Cancale in time for a late lunch they decided to leave the car and continue on foot along the coast toward *la Pointe du Grouin*. The breeze from the English Channel brought them a refreshing tang of salt. In the quiet of the countryside they followed the rugged coastline, scrambling down from time to time on rocks jutting out into the sea.

From a village store they chose slices of sausage, a baguette, a chunk of camembert and a bottle of *cidre mousseux*. Just at dusk their trail led to a rocky summit overlooking a bay. Sprawled out on their sleeping bags they munched their sandwiches, watching the sun sink into the sea, spreading bands of purple and orange where the western slope of sky rested on the water.

Bill lighted the chemical stove and heated water from his canteen to make instant coffee.

"Good Lord, I'm cold." He swallowed his drink and rubbed his hands together. "Who thought of this anyway?"

"You did. Remember? Right in front of my warm fireplace you said, 'Let us go hiking in Brittany'."

"So it was my idea. But you're here aren't you?"

"I was not certain it was a good idea."

"Yeah. But you were more worried about personal relations than about being cold." Bill rinsed the cups and stowed them in his pack. "Well, let's get moving."

They struck out across a rocky field to the road and stopped at the first farmhouse to ask directions. A dog started barking as they entered the yard and several others joined in, setting up a chorus in the quiet of the country night. Before they could knock a bearded face peered out from the slit of light.

"Who is it?"

"*Bon soir, monsieur*," Colette called. "We are hiking and would like to find a hotel for the night. If you please, could you direct us to the nearest village with a hotel?"

"No hotels around here," the voice answered as the door opened a trifle wider.

"We do not know the roads here."

"Nearest hotel St. Malo."

"Which direction?"

"*Par là.*" A hand pointed out the door. "Long walk."

"*Merci, monsieur,*" Colette said quickly as the man closed the door.

"Talkative type," Bill remarked as they continued down the road.

"There are not many strangers who walk around these parts at night. Brittany can be very isolated. Many of the older folk speak Breton but speak no French at all."

"Well, I don't know what he meant by a long walk but I'm running out of steam. We may have to sleep out tonight. The sky is clear."

"If you wish." Colette shifted her pack.

"How do you say 'to sleep out'?"

"*Dormir à la belle étoile.*"

"Most poetic."

"It would sound a lot more poetic to me," Colette said, "in July."

"We'll find somewhere out of the wind."

They started looking for a place sheltered from the sea. For the next hour the road followed a beach that sloped down to the water. Finally the road led to higher ground where Bill spied a haystack in the distance. They headed for the dark mound in a rocky field.

"Not very big," he said when they came up to it, "nor expensive. I think we can keep out of the wind here."

They dumped their packs and Colette sat down while Bill scooped out two hollows on the leeward side, spreading out the dry hay. Then he unrolled their sleeping bags and packed more hay under them for a mattress.

"Your canteen full of water?" he asked.

"Of course."

"Good. We can save that for morning coffee. We'll share mine tonight."

"Sorry," Colette said after they had brushed their teeth, "this cold air does not inspire light conversation. I'm going to retire."

In her sleeping bag she pulled tight her *écharpe* around her neck. Bill made a pillow of his ski jacket and scrunched around to find the most comfortable position.

He cursed himself for not having put the sleeping bags closer together.

"There are usually field mice in haystacks," he called out. "Are you afraid of mice?"

"No. But if you are, you can come closer."

He detected a tone of amusement in her voice. "Helmer," he told himself, "that is no way to be masterful, you bungling idiot."

"You have an expression in English," she said. "How do you say it? A man or a mouse."

"I wouldn't mind being a mouse right now. I could crawl in with you and be warm."

"Yes, but a mouse would be unable to unzip my sleeping bag."

Bill rolled over until he was beside her and opened her sleeping bag with one pull.

Colette lay on her back and feigned sleep.

"If you need help in your dreams, I'm here." Bill told her as he crowded into the sleeping bag.

"I could use some heat but a stove would be better and less personal."

"I'll turn the burners on high.."

When he put his hand on her shoulder she rolled over against him in a tight embrace.

By morning, they were pressed together in one sleeping bag with the other blanketing them for extra warmth. Bill awoke with an impression that a cloud of insects were around his face picking at his eyelids and ears. He opened his eyes to see Colette standing against the sky, laughing down at him and throwing bits of hay into his face.

He jumped to his feet and chased her around the haystack twice before he could catch her.

"Ready for a morning dip?" She took his hand and pulled him toward the beach.

"Sure. I'll race you out to the mouth of the bay and back."

"Wait a minute." She turned toward her pack. "I have a towel here."

Bill thought she was kidding. It was early morning and the April chill was penetrating. The ground and rocks were covered with dew and the gray-green sea looked icy under a sunless sky stretching over the channel.

"I am not going to get my clothes wet," Colette said when they were standing on the beach. "If it does not shock your American modesty I will take them off."

"Go right ahead. I don't shock easily."

To his astonishment she started stripping. Swimming in that cold gray sea was the last thing in the world Bill wanted to do at that moment, but he was ashamed to back out. He started to undress still hoping that she would not dare go into that frigid sea.

"Come on." She took his hand. "One, two three..."

The water felt like ice on his legs and the spray they kicked up made a burning sensation wherever the drops hit his skin. After a few steps he stumbled, losing his grip on her hand plunging into the icy gray water. The shock was paralyzing. White-hot stabs of pain penetrated his chest and he fought for breath.

He started splashing, moving his arms with difficulty as the muscles tightened. He shook his head vigorously from side to side trying to take a deep breath but his chest seemed frozen. After thrashing a few strokes, he groped for the bottom with his feet and scrambled out onto the beach. The morning air now felt warm and soothing on his body.

Colette came running up flinging drops of water at him. They ran around in a circle rubbing each other briskly with the towel. Then they pulled on their clothes and ran hand in hand the full length of the beach.

"Wow," Bill was panting. "I'm beginning to feel almost normal. For a minute I thought I'd never breathe again."

"I feel wonderful," Colette said filling her lungs with air and exhaling slowly, "except for my head. It is like a lump of ice."

"Good Lord." Bill squeezed her wet hair. "We better build a fire right away."

With chemical tablets for the portable stove he started a fire and fed it with hay. Colette lay in her sleeping bag and kept her head close to the smoky fire as she sipped at a steaming brew.

"Better than *les Champs Elysées.*"

They had a glorious week of vacation, scampering about the countryside. They threw stones into the sea, hunted shells along the beach and climbed the rocks. At Trégastel they spent an entire day wandering among the strange rock formations fantasizing about the gigantic boulders shaped like prehistoric monsters.

"You know," Colette stared at him, "that rock looks like you. It reminds me of an American story I once read, '*The Great Stone Face*' by James Fenimore Cooper I believe."

"Nathaniel Hawthorne wrote that story and I don't look like that rock with a great protuberance for a nose."

"Don't be so literal, *Chéri*. That rock has a rugged clean-cut American look." She bent down to examine a shell. "Hawthorne also wrote "The Scarlet Letter" did he not?" She dropped the shell into Bill's pocket.

"Yes."

"After this trip I should wear a scarlet letter."

"Don't say that." He caught her roughly by the wrist.

"Let go. That hurts." She tried to break away. "You are just a Puritan."

"Dammit, Colette, I am not a Puritan. I just don't like to hear you say that." He released her.

"A scarlet letter like cheerleaders wear at school might be attractive."

Bill couldn't help laughing. "You better not make a remark like that at a P.T.A. meeting."

"I love these big rocks," she said. "I came here once with my family when I was a little girl. I knew how Alice must have felt when she walked through the looking glass."

Bill had never felt so relaxed and Colette had never found him so charming. They both hated to see their vacation end. Back at Cancale the last day they arrived in time for dinner.

"We can get a hotel room," Bill said.

Colette nodded.

After some hesitation Bill asked the clerk in the small hotel if he had two single rooms.

"Yes, but one double room would be cheaper."

"A double room then," Colette cut in decisively.

"I don't like the way he acted," Bill said later.

"The double room is cheaper."

"That is not the point. It was his attitude. That's typically French to assume a double room and not take my word for it."

"If we had two rooms would you have stayed in yours?" she inquired.

"Perhaps not."

"We are simply more practical and more honest."

Bill was too happy to nurse his ruffled ego. He was certain now that he loved Colette. When they returned to Paris he would ask her to marry him.

Next morning when Colette awoke she lay in bed, studying the wallpaper in the early morning light. It had been a marvelous week. She watched the curve of Bill's back as he hunched over the washstand. She thought of Jean.

Jean would not have slipped quietly around the room to avoid waking her. Sometime she wished Bill were more impulsive. What would it be like to live with him? She could imagine what Jean would say and the look of scorn on his face. She hadn't seen him since that terrible Christmas party. What would he think? Anyway that was all finished. She tried hard not to think of anything. Then for no apparent reason she was sitting in the bed crying.

"Darling, what's the matter?" Bill came over to sit on the bed.

"Nothing. I'm all right. I'm just a little bit tired and I would like to be alone. Just a little while, please."

"Sure. Sure. I'll go out for a walk and give you a chance to get dressed. I'll come back in about an hour and we can go down to breakfast. O.K.?"

"You are kind and very understanding."

It was natural for her to feel upset, Bill told himself as he walked down the street. I've acted badly. But I'll make it up to her when we get back to Paris. All the same he wanted to make some gesture. He thought for a moment. Flowers! He would get her some.

In a square at the end of the street he found a flower shop but it was closed. He knocked on the door.

"She's not open yet." A woman came out of the café next door. "Do you need flowers for someone who is sick?"

"No. For somebody in love," Bill answered.

"Perhaps Françoise will come down." She called up to a window.

"I'm eating breakfast." A voice replied.

"There is a young man in love down here," the woman in the street said. "He says he needs flowers."

"I'll be right down."

"I can wait," Bill called but she had already shut the window. In a few minutes she appeared in bathrobe and slippers.

"For love and death I will open my shop," she said cheerfully. The lady from the café next door had followed her in.

"Please don't go to all that trouble," Bill said but she was already busy. Minutes later she reappeared with a bucket of red roses.

"That's fine," he said. "I'll take a dozen." He reached for a flower.

"No, that is in full bloom" the café lady said. "It will soon be faded."

The two women picked out the roses, chattering over each selection.

What a wonderful place the world is Bill thought as he walked back. When he reached the hotel Colette was dressed. In her dark sweater and slacks she looked tiny and beautiful.

"Here are some flowers for you." He watched as she unwrapped them.

"Oh, Bill. You mustn't do that." There were tears in her eyes.

"I wish I could give you something nicer. I love you, Darling." Damn. He hadn't meant to say that just then.

Colette started to cry again and Bill took her into his arms.

"Please don't cry, Darling. I do love you. I want to marry you."

"No, Bill. Please, not right now. Don't ask me now, please."

Bill realized that it was the wrong time and place. He had planned to ask her after a dinner with champagne and flowers. Of course she was disappointed.

"You are sweet, *Chéri.*" She cupped her hand against his cheek.

Nevertheless, Bill felt like singing when they went downstairs to breakfast after Colette had pinned a rose on her sweater. He ate four croissants with his *café au lait.*

Chapter 25

Kay was sitting on a bench near the monument at the *Porte de Saint Cloud* trying to study her French assignment while waiting for Tony. When Mademoiselle Bernard read *l'Avare* aloud to the students her eyes sparkled. Her voice was warm and exciting. The way she acted out the scenes made everyone in class burst out laughing. Kay loved those moments.

Now Kay was starting Act II but by the time she finished a speech of *La Flèche* she had forgotten what *Cléante* had said to him. Her mind just would not focus.

That man had upset her a few minutes ago, a middle-aged man whose manner she had not liked from the start. He had sat down beside her and started talking about *Molière*. She answered him politely. As they talked he moved closer and unexpectedly placed his hand on her thigh. Kay had jumped to her feet and fled, terrified. She walked up le *boulevard Murat* and crossed the street. When she looked back the man had disappeared. I wonder, she thought, if that happened because I have sinned. Maybe that changes you, makes you look vulnerable. The idea frightened her.

She returned to her bench that faced the Route de Versailles bus stop where she hoped Tony would soon be arriving. She looked up from her book each time a bus came in, worrying about Tony getting her message. That morning she had been determined to tell him but she lost her nerve. When finally she got up her courage after school he was in the boys locker room dressing with the track squad. Jack had promised to deliver her message but she didn't trust him. Oh God, she prayed silently, give me strength to tell him and please God, don't let him be mad. Please don't let it hurt him.

"Hey, what's the big idea?" a voice behind her said.

"Tony. How did you get here? I was watching the bus stop all the time."

"Jack brought me down in his car, but what's so special? This was an important turnout. Coach was going to time me tonight. What's so hot it can't keep?"

Kay felt her courage melting. This was all wrong. It wasn't the way she had planned it. She had carefully rehearsed what she was going to say. She would see Tony walking across from the bus stop and hold out her hands to him. Then she would look directly into his eyes and tell him, right off. But now he was standing with one foot on the bench looking angry and disappointed.

"Tony, I just had to see you."

"For cripes sake, you saw me a dozen times today. We ate lunch together in the cafeteria, didn't we? Making me miss a track turnout. Well what do you want?"

"Tony, I…I…Tony, please sit down here beside me."

"For the love of Pete. Did you want me to miss a track practice and come half-way across Paris just to sit by you?"

"Tony," she said trying to be casual, but her voice quavered a little. "Tony, I think I'm going to have a baby."

"Just to think—WHAT? What did you say?"

"I think I'm going to have a baby. Tony, please don't be mad."

"Cripes, what did you have to go and do that for?"

"I'm sorry, Tony. Really I am."

"Jeepers, how do you know? Are you sure?"

"Almost sure. I haven't…I don't…well, I mean nothing has happened to me now for more than two months. I asked Martha. She knows a lot about these things and she said that was a pretty sure sign."

"Cripes. Now we've had it. We've really had it."

"What are we going to do?"

"I don't know."

"Tony, I'm scared. My father will kill me. And if he doesn't I'm sure God will punish me. Do you believe in God?"

"I don't know. Sure I do, I guess."

"But I mean really believe. Do you ever think about it?"

"I used to be an altar boy at church. But I don't often think about God, never at school."

"Do you suppose God will punish me?" She started to cry.

"Aw, jeepers, Kay, don't cry. Please don't cry." He put his arm around her.

Kay had resolved to be brave but she just couldn't help herself. She leaned against Tony's shoulder sobbing.

"But it's such a sin. Not just a little sin like telling a lie or maybe drinking a glass of wine. This sin is…" she paused for a moment. "This sin is …well, just awful…really awful."

"I don't know if it's so bad, Kay it's not like we…well, like we did it just for fun or something. It's not like I didn't love you. It would be a lot bigger sin if I didn't love you," he said positively, feeling a sense of relief at the logic of his argument.

"Do you really love me?" She was trying hard to stop crying.

"Sure, I love you. Gee, I've told you so before."

"But all the couples we go out with say that. It's the sort of thing fellows say to their dates."

"Yeah, but that's not why I said it."

"You don't say it very often. You never talked to me much about it."

"Cripes, if I tried to tell you how I feel, it would sound…well, sort of goopy. You know—strictly corn. I'm not good at that, but gee, you know how I feel, don't you? That's what's important. I am so proud that you want to be with me. I really feel it, Kay, honest I do."

"But it's still a sin, even if we do love each other."

"It's not like I didn't want to marry you."

"But that's why God wants people who love each other to get married first, so they won't sin, I mean."

"We will get married, maybe just tell our folks we plan to get married later. Then the baby won't be quite so bad, if we're going to get married anyway. Most married people have babies. Why should everybody get all hot and bothered and blow their fuses about that?"

"Oh, no. We can't tell our folks." She was trembling.

"I think I could tell mine. Ma would really holler, though. She's a good egg, but that would be a strain on her. She'd get mad like she did the first time I got kicked out of school. You could hear her for miles. It scared me, and Pop just got real white and choked up like he does. He was just busting to clout me, but he didn't. He never does. Funny, Ma blew her top the first time I was suspended. Now she saves up work around the house for me when I'm out of school." Tony had almost forgotten his immediate problem.

"Well, I can't tell my folks. You don't know my father, Tony. I've seen him when he talks about women who sin like that with a look on his face that is…that really scares me. I could never tell him, never. I've been told about sin all my life. My father is a religious man, really a Christian. He could never understand how his daughter could do such a wicked thing."

"Maybe we could get married right away, but I don't think we're old enough unless our parents sign a paper or something. They would have to know."

"Couldn't we run away and get married?"

"Where could we run, Kay? It takes a lot of dough to go back to the States. Where could we go in France? Takes beaucoup de loot to live in France, too. I only got about ten bucks."

"I guess you're right."

"Look." His face cleared. "I've heard about doctors who can do something about babies…who can fix you up, I mean. They know how to…well, how to stop them from coming. See what I mean?"

"Oh, what a terrible idea, Tony. That would be just like killing something…alive, like killing somebody. That would be the worst kind of sin. How could we live with that?"

"It was just an idea, that's all. What do you want to do about it?"

"I don't know."

They sat without speaking. The six o'clock rush was pouring a stream of vehicles into the traffic circle around the Porte de St Cloud where they were. Trucks and buses, their turn signals waving, tried to break out through the cars that were circling the outer rim in an endless revolving ring. Against the rhythmic hum of tires and motors there was a symphony of whistle blasts, shouted insults and squeaking brakes.

The sunset crept up from the horizon silhouetting the hill at St. Cloud. And still they sat there. Kay was gripping his hand, squeezing it so hard it hurt but Tony didn't want to pull it away.

"Look," he said finally, "we must do something. You have to see a doctor, anyway. It's just a matter of finding out where to go. Maybe I can ask Jack. He knows a lot of things."

"Not Jack," she answered. "I don't like him."

"Okay. Who shall we ask?"

"We might ask the counselor, Miss Serinac…but then I guess we couldn't do that. She's nice but you just couldn't talk to her about that."

"That's not her job."

Tony thought for a moment. "Here's an idea.. Mr. Helmer understands a lot of things, but gee, he's a principal of the school. We couldn't ask him something like that."

"I suppose not."

"Well, it looks like Jack then. It doesn't cost anything to ask, and we got to do something."

"All right," she said.

"Just think of you being a father," Kay said as they walked over to the bus stop.

"Me? A father. That's a good one, really cool." Tony laughed so hard tears came to his eyes. He stopped abruptly when he saw the hurt look on her face.

Unexpectedly the idea penetrated into his consciousness. Just think of that—him a father like his dad was a father, something of his own flesh and blood from the seed of his own body.

"Cripes, Kay." He put his arm around her tenderly. "Me a father, cripes."

Chapter 26

Bill scanned record jackets seeking a gift for Colette at the Post Exchange. He wished he knew more about Bach. What did the man compose? Maybe he could find a list...

"Hello there, Mr. Helmer."

"Oh, Mrs. Manick. How are you?"

"Fine, thank you. I'm so glad I ran into you. I wanted to apologize for not coming to the meeting last night."

"What meeting?"

"Why, the one at Mrs. Breen's house. Didn't the P.T.A. council get together last night?"

"I didn't know a thing about it."

"Oh dear, I hope I'm not telling tales out of school. Anyway, if they were going to discuss the high school I think you should know about it."

"So do I. And I thank you for telling me."

Bill called Peg Callahan that evening. Josette answered the phone and said that the Callahans were out. He had no sooner arrived at school the next morning than he received a call from Mrs. Callahan.

"Bill," she said, "I want you to come out to dinner tonight."

"I'm not sure I'll be free, Peg. I'll be working late and Hal Evans planned to help me."

"Can't you possibly change your plans?"

"Well, yes, I suppose I can."

"I know this is short notice but it's important that you come."

185

"I'm sure Hal will understand. I wouldn't want to miss one of your good dinners, Peg."

"Better not miss this one. See you tonight about seven."

"Hello, Peg, hello. You still there? Do you know anything about a meeting at Mrs. Breen's house?"

"That's why I want you to come out tonight, Bill, but I don't want to discuss it on the phone. Bye."

Bill stopped in a toyshop to buy presents for the children. The tree-lined road lifted his spirits as he drove up to the chateau where the Callahans resided. He ran up the stone steps and lifted the brass knocker.

"Hi, Bill. Come in." Peg Callahan was standing in the doorway.

"Mamma, it's my day to open the door," a voice called from the long hallway.

"Oh, oh." she said. "I'm strictly out of channels. You'll have to go back outside."

As Bill backed out in confusion she firmly closed the door. Seconds later four-year-old Tojo opened it, straining with all his force to drag the heavy slab back on its hinges.

"Enter," he said.

"Hello Tojo. How are you?" Bill stepped over the threshold.

"I'm fine," Tojo replied shaking hands. "What did you bring me?"

"Tojo, you are not to ask people for presents," his mother said.

"Perfectly natural." Bill turned toward the boy, "Here is an automobile." He handed him the toy car.

"What kind is it?"

"A Simca sport."

"Does it have a horn that makes a noise?"

"No. I'm afraid not."

"Colonel Carpenter gave me a car with a real horn that blows."

Bill smiled. "Well, I'm not yet a full colonel. That is not bad for an underpaid civilian."

Tojo put the car on the floor and rolled it along.

"Anyway, the wheels turn," he said. "Thank you very much."

"Come in by the fireplace. Even in spring a blazing fire feels good. Tom is shaving. He'll be out in a minute." Peg excused herself and reappeared with a tray of cocktails.

They sat and talked in front of the fireplace while Josette fed the children at a small table set to one side.

When Josette had finished giving the children their supper she took them into the playroom and returned to help Peg serve dinner. She enjoyed needling Colonel Callahan about the American occupation of France.

"If the Romans had developed supply lines like the Americans," Josette remarked, "we would still be speaking Latin."

"You'll doubtless be speaking English in a few years," Tom told her.

"Because your civilization is so superior?"

"That has nothing to do with it. Because of our productivity. Just look at Peg. She has four kids and she wants four more. We will just naturally out produce you."

Bill looked at him. "If that's going to be your criterion for the universal language of the future," Bill said, "you better start teaching your children Chinese."

"I don't care about building a brave new world," Peg said. "I just want lots of children. Four kids are so much fun that eight should be twice as good. We're still young."

"Not for long," groaned Tom. "Maybe Congress will give me a medal. With enough people like Peg our superior numbers could force the Russians into a little corner of the Arctic circle."

"That's what I'm doing for democracy."

"I'm doing my share for democracy in more ways than one." Tom turned to Josette. "Where else in the world could you find a full colonel standing for half an hour outside the bathroom door while the French maid fixes her hair."

"Please. I am not a maid. I am a governess."

"I get pushed around by women in this house like Dobuan men by their mothers-in-law. There is no time limit on Josette's ablutions. She's *très caline*."

Josette and Bill started laughing.

"I said something funny?" Tom looked at them.

"You better not tell your office staff that your French governess is *très caline*," Bill told him.

"Why?"

"How would you say that in English?" Josette inquired.

"Caressing or cuddling. You would usually say that for children. I think you mean *coquette*."

"Oh, yeah, but I don't see much difference."

"In that case I better keep an eye on my household," said his wife.

Tall tapers lighted their dining room. Josette excused herself to put the children to bed.

"Tom, I can't understand," Bill said as he finished his wine, "why a man with your background in anthropology would stay in the Army."

"Well, along with our children we can see a lot of the world inexpensively while enjoying our family. I can retire young and still do some work in anthropology. If we raise eight kids I can probably start sifting the ruins of our own house."

"Think of the field work experience Tom is getting," Peg added.

"Your question, Bill, implied that it's unusual for an educated man to choose a career in the armed forces. You think most career military men have low I.Q.'s and couldn't do other skilled work. That's a dangerous blind spot for a man in your position. There are a lot of intelligent officers in this community and you better be finding out who they are. You may need their support one of these days."

"That's right, Bill," said Peg. "Now we can get down to the reason I wanted you to come over tonight."

"Oh yes. I'd almost forgotten. The P.T.A. is a hell of a dish to serve after a wonderful meal like this."

"While Peg clears the table, I want to try out an idea on you…"

""No you don't, Tom Callahan." Peg came in with a dessert tray. "Both of you are good for all night if you get started. No primitive male club idea where the gentlemen retire to the library for liqueur and cigars. We both have business to discuss with Bill."

"You see, Bill, how the patriarchal system has been weakened."

"Don't browbeat me," Peg said. "I've studied anthropology, too. That's why I married Tom. I couldn't resist that combination of a dolichocephalic head on a Celtic type."

Tom grabbed at her but she stepped aside.

"I would like to have you fill me in on what is happening, Peg. I seem to be the last one to know about the doings of the P.T.A. these days."

"Why does Mrs. Breen have the axe out for you, Bill?"

"I had to discipline her daughter once."

"Well, I have my personal intelligence service now. I can give you a full report on the meeting. Mrs. Breen is on a youth activity committee. She called an informal group of interested parents instead of having an official meeting, so she could avoid asking you."

"I'm offended. They probably had ice cream and cake. What happened?"

"The meeting turned into a gripe session against the high school and especially against you. Chaplain Selner established himself as a leader. From all reports Captain Murphy doesn't love you either. They may have ideas of lining the P.T.A. up against you."

"They plan an attack at the next meeting?"

"You underestimate them," Peg answered. "Here roughly is the strategy. They plan a quiet but active campaign against you during the rest of this year. When next year's officers are selected at the end of the semester they hope to vote in an anti-Helmer slate. Then, when the new council meets for the first time after school is out, they plan to present a petition in the name of the P.T.A. requesting headquarters to transfer you to another job, in the best interest of the Paris High School. They will try to get the Old Man to sign it but if he doesn't go along with it they'll present it anyway. That way they can avoid discussing it in an open meeting."

"That would probably be fatal," Bill said. "My headquarters doesn't like me too much as it is. The school inspector, Carlson, would just love to get a petition like that."

"Captain Murphy promised his support, but doesn't want to get directly involved in school politics. He's afraid of the Old Man."

"Smart boy."

"He's asking for trouble," Tom said. "Junior officers don't get ahead that way unless they're a lot smarter than Murphy."

"Well, I'm not going to sit around and do nothing about it," Peg said. "They got my Irish blood roused and I'm starting my own campaign right now."

"Peg's bored anyway," Tom added, "with nothing to do but sit around and take care of four kids."

"Peg, you are wonderful," Bill looked at her. "What do you think we should do?"

"I don't think you should do anything about it in a direct way. Just keep in contact with me. I may need a bright idea for enlisting parents on our side. A lot of them appreciate your leadership, Bill, but the satisfied ones don't make much noise. We have to dig them out."

"I can't tell you how much I appreciate your friendship and help," Bill told the Callahans as he was leaving. "This briefing should help. Is that the complete report from your intelligence, Peg?"

"Well…." She hesitated and turned to her husband. "Do you think I should tell him the rest of it?"

"Sure. Bill needs to be fully informed."

"Bill, we're good friends so if you think I am out of line please tell me. I hate to carry tales to you about your own faculty but from what I hear, a couple of your teachers are helping this movement. I don't have any proof but I think you should be careful."

"Some of the teachers gripe a lot but I don't know who would do a thing like that."

"Watch Mr. Jackson for one. I have reason to believe that he is a source of discontent."

"That surprises me. I've had some run-ins with him the last couple of years but I never thought he was that unhappy."

"I might as well give you the works. The final charge is that you go overboard in being pro-French. They are trying to interpret this as being anti-American. One point is that you give too much attention to Franco-American relations in the school program and in your personal relations with one of your French teachers."

"Damn it all, that's my own business. Nobody else can tell me whom I can associate with."

"Calm down, Bill. I'm just telling you."

As Bill drove home the warm glow of appreciation he felt toward the Callahans changed to anger when he thought of the coming battle. As he drove over the crest of the hill at Saint Cloud, the lights of Paris lay below him like a valley of brilliants. Powerful light beams sculpted the monuments, *le Tour Eiffel*, the dome *of Sacre Coeur* and the twin towers of *Nôtre Dame* backlighting the delicate spire of *la Sainte Chapelle*.

Through this pattern of lights he could see the Seine, as if an artist had added a long curving brush stroke across his canvas. For the first time he felt a personal connection with the signs "Americans Go Home".

Following the twisting road into the city he knew that any fight to stay in Paris was worthwhile.

Chapter 27

Bill waited for the fourth ring before deciding that Maria must be out of the office. He picked up the telephone.

"Paris High School. Helmer speaking."

"Red Rodger from Comco."

"Hello. What was that?"

"Repeat. Red Roger from Comco."

The voice sounded familiar. Was that Murphy?

"I don't get it."

"Don't remember the security code, do you Helmer?"

"No, I don't."

"I figured you wouldn't. You're supposed to know it."

But Murphy was too excited to push his advantage. "That means this Security Plan B is in effect as of right now. That's straight from the Old Man, himself."

"What am I supposed to do?"

"It's a little late to find out what you are already supposed to know but you better damned look at that plan and see me right away. And I mean right away."

Bill opened the safe in his office and started pawing through the papers. Maria couldn't help him because this was a classified document which he vaguely remembered hiding but had absolutely no idea where. He couldn't even visualize what it looked like. When he found it under a pile of papers he brought it over to his desk.

He leafed rapidly through the pages. Let's see…"A Statement of The Purposes of Security Regulations. That's not it. "Security Plan A…There it was…"Security Plan B.

Plan B provided for emergency transportation of school students from the school to their homes in unmarked civilian vehicles by the shortest and safest routes under the direction of Security Services acting for the Commanding Officer. Adults were to prepare a list of items—blankets, flashlights, maps, jerry cans of gasoline, etc…and then they were to wait in readiness for a more advanced phase of the plan which might require meeting at pre-designated rendezvous points for a total evacuation of the civilian population.

Bill slammed the safe door shut and dashed down to Murphy's office. The place was jammed with officers.

"We have information," Murphy said, " that the Communists plan to put up road blocks for the school buses today when we take the children home from school."

"When does this security plan go into effect?"

"We are on alert right now."

"I mean when do you plan to take the students home?"

"We're waiting to check with the Old Man. He should be here in a minute. What do you think?"

"I have no idea how long it will take under this system."

"I believe," said the Transportation Officer, "that we should proceed immediately. No use taking any chances."

Colonel Carpenter was of the same opinion. Get the students home as quickly as possible. He wanted to check out some details personally and he asked that Bill be ready at any moment to call the student body and faculty together for instructions.

Bill sent a bulletin around to all teachers warning that a special assembly would be called on short notice during the morning. Then he went back into his office.

About ten thirty word came that Colonel Carpenter wanted students and teachers in the auditorium. When Bill approached the stage the colonel was already in place before the microphone of the P.A. system that had been turned on and tested.

Bill had no intention of being upstaged by the Old Man in an emergency. Dammit, it was his school, wasn't it? As the last students filed in he moved up beside the colonel and calmly reached for the microphone. Pulling it over to a convenient spot he opened the assembly.

"Your attention, please. We have called this special assembly as part of an emergency plan. Our commanding officer of the support unit will now explain to you what is to be done. Colonel Carpenter."

Bill had never heard the auditorium so quiet. Students sat straight in their chairs sensing that something unusual was happening. The Old Man took the microphone and looked out over the room.

"May I ask that any persons in this room who are not American citizens please leave."

Colette and the other French teachers, sitting near the front, rose and departed under the suspicious gaze of some students. The colonel waited until the doors at the entrance closed behind them before he continued.

"First of all, I think there is no need for alarm. Our Security Services have information that there may be some trouble today during our return bus runs. We plan to take you home by small groups in civilian vehicles. We must have the strictest kind of military discipline. We expect you to obey orders. When loaded in cars you will be expected to sit far back in the seat and as low as possible. The less you can be seen from the outside the better. You will take with you nothing but your clothing and personal effects such as lunch boxes. The driver of the car will be a soldier and he will be in command."

Nobody had thought of what to do next. An officer went outside to watch for the arrival of the cars. Bill wanted to send students back to the classrooms. Murphy was against that idea but, when pressed, admitted he had no plan as to how students would be loaded. Bill suggested that they talk with Henry Bennett, the bus dispatcher.

"Bennett is British. We can't let him in on a security activity."

"Good God. Henry runs the bus operation. He knows every route. He has a roster of kids on each bus."

"I see no harm in consulting Bennett," Colonel Carpenter said, "so long as you give him no details of the security plan."

Murphy started away and then turned back suddenly.

"Hey, what about the French teachers?"

"Well, what about them?"

"We should send them home right away, get them off military property."

"Why?"

"They are French, that's why. They ain't U.S. citizens. I don't trust any of them."

"That's ridiculous."

They both looked at the Old Man.

"I hadn't thought of that." He turned to the Security Officer. "They surely must have security clearances."

"Yes, sir, they do. But they are cleared by French security and I don't know for sure what that is worth."

"Look," Bill said, "if you send them off like a pack of criminals they'll never have any control over the students."

Control and discipline were arguments the Old Man could understand. He scratched his head.

"You have a point there, Mr. Helmer. Possibly we could restrict their movements. Where are they now?"

"Probably in the teachers' lounge."

"I protest. That's humiliating for the professional staff."

"This is an emergency, Mr. Helmer. Please ask them not to leave the building or go near the military offices on the first floor corridor."

"Fair enough."

During all this time the students sat quietly but now they were becoming restless. Somebody called out, "Are there bomb shelters at school?"

Colonel Carpenter walked back onto the stage.

"You might as well know that we think this may be a plot of the French Communists against the Americans. That is all I can say. Good soldiers don't ask questions. Now I want you to honor the American tradition of courage and discipline under conditions of danger. You are representatives of a great nation."

Bill left Hal in charge and went into the office to check with Maria. Half an hour later Hal came in.

"Bill, no cars have showed up and it's almost noon. Did anybody check with the cafeteria about lunch?"

"Not as far as I know."

"These kids are getting hungry. We should let them eat."

Murphy didn't want to let anybody leave the auditorium but it was noon and the civilian vehicles weren't there, so the captain finally conceded that the students could eat under the supervision of the teachers and Military Police.

After lunch the students and teachers reported back to the auditorium. Soon Hal appeared in the office with Irene Young.

"The kids are getting pretty restless. What do you think we should do?"

"No signs of transportation?"

"Nope."

"This is ridiculous. We should send them back to classes. I'll see Murphy."

"We have to send these students back to classes," Bill told the captain. "They're getting bored sitting in the auditorium with nothing to do."

"How long would it take to get them down here from the classrooms?"

"Fire drills take about one minute twenty seconds. That's par for the course."

"All right, Helmer, but goddamit this is on your neck not mine."

Bill made a tour of the building to see how classes were going. He checked out the teachers lounge on his way back to the office. Colette was the only one there.

"Classes are back in session."

"I know. This is my prep period. Bill, you and I have talked of this but I still do not understand why Americans are so afraid of Communists. Some of the teachers are almost in panic."

"I suppose it's the Army's job to expect the worst in any situation."

"I am not a Communist. I do not like their politics. But I cannot see why anybody is so afraid. I do not believe French Communists would harm school children. Do you think there is a great danger?"

"At this point I think the whole thing is a colossal false alarm. But I also think we should take no chances. I only want to get the students home and the U.S. Army does not seem capable of such a simple operation."

Murphy came to the door and stopped when he saw Colette. She started to leave.

"Stay right where you are. I'll step outside a moment with the captain."

In the hallway Murphy looked about them and spoke in a low tone.

"I just found out that the cars won't be here for another two hours at least."

"Two hours? Good God! What happened?"

"There aren't enough black command cars. Most of them are the official Army color. They got some Embassy limousines and we finally got some Hertz cars rented. The Contracting Officer just called."

" The guys who dreamed up this security plan should have thought about the cars."

"The G.I. drivers showed up in uniform and had to go back for civies. They are taking elementary kids home first and that will take another couple of hours."

"Two hours? It's four o'clock now. Why that will be six before they even start."

"Nothing I can do about it. Better keep the kids in class."

"We can't do that but I am willing to ask the teachers to supervise them for some recreational activity. But we can't keep them in the classrooms."

"We can put a perimeter guard of M.P.'s around the athletic field. But nobody goes off the field."

"All right with me."

"One minute, Captain," Bill said as Murphy started for his office. "What provisions have you made for these people to eat? We can't keep them here without food."

"The cafeteria is closed. How in hell can we feed this many kids?"

"We could get milk and sandwiches. That's better than nothing."

"Who would pay for it?"

"That's a military problem to feed people."

"I'll check with the Security Officer."

"Captain, I'm going to call and order stuff even if I have to buy it myself."

Bill marched into his office and picked up the phone. He dialed and dialed but could get only mechanical sounds.

"The telephone has been out for two hours," Maria told him. "The military switchboard was swamped with calls."

He ran down the hall to the military office. "Murphy the telephone is out."

"I could have told you that."

"What about food?"

"I'm sending a couple of the boys out right now for sandwiches and milk."

Two shipments of food arrived about six o'clock, one from the PX Snack Bar and one from the Noncoms Club. A jeep and an Army truck unloaded sandwiches and cartons of milk. They were immediately surrounded by whooping students elbowing each other to get at the food. Teachers took sandwiches into the building to eat in a more relaxed atmosphere.

The first civilian cars arrived and Murphy was occupied with the loading. Students were brought out in groups of five and loaded into the cars as they pulled up in front of school. Bill was watching when the counselor came up to him.

"Kay Selner isn't feeling well, Bill. She's lying down in the sick room. Can we load her in the next car?"

Kay's face was drawn and she leaned heavily on Mary's arm.

"Maybe you should go down for a check at the military hospital," Bill suggested.

"No! No! I don't want to go to the hospital. I won't go there. It's just an upset stomach." She was almost hysterical. "Mr. Helmer, please don't let them take me to the hospital."

"All right, Kay."

The counselor patted her on the shoulder. "You'll be home in a jiffy, Kay. Everything will be fine."

"What's going on here?" Murphy came up and saw the student standing there.

"Mr. Helmer loaded somebody else and told me to wait for the next car."

"Who in hell is running this show?"

"Murphy, we had a sick girl and loaded her first. Want to make an issue of that?"

"Helmer, I wouldn't refuse to load a sick kid first. What the hell do you think I am? I'm just trying to keep some order in this operation."

Shortly after midnight the last students were loaded. Bill found Murphy at his desk looking haggard. "I guess we got them all home."

"Yes, thank God. The army has a lot to learn about emergency transportation for school kids."

"Listen, Helmer, we're both going to hear about this. The civilians in this school better get with it on security procedures."

Too tired to argue Bill joined Hal and Colette who had stayed to help until the last minute. As they left the building he stopped and pointed.

"Maurice is still open. I don't think I can make it to town on an empty stomach. Let's see if we can get something to eat."

Maurice was closing the café but he thought he could fix them a steak.

"That would be the greatest contribution to Franco-American friendship since Lafayette," Hal said.

"Something wrong at school today?" Maurice asked.

"No. Nothing wrong. The Army just tried a new way to get students home."

"I wish they would use the same plan for bringing them to school."

Colette yawned. "Then I could sleep until noon."

Chapter 28

Sitting at their sidewalk café Kay and Tony looked out into *le Jardin du Luxembourg*. From the double gate a tree-bordered *allée* led straight to the sparkling fountain, set in bands of circular flowerbeds. Chestnut trees lined the pathways into the park. From his little white wagon an ice cream vendor was carrying on a brisk business. Nearby a stout woman was holding firmly to a cloud of colored circles floating against the sky.

"Hey, get a load of that," Tony pointed.

A man in a frock coat over his sweatshirt approached the terrace of the café waving a battered top hat..

"*Messieurs-dames, attention s'il vous plaît.* I have the gift of making things disappear. Now for your pleasure I shall show you my magic. May I borrow that package of *Gauloise* for a moment, my friend?"

A man smiled and handed him the cigarettes.

"*Regardez.*" He held high the empty hat for everyone to see . "There Is no trick. I put the cigarettes in the hat and. . ." he waved his hand gracefully, "presto—they are gone." He turned the hat over, shook it and pounded the top. An *agent de police* quietly walked up behind him and stood watching.

"Now I shall do something more difficult. Will somebody..." he paused, sensing the attention of his audience behind him. He glanced over his shoulder then bowed low. "Now for the best trick of all. I shall make myself disappear." He ducked under the outstretched arm and ran around the corner. The policeman stood laughing with the crowd.

"Cripes, I never saw so many characters in my life. It's better than a movie."

"Mademoiselle Bernard brought us on a field trip once to see the Latin Quarter. She said that long ago everybody spoke Latin. Courses were taught in Latin. You heard it on the streets."

"Gee, all the Latin I know is *e pluribus unum*. How long ago was that?"

"I don't remember exactly but she said the Sorbonne was started in the Middle Ages."

"Holy smokes, that's even before the Pilgrims."

They sat there watching the people go by. Both were quiet, not wanting to be reminded of their problem. Tony finally broached the subject.

"Guess we better go pretty soon. According to Jack the place opens at three."

"Sure you know where it is?"

"I got it written down here. I looked it up on the map, too. It's not far."

"I kind of hate to start. Wish we could sit right here all afternoon."

"Me too. Say, Kay, when can you tell that somebody is going to have a baby, after how many months, I mean?"

"I don't know. I've heard my mother talk with different ladies about it. I guess there are some people who can tell real soon, even before you start getting big. I doubt that my mother can, though. Her father was a minister and she is real dumb about things like that."

"There's a lady in the apartment next to us. She's going to have a baby. I think Mom said she was six months pregnant and it really shows. Boy, does she stick out in front."

"Tony, that's not a nice thing to say. Gee, six months. We haven't got much time."

"You know," Tony said as they walked down the street, "you're a lot prettier since…well, lately, since the business about the baby."

"You think so?" She put her head on his shoulder as they went along.

"Cripes, don't get drippy about it. You're the prettiest girl in school. But there's no need to start drooling all over the place about it."

They turned off le *boulevard St. Michel* and toward the Pantheon, passing in front of *Lycée Henri IV* and entering a maze of narrow streets. But for today they had no eyes for history and monuments. They were hunting an address.

The nameplate beside the door said simply "Mme. Bouganet". Tony pushed a button to open the door and entered a passageway leading to an ancient courtyard. On the wall another sign with an arrow indicated a dimly lighted corridor. Advancing to the far end they found the door. Kay took a deep breath. Tony pulled the bell cord.

"*Entrez*," a voice called, so they pushed open the door and stepped into the tiny reception room. Sitting on a wooden bench a woman was crying, her shoulders moving rhythmically. On the wall above her head a large 1937 calendar bore illustrations of the signs of the zodiac. Tony and Kay sat down. The woman raised her eyes to look at them and went on crying.

After a few minutes a woman in a print dress came into the reception room. She stood there for a moment, her eyes darting around the room. She bobbed her head at the crying woman who rose and walked into the office. Madame Bouganet nodded at the young couple and closed the door.

Kay and Tony exchanged looks. They had never dreamed of anything like this. Kay had pictured maybe a gray-haired lady in a spotless white smock. She would be a kindly person with a sweet smile and a gentle voice. They would sit in her office and tell her the whole story right off.

They hoped she would have some suggestions as to how they could have their baby, or how best to tell their folks. If it were necessary to do something else she could tell them how to make their plans. Kay sat there staring at one of the pictures on the calendar, an animal sucking the breast of a woman. VIRGO. She grabbed Tony's hand.

"Tony, let's get out of here."

"Okay, if you—oh, oh, she's coming now."

Madame came out of her office and led Kay into a small room. It was unlike any medical facility she had ever seen. The space was neat enough but not as sanitary as she expected. Faded linoleum covered the floor. A high single bed occupied the center of the floor. The woman seated Kay on one end of the bed before asking her some questions, speaking very slowly.

"What age have you?"

"I will be eighteen this year,"

"Are you in good health, no chronic medical conditions?"

"Yes."

"No illegal drugs?"

"I have never taken any."

She nodded. "*Bien.*"

Out in the waiting area Tony sat studying the astrological designs. The only other information available was a pamphlet entitled *L'interruption de Grossesse.* It was hard to make out the words of a text printed in thin italic type. Without a dictionary he was lost. He sat wishing he had insisted on going in with Kay. What could that woman be doing to keep her in there so long?

Meantime Madame Bouganet had Kay lie back on the bed and with her fingers gently probed the lower parts of her body.

"Since how long?" she asked.

"A little more than two months."

"If you wish to end your pregnancy you should not wait much longer."

"How do you do that?" Kay asked.

"*Dilatation et curettage.* I show you." She reached for an illustrated card on her desk nearby.

Sitting again on the bed Kay was pale and shaken. She wished desperately that Tony were with her.

"Can my friend come in now?"

The woman opened the door and beckoned to him. Kay looked so miserable that he stood by the bed and put his arm around her.

"*Quand?*" the woman asked.

Kay looked at him. "She means when, when do we want to…"

"*Faut pas attendre.*" The woman gestured. "Must not wait."

"How much does it cost?" he asked.

"*Trente mille francs, monsieur, mais il faut faire bientôt.*"

They told Madame Bouganet they would let her know about a date soon and left.

"Gee, thirty thousand francs," Tony said. "That's beaucoup de dough, almost a hundred bucks."

"Oh, Tony." Kay clung to his arm. "I don't ever want to see her again. She was polite but very business like. She knows some English."

"Yeah. Creepy place, huh? But Jack told me that some of his French friends said she was good. He thinks a society doctor would be afraid to do that for a foreigner unless he got a lot of money."

"I thought she was a doctor."

"I didn't know what the deal was."

"Wait, Tony." Kay stopped and leaned on his arm. "I feel kind of sick to my stomach."

"Let's find a café somewhere and sit down."

"I think I'll be all right. But, please, let's walk real slow."

"Sure." Tony put his arm around her.

"There's a church, Kay." He pointed across the street to *Saint Etienne du Mont*. "Want to go inside and sit down for a minute?"

She nodded.

The church was empty. Sitting there in the cool silence Kay put her head on Tony's shoulder and closed her eyes. When finally the dizziness passed she looked around. Over on one side the stained-glass window floated in the dark interior. She got to her feet and took Tony's hand.

They stopped to study the design depicting the Nativity, outlined in the clearest blue Kay had ever seen. For an instant it seemed to her that all the beauty in the world was concentrated in that vibrant blue, filling her vision and throbbing in her temples. You can *feel* color, she thought, as she looked, like you can feel a pure phrase from a violin sonata. That blue is so deep it hurts.

"Hey, look at this," Tony whispered, but she was no longer beside him.

He looked down and saw her kneeling at a prayer bench her forehead resting on her arm. He stood there quietly waiting. When she came back to him he slipped his arm around her and held her tight. Kay took his hand and pressed it against her stomach.

After leaving the church they walked for a long way without saying a word.

"Tony, don't you ever pray?"

"Not in a Catholic church. I'm not Catholic."

"Neither am I. But that church—it's so beautiful that you just know that God is there. Besides, I'm sure He can hear you wherever you are."

Now that the spell was broken Tony's mind came back to the problem.

"Cripes, if she charges that much it must cost a lot more to have a baby."

"Oh, I think it does."

"Look, why don't I tell Ma and get the money from her? Even if she gets mad she'd come through with it."

"No. If you told your folks they'd tell my father. I know they would."

"I'm trying to think of something."

"I want to have that baby, Tony, more than anything else. Maybe we can figure something out without letting my father know."

"You can't do that, Kay. He'd have to know."

"I suppose so."

"Let's see. Pop gives me five bucks a week to spend. I got about forty saved for summer vacation. I can sell my cigarette ration card at *Pigalle*, maybe sell some of my stuff at the *Marché aux Puces*. But thirty thousand francs—that's still a lot of dough."

"Please, Tony, let's try to think of something else, anything else."

"Okay." He kicked at a pebble. "Gee, the world is a stupid place. It wasn't made for kids, that's for sure."

Chapter 29

It was the first of May. "Today Paris is the world's most delightful city." Bill took a deep breath.

Colette smiled. "When it turns warm, people are happy,"

This bright blue sky enlivened the streets crowded with holiday travelers. An assortment of people, children and little old ladies were selling bouquets of *muguet*. Bill and Colette passed the bookstalls of le *quai Anatole France* stopping to study illustrated maps and watercolor sketches hanging from clips.

In the Latin Quarter the quay became even more crowded.

"Let's go down and sit by the river for a few minutes to get away from the people," Colette suggested as they crossed *la Place Saint Michel*. "I love to watch the boats."

They descended the steps to the *berge*. Across from them were the vine-covered walls of the Nôtre Dame gardens.

"Here." Bill spread out a newspaper on a cement block. "Sit on that, my lady."

"*Merci, mon ami.*"

From up in the park across the water came the shouts of children at play. Before their eyes the reflected cathedral rocked gently on the surface of the Seine.

"I never told you that my mother and father were married at Nôtre Dame."

"You never said much about your folks."

"My mother died when I was a baby. My father I remember was an exceptionally kind man and he was always gentle with us. He became angry about politics. Papa loved the government of France but often he was upset with the people who ran it."

"He sounds *sympathique*. I think I would like him."

A *bateau mouche* gliding down the river past the island was crowded with passengers who waved to them as the boat passed.

"We should go soon, Bill."

"I know you aren't keen about the parade. We don't have to go if you would rather not."

"Oh, no. I think you should experience this special day."

As they walked onto the *Pont Sully Morland* they could see the monument and the broad boulevard leading to the famous *Place de la Bastille* which was already thronged with people. The big circular Place was ringed with police and police cars.

Bill looked around them. "Never saw so many *flics*."

"This is where history takes place." Colette pulled his arm. "Let's go this way. The parade will start at *la Place de la Nation* and proceed along *le faubourg Saint Antoine*."

They were moved along by the crowd and found themselves pushing and squeezing like everyone else. Getting onto the sidewalk proved to be perilous despite police efforts to clear a passage.

"I see no American military here," Colette remarked, "Why?"

"One reason may be that the Army puts out orders for all military personnel to wear civilian dress today," Bill replied. "They also request that civilian vehicles with military plates be kept off the streets."

"Why are you so frightened?"

"No use asking for trouble."

They were now standing in a crush of people unable to move. Bill began to realize that he was enjoying this and had no fear. It was an adventure and he was prepared to be a part of this event.

"Colette! Colette!"

They looked around and could see nobody they recognized.

"Somebody was calling you."

"There are thousands of French girls named Colette." She laughed.

"Colette, here we are."

A slim blond woman and a tall black man were thrust upon them, almost into their arms.

"Marguerite. Larry. Quelle chance!"

"Who are they?" Bill asked.

"Friends of Ken. Remember meeting them at your Christmas party?"

"Oh yes I do now. Join us."

Turning their backs toward the sidewalk, Bill and Larry managed to push backward from the center of the boulevard taking the girls with them.

"Listen. It has started."

They could hear the chanting marchers as they struggled to keep near the front. Hundreds of young people marched along in groups singing, waving signs and exchanging shouts with spectators along the street. Crimson banners under the blue sky and billowing scarves turned the long column into a ribbon of color.

"*Ri-cains en A-mé-rique.*"

"*A-mer-loques en A-mé-rique.*"

Bill listened. "That's us?"

"Of course."

"*A bas les dix-huit mois.*"

"And that is against military service in Indo-China."

"*Libérez Henri.*"

Placards bearing photos of Stalin and Maurice Thorez marched by.

Then. "*A bas Baylot. A bas Baylot.*"

Bill leaned close to Colette's ear. "Who is that?"

"*Le Préfet de Police.* Nobody likes him except maybe his wife. His officers harass political demonstrators."

"*A-mé-rique c'est la guerre.*"

A youth group came along marching under a gigantic red placard on a bamboo pole. When they drew abreast Bill recognized the leader.

Marguerite waved her scarf. "Jean."

The young man passed his sign to a companion and ran over to greet Bill and Larry and embrace both girls.

He turned to Bill. "You like the parade?"

"I think so."

Jean put one arm around Colette and his other arm across Bill's shoulders. He pulled the two of them along into the parade as they hurried after the tail end of his group. Surprised, Bill automatically grabbed for Colette's hand and swept along with them, carried by the momentum of the marching column. He saw spectators watching them as the chant started up again. "Americans go home!"

"Good Lord. Let's get out of here."

He reached for Colette's arm and broke away from Jean. As Bill pulled her over to the side Jean looked back and laughed, waving before breaking into a sprint to catch his group.

"Well, I'll be damned."

"You looked amazed." Colette roared with laughter. "Were you shouting for Americans to go home?"

"That's no joke. And now we have lost Larry and Marguerite."

"The best thing to do is stand right here and perhaps they will come along."

They found Larry and Marguerite half an hour later as they inched along the line of spectators toward the Bastille.

"I don't know about you but I've had enough."

"Me, too," said Larry.

"Let's go."

Colette looked at them. "This is the most orderly May Day I have seen."

"But it is not over yet," Marguerite said. "The police will find an excuse to do some clubbing before they finish."

Larry nodded. "Just like when I was a kid in Harlem."

"Come over to my place for a while," Bill said. "Your friend Ken will be there."

"*Bonne idée.*"

When the drinks were served back in Bill's apartment Larry proposed a toast. "Everybody is telling Americans to go home and that's just where I am headed next month. Shall we drink to Uncle Sam?"

Ken looked shocked. "You're going to the States?"

"I got my orders yesterday. Had a year's extension already. When I tried for another one I had no luck. We will be leaving the first week in June."

"You going together?"

"Wives are not included. I want Marguerite to go by ship but she prefers the airways."

Bill sat down with his drink. "I thought families always went together by ship. I didn't know the Army gave you a choice."

"They don't when they pay the bill. Only sergeants and higher get dependents shipped. I have to pay for Marguerite and the baby."

"And where will you be stationed?"

"I don't know but I sure as hell hope it won't be Alabama. First I'll ship to Fort Dix."

"Think you'll like the United States, Marguerite?"

"I'm rather frightened but as long as Larry is there it will be all right."

"Let's honor this event." Bill put his arm around Colette. "I'm inviting all of you to dinner tonight. We'll find a good restaurant. You'll have time won't you, Ken, before you're due at the club?"

"Great idea, Bill. And then after dinner you all can be my guests at the club."

In high spirits they sat around the dinner table savoring the occasion.

"I enjoyed the parade." Marguerite looked at Bill.

"Frankly, I thought the chanting got a bit monotonous. We have a song, Ken, that French marchers could dedicate to Americans on May Day."

"We'd Get Along Without You Very Well."

"Didn't Johnny Mercer do that one?"

After dessert Ken looked at his watch. "I hate to break up this beautiful moment but I'm booked for the evening. Let's go."

For the first time in months Bill was able to forget the school. Never a great dancer he often avoided the dance floor. But when they were seated at Ken's club the graceful Marguerite refused to take 'no' for an answer, guiding Bill along with her.

"*Mon ami*," she said as they whirled around the tiny square of space, "you can bend without breaking."

"What?"

"You have fine rhythm but you are so stiff. Let go." Doubling her hand into a fist she pressed it sharply into his back.

211

"Ouch. That's like a rabbit punch." He relaxed as the fist was removed.

"Much better. What does Larry say?—sweeng eet, baby."

Bill soon discovered that dancing could be fun.

"When he loosens up," Marguerite told Colette as they returned to the table, "he's a good dancer. Try him."

Larry lifted his trumpet to his lips to warm up slowly with Saint Louis Blues. Then he stepped up the tempo. Conversations died at the tables and dancers stopped to listen.

Ken found someone to sit in at the piano and danced with the girls. Joining them for a quick drink during an intermission he introduced a blond French girl to them as Blossom, a sometimes singer with the Trio.

"In honor of this evening Blossom and I are going to sing a new song I wrote. It's called *The Kinsey Report*."

Ken returned to the piano and went into a huddle with the other boys in the Trio before they started to play.

Meanwhile some newcomers approached the next table. The two couples were obviously Americans. The older man was burly. Dressed in a plaid shirt and string tie, he wore a ten-gallon hat which he had refused to surrender at the check stand. He turned to the waiter.

"Give us the best damned table in the house, sonny."

"*Oui, monsieur.*" The waiter set them up next to Ken's party.

It was hard to ignore the booming voice and Bill found himself extremely irritated.

The man caught the attention of the tables around him and when a woman looked curiously at the big hat he tossed it over to her.

"Try it on, sister."

She placed the hat carefully on over her hairdo and posed while everyone applauded. Then Bill began to hear snatches of conversation that made him feel uneasy.

"Sure, they're here together."

"That's probably why so many of them come to Paris."

"She probably likes it. Some of them come over here to get studded by a big black boy."

"Bill." Colette was tapping his arm. "Ken's song."

Ken and Blossom were at the microphone ready to swing into their calypso rhythm.

> *Do you sleep in bed, he said*
> *With a pillow under your head*
> *When I am led to bed, she said*
> *My bedmates all have habits*
> *They are very much like rabbits*

"Why doesn't she make love to that Jig right on the spot," came from the next table.

"Not so loud, Jake," one of the women at the table said. "People will hear you."

"I don't give a damn who hears me. I'll bet those niggers are American."

The trio had stopped playing and in the quiet of the club this comment was meant for all to hear.

Bill experienced a familiar electric feeling in the hair on his neck. He surprised himself by standing and facing the next table.

"Sir, my friends are American, and your language is extremely offensive."

The man took a quick step toward him.

"Nobody can tell me..."

Two waiters pulled the man back and attempted to sit him down. With a sweep of his arm he sent one of the waiters staggering backward. Bill had clenched his fist ready to swing but the man was no longer there. Louis, *le patron* of the club. arrived in a flash with a waiter and they escorted the big man through the door. His friends looked at each other in confusion. Then they followed him out.

An uneasy silence hung over the club. During the scuffle Ken and Cotton had finished their number. Larry was well launched into a trumpet solo with "Body and Soul". He returned to their table when he finished.

"That was great, Larry." Bill gave him a thumbs-up.

As they all sat there in silence Louis appeared at their table with glasses and a bottle of champagne in a silver bucket. He placed a tray in front of Larry.

"Compliments of the house."

"We should drink to something," Ken suggested.

"To Larry," Colette raised her glass. "Health, happiness and luck."

"Thanks, baby. The luck I might need."

Bill and Colette were silent in the car driving home. Bill tried to think of something comforting but his imagination was bone dry. After he had pulled up to the curb he and Colette watched Larry and Marguerite walking up the front steps. With his arm around her Larry opened the door and they turned to wave before disappearing inside.

Chapter 30

Kay Selner had always done what her parents wanted her to do with one notable exception. At age 14 in the eighth grade of her church school she was seated next to a girl named Emily. A chief rebel of her class, Emily was frequently in trouble. Kay started eating lunch with Emily. They became friends and shared their secrets.

Emily's biggest secret was that her father beat her and one time hit her mother. Once when they were together in the girls' toilet Emily showed some of her bruises. On one occasion she had been placed in a shelter for abused children.

When the teacher caught them exchanging notes she scolded them before their classmates, threatening more severe punishment. After school the girls hugged each other and decided to walk around for a while.

They joked with men repairing the sidewalk and visited some shops. Emily conned a store clerk into giving them candy bars.

"I have never had so much fun," Kay remarked as they sat on a bench chewing on the bars and watching the street life of the nation's capital.

Emily persuaded Kay to consider running away with her. She had once seen a western movie and thought they might hitchhike west to see real cowboys. Kay found that exciting but really frightening. At nightfall Emily led them to the shelter for abused children.

Blanche, the housemother, greeted the girls warmly and gave them a hot meal. The two girls were given adjacent cots in a crowded dormitory.

The next morning Blanche, who already knew Emily, called the school to find Kay's parents. Kay's father came for her immediately. As he hurried her away Kay broke his strong grip on her arm to stop and give Emily a parting hug.

Emily was removed from the school and until the end of the semester Kay's mother came every day to escort her home or to her violin lessons.

At the age of seven Kay had been started on violin lessons. She had no special interest in the instrument but she practiced faithfully each day. Music lessons had the same importance as schoolwork, Sunday school, and prayers. Her ability to play increased during the next four years. For her the violin was simply an instrument her folks had wanted her to play—until she met Mr. Nicotelli. Then it became something sacred, on a level with her feelings about God, only more real.

The change came about after her father was transferred to Washington D.C. Her folks looked for a violin teacher and arranged for her to study with Mr. Nicotelli, a slender man with nervous fingers vibrant with the intensity of his commitment to music. It was her first contact with genuine human emotion. At first he frightened her. He would knock the violin out of her hands with a sweep of his arm and catch it in midair to demonstrate that she was not holding it properly.

"No! No! You would not let me remove your head, no? When you play the violin it is a part of your body like your head or your heart."

He was unrelenting, tough. He made Kay cry more than once, and sometimes she felt like a dunce who should have studied the mouth organ instead of a more delicate instrument. This was how she felt until she came to know him better. Then she discovered an inspiring friend.

The violin became a passion with her, all the more exciting because she had someone with whom to share it. She made phenomenal progress and Mr. Nicotelli began to talk with her about a concert career.

"The thing to get is tone, tone, tone. Technique is nothing. Anybody with muscles can develop technique."

Kay had to smile, thinking of the difficult hours he had driven her to develop posture, ease, and technique.

Another time he told her, "You have a beautiful soul," in the same matter of fact way he might compliment her on a dress she was wearing. "It comes out when you play. You are beginning to develop tone. It is your soul speaking out. You are young but already you have something to say. You feel things. Yes, you are one of those, capable of sorrow. As you grow your soul will become full of tears and if you work hard you will be able to project them into the tone of your violin."

Until she met Tony, Mr. Nicotelli was the only person she had ever loved. Kay went to tell him goodbye when she left Washington and they both cried.

Mr. Weinberger, the instrumental teacher at school, had listened to her play and said frankly that he couldn't help her very much. He counseled her to find a skilled teacher, perhaps at the *conservatoire*, and to take advantage of the concerts that could be heard in Paris.

Since she met Tony music had a new meaning for her. Playing the violin was satisfying as it had never been before. So strong was her urge to play that she could scarcely wait to get home from school in the afternoon. She was working on two Beethoven sonatas.

At this moment she was practicing a sonata for her solo in the spring concert to take place at school the following week. Mr. Helmer had suggested that Mr. Ken Wilson might be willing to play the accompaniment for her. She was thrilled at the idea. They had practiced together the day before and he was enthusiastic about her playing. Kay wanted to be worthy of his praise.

She tucked the violin under her chin.

"I hope you're not neglecting your other studies for the violin," her mother remarked that afternoon. "Perhaps too much music isn't good for you. You look peaked."

"I'm all right, Mother. I must practice for the concert." She wished at all cost to avoid discussing her health or her appearance.

After the night with her classmates and Tony at Pigalle when her parents were away she lived in an agony of guilt exceeded only by the fear of discovery. Every ring of the telephone shattered her composure. Martha's mother might be calling and say something revealing that Kay had not spent that night with Martha. But her parents were so habituated to her obedience that they never thought of checking on her. And now the fear of exposure had been replaced with a more compelling problem that filled every corner of her consciousness and kept her nerves as taut as the strings of her violin.

Her mother was still hovering at the door.

"Just the same, you don't get any exercise. You hardly went outdoors during Easter vacation."

"Well, when you and Daddy go to the conference, I'll stay with Martha and we can play some tennis or go for a long walk." She waited, breathless, to see if this plan would be accepted.

"You know, dear, I don't like the idea of leaving you for a weekend like that. Your father doesn't either. We've only done it once before."

"But I won't be alone, Mother. I'll be with Martha. We can have so much fun."

What a terrible liar I'm getting to be, she thought. Fun was hardly the word for her appointment with Madame Bouganet a week from Friday. The old woman had said that if she could stay all night and rest Saturday, everything would be fine. It was more luck than she could have hoped for, that her folks were leaving for a weekend.

"Well, you must promise to be a good girl and offer to help Mrs. Luten with the dishes."

"Of course, Mother." Kay breathed a silent prayer of thanks. She couldn't wait to tell Tony. She thought of calling him from Martha's house but he was probably out practicing with the track team.

The track squad had gathered at the far end of the athletic field and the boys were milling about waiting for Mr. Parsons to come and start the try-outs. Tony was horsing around with a shot-putter named Larry, a husky senior. Larry caught him off balance with a shoulder butt that sent him spinning into a couple of teammates. Tony struck one of the boys full force and the two of them toppled to the ground.

"Watch what you're doing, Mosca, or I'll pin your ears back." It was Chuck Mason.

"You and how many divisions of infantry?"

"I can knock you on your big fat ass without..."

"All right boys, all right." The coach came running up. "Gather round and make it snappy. We got a lot to do tonight. You boys know the score," Mr. Parsons said. "The All-Star track meet for American high schools will be held in Frankfurt, Germany the first week in May. That's just ten days off. Each school is entitled to one and only one entry for each event. You know what that means. We have to choose. That's why we're here. I don't want to hear no squawks afterwards. Maybe you won't do your best and figure you should have another chance. Well, that'll be just too bad. Tonight is final."

Holding his hand toward the boys to keep their attention, he said something to Mr. Evans as he gave him a stopwatch.

"I brought Mr. Evans with me to help time and judge the winners. If he and I disagree, we'll run the event over. If we agree, that will be it. We'll run the field events first and then the track events, starting with the dashes and working up to the mile. Track men, take off your sweat pants and start warming up on this side. If you finish before your race is called, be sure to put your sweats back on. Don't get cold. Snap it up now. Good luck everybody."

"Too bad you have to miss that trip to Germany, Mosca."

"Save your sympathy. You may need it yourself."

"We'll see."

"After track season," Tony told him, I'll be around to settle with you."

"Yeah." Chuck stopped running in place. "Like you did before. Hit me with a carton of milk when you knew the principal was around to stop it before I could fix your clock."

"I don't like the way you shoot off your mouth." Tony started doing deep knee bends.

"You're getting a might finicky since you've been running around with your precious chaplain's daughter."

"Leave her out of this." Tony straightened up abruptly. "Or you'll get something you don't expect."

"Sweet little Kay. Thinks she's so high and mighty. You know why nobody likes her, don't you? She's so good she stinks."

Tony swung hard with a right, a straight punch starting shoulder high. But it never landed. A hand caught his wrist in a crushing grip, forcing his arm down to his side so hard he felt the pain in his back.

The hand quickly shifted to his shoulder where the fingers dug into his muscles. He swung around furiously, ready with his left. It was Mr. Evans, whose other hand was on Chuck Mason's shoulder.

"If you girls are angry with each other, why don't you try pulling hair?"

The two boys stood there squirming.

"Any more of this and you're off the squad. I'll knock your heads together and drag the bodies over to Coach Parsons. After track season if you two want to slug it out I'll get some six-ounce gloves and referee for you. But if you want to run in the All-Star you better stop acting like grade school kids. Now get out there and warm up."

Releasing his hold, he gave each of them a clap on the back. Then he turned and walked across the field toward the jumping pits.

When the hundred-yard dash was called some time later there were two candidates, Tony Mosca and Chuck Mason. Tony knelt on one knee at the line, carefully measuring his distances for starting holes. He pushed his spikes against the backs of them to test the angle.

"All right," Mr. Parsons announced. "You each have one false start, then you're through. Remember what I told you about straightening up too fast. Come on let's go."

Tony wished he hadn't smoked so much lately. He promised himself not to touch another cigarette until after track season. "Oh God, please let me win just this once, please let me win."

"On your marks." Tony knelt, carefully placing his feet in the starting holes.

"Get set." He was up with most of his weight on his hands and with his head down.

The pistol fired.

"No, No," the coach shouted. "False start."

They came back to the line.

"You jumped the gun, Tony. Watch that. It'll disqualify you in an official meet. This'll be your last chance." He handed the pistol to a student assistant. "Here, you start them but give me long enough to get up to the finish line with Mr. Evans. I better watch this one from there."

"On your marks. Get set."

Crack.

It was one of Tony's best starts. He had all his weight balanced on his hands and he kept his head down. With weight thrown forward he didn't come out of his crouch until the fifty-yard marker. He put everything he had into each thrust of his legs, keeping a balanced rhythm to his arm swing. Mason was right beside him but he couldn't tell who was in the lead. He had a feeling that Mason was slightly ahead but he was afraid to look. Looming before him the tape seemed blurred. He lunged forward with all the force he had left.

"What was your verdict on that one?" the coach called across to Mr. Evans.

"I had Mosca by about two feet."

"It was closer than that but Tony hit the tape first. No doubt about that." He made a note on his record sheet and called out. "Mosca for the hundred yards. Mason will be alternate."

"What does that mean, coach?" Chuck panted as he and Tony came back to the finish line.

"That means you replace Mosca for the All-Star if he's not able to go."

Chuck Mason came up along side as Tony headed back to the locker room. He spoke softly because the coach and Mr. Evans were close behind them.

"I'm going to fix you but good."

"You don't have to send any engraved invitations, pal. I'm ready any time, just any time."

Tony's anger was mixed with elation at his triumph. He couldn't wait to tell Kay about it.

Chapter 31

"I hope you didn't mind waiting, *ma cherie*. I was helping Hal finish a final exam schedule. I didn't think...Fool!" Bill swung the wheel sharply barely missing the motorcycle.

"Those things frighten me. I hope you never ride one."

"Don't worry. I like life."

Colette settled back in the seat. "Friday is always a beautiful day."

"True."

"You notice there is no French word for weekend, an American invention I like."

"Glad you approve."

"Especially this year. Our weekends have been marvelous." She put her hand on his shoulder. "Can we drive through the woods, *chéri*?"

"Of course." Bill swerved off the highway into a road winding among the trees.

Colette rolled down her window and breathed deeply.

"Only two more weeks," he said. "We'll really have to hang one on."

"Hang what?"

"You know, a real celebration—champagne and dancing."

"Well, I would like to celebrate by exploring these beautiful woods."

"This weekend?"

"Or possibly live here forever and ever."

"Without sleeping bags?"

"We can dine on herbs and roots and sleep on Spanish moss."

"Where is the Spanish moss?"

"*Chéri*, you cannot see any but it is there. So are the wood nymphs and elves."

"In our *Bois de Boulogne?*"

"Naturally."

Bill reached for her hand. "We'll find a dignified old praying mantis to marry us under a big oak."

"You think we should be married?"

"What do you suppose I've been trying to tell you since Easter?"

"I thought you only wanted to renew my contract at school."

"Damn you, Colette. I'd like to take your pants down and spank your bare butt."

"I would resist."

"Just you wait until school is out."

He pulled out into the heavy traffic near Colette's place. When he parked in front they sat still for a moment. He made no move to get out of the car.

"Can you come up for a while?"

"If I did I might not make it out to Callahan's."

"You are having dinner with Mrs. Callahan?"

"Yes, with the family."

"Bill, you never mention the P.T.A. election."

"I would rather not think about it."

"What will happen if your friends do not win?"

"Well, they may transfer me to Siberia or back to Oregon."

"They want to punish you?"

"Well, we have some unattractive school jobs. They could make me a teaching principal in a junior high school in central France or Germany."

"Is that possible?"

"Oh yes."

"Then you could not stay in Paris?"

"Well I might be a *clochard* and sleep under a bridge."

"You are not worried?"

"I can't worry about two things at the same time. I've been worried about you."

224

"Are you now?"

"Of course," he said, "but the next two weeks should break down your resistance."

"When you take down my pants." Colette opened the door.

"You're having dinner with me tomorrow night," he reminded her.

"Yes. Perhaps we can suspend something. How did you say it?"

Bill looked puzzled then laughed. "Hang one on, you mean?"

"That sounds *très grave*."

"Just the opposite. You down bottles of whiskey or champagne, if you happen to be in France. It is most helpful."

"Like Hal and Mr. Jackson at your Christmas party?"

"Exactly."

"*Très bien*. We will hang one if you wish, but I may get foolish."

Bill smiled. "I hope so."

When Bill arrived the Callahan clan was engaged in a game of badminton. He declined the proffered racket but gratefully accepted the iced drink Josette brought him. As soon as Tojo was satisfied he had more points than anybody, Tom and Peg joined Bill.

"We're eating picnic style, Bill. Tom found some thick steaks in our own little nearby *boucherie*. We'll just throw them on the charcoal and let everybody help himself."

"Tonight I can do justice to a steak."

"What's happening at school?" Peg asked as they sat after dinner in the twilight of a balmy spring evening.

"I feel I've been letting you down, Peg, on this P.T.A. thing. I'm up to my ears."

"Frankly, the campaign is getting nasty. Have you seen any of the literature Mrs. Breen is putting out?"

"I saw a couple of posters. Matter of fact there's one on the bulletin board in the front hall of the school."

Peg went into her library and came back with some paper, mostly mimeographed mail-outs. Tom stood.

"No light here. Let's go up on the porch where Bill can read and have some more coffee."

The literature from the Committee on Christian Education implied that the school children were not getting a proper "American" education. Bill presumed that Chaplain Selner meant the kind of teaching now being offered in the American High School.

"Jingo patriots have always waved the Bible and the cross. However, I didn't expect anything quite so crass, Tom."

"Don't forget, Bill, this is a military community where patriotism is all important."

"This Christian Committee gets under my skin," Peg added. "Just look at this little gem of Charlotte Breen's." She handed Bill a neatly mimeographed bulletin:

P.T.A. ELECTION BULLETIN
VOTE FOR

Major Charles Banks (Army).....................President
Captain Matthew Long (U.S. Navy)............ Vice President
Mrs. Charlotte Breen .... Treasurer
Lt. William Mason (USAF).........................Secretary
CAST A VOTE OF CONFIDENCE IN THE FUTURE OF OVERSEAS CHILDREN

We want the best schools in Paris for the Nieces and Nephews of Uncle Sam:
LET'S GIVE OUR STUDENTS A BREAK.

"There's something there for almost everybody, at least for the people who've been opposing me this year."

"How's that, Bill?"

"Mrs. Breen and Chaplain Selner are working together on this committee."

Bill studied the list. "This is what you call a balanced ticket. Gets every major branch of the service."

"Never mind." Peg handed him a bundle of papers.

"More coffee, Bill?" Tom filled his cup and put the pot down on the flagstone terrace beside his chair. "This Americanism bit worries me. I hate to ask you this, Bill, but did you ever have any trouble with your security clearance?"

"Not that I remember. Why do you ask, Tom?"

"I'm not supposed to tell you this but a man was around from the Security Section checking on you just last week. He sounded as if your security status has been opened up again."

"I can't imagine why they would do that."

"There was also a man from French *sureté* asking about the French teachers and seemed especially interested in Mademoiselle Bernard."

A flash of fear made Bill's skin tingle. If they dug enough into Colette's friends and found Jean, it could reveal damaging security information.

"Dammit, Colette is a fine teacher. I don't see what security has to do with it."

"It has a lot to do with it, Bill."

"Many French people have Communist acquaintances. Colette probably has. After all, there are five million Communist votes in each French election."

"This is tricky stuff. It pays to be careful. I believe the topic is more a personal project of Murphy's than a plan of the committee, Bill."

"How do you know that, Peg?"

"I have my inside intelligence. Mrs. Breen is onto the American angle but she just thinks you love the French too much."

"This could be real dynamite." Tom shook his head.

"Well, there isn't a hell of a lot that I or anybody else can do about their past friends and acquaintances. I would stake my honor on the fact that there are no Communists on the school staff."

"That's not the point. You don't have to be a Communist to be a security risk from the military point of view. This has me worried."

"Incidentally, do you have American flags in all the classrooms?"

"No, but I'm well covered on that. They have been ordered a long time."

"I got myself on the committee to count ballots," Peg added. "And it wasn't easy. I can't figure out why they made such a great fuss over having a mail ballot. Maybe I'm just not bright but I don't see any particular advantage to them."

"Elementary, my dear." Tom checked off the points on his fingers. "First, if it's a nice evening not many will come to a meeting. Second, the ones who do come are worried about their kids and want favors from the school. Third, the Old Man will be there. If he smiles on Bill it would influence voting."

"That's sound strategy, Peg. They're not stupid."

"The mail ballot was Chaplain Selner's idea. He's quite a politician."

"The early missionaries came over to make Christians out of Americans," Tom remarked. "What really happened is that America has made politicians out of the Christians."

"The election is next week and I'll be glad when it's over."

"What deadline did you set, Peg?"

"The count will be announced the day after school is out."

"Wow, it's almost midnight. I better go."

"We're rooting for you, friend."

"Thanks for the dinner."

Standing in the drive Tom stifled a yawn. "We'll have to celebrate when this school year is all wrapped up."

"That's what I was telling Colette today."

"You know I never really talked with Colette until the last P.T.A. meeting. What a charmer, Bill."

"I think so myself. In fact I'm trying to persuade her to marry me."

"Why didn't you tell me? I had no idea. You can't leave on a line like that. If I had known I would have invited her tonight. "

"I will invite you over to my place. I'm not much of a cook but Ken is a real chef. We can both mix drinks."

'Oh, yes, Bill. I almost forgot. What do you know about Ken's politics?"

"Why do you ask, Tom?"

"The security man asked me about him."

"He has no interest in politics. But what business of the Army's is that?"

"To be perfectly honest about it, Bill, the fact that you are sharing your apartment with a black man is not in your favor."

"Why, Tom! How in the world can you say that?"

"That is not my opinion. You know that, Bill. I'm merely stating a fact."

"I still don't see what that has to do with the price of eggs."

"The Security man who talked to me had a Southern accent a mile broad. Living with Ken isn't a material fact. It would never go on the record. But it's prejudicial all the same. Don't be naïve, Bill."

"I'll choose my own friends, thank you, and they can shove their goddam job."

"You are dead wrong there, Bill. We could all pull out on some high sounding principle and nothing would be gained. Government service needs people like you—like us. We can do some good if we keep fighting and don't run away."

"Is Tom right about playing along with the system so you can stay and fight," Bill wondered as he drove home, "or is that just an excuse, an easy way out?"

Swinging left on the outer boulevard Bill headed for *Montmartre*. He decided that he would drop by the club for a drink with Ken before he went home.

Chapter 32

The student recital had been long. In the heat of the school auditorium the audience became restless. Ventilating fans in the back were switched on between numbers but they were so noisy they had to be turned off during each performance.

"Our last presentation," the student announcer said, "will be a violin solo, Beethoven's Sonata Number 2 in A, played by Miss Kay Selner. She will be accompanied at the piano by Mr. Kenneth Wilson, American pianist and composer."

It was good of Ken, Bill thought, to dig himself out of bed after playing all night at the club. He had come out several times to rehearse with Kay. In the spirit of the occasion he even donned formal dress to give a concert touch.

Kay appeared on stage and stood there while the student announcer adjusted her music stand and microphone. Tony put away his pocket book and straightened up. How lucky can a guy be to have somebody like Kay in love with him?

He was glancing around to see if people in the audience were watching Kay. Mrs. Stepanovic, sitting two seats away, caught his eye and smiled at him.

Kay wore a white evening gown with simple lines. Her classmates, long accustomed to backless and strapless dresses, found nothing exciting about her robe, but her father had. He had almost forbidden her to wear it at the last minute. Kay wondered as she stood there in front of everybody if the dress were indeed vulgar as he had said. She looked out at the audience. Mr. Nicoletti would have been upset had he seen her so uneasy before starting to play. Poised with her violin in place she nodded to Ken.

Ta da, tada, tada…Piano and violin swung briskly into the opening measure as one instrument.

Mr. Weinberger, relieved that the recital was almost finished, made his way out to check on refreshments. Then he turned to listen. When she started the second movement he reached for a chair. He had no idea the girl could interpret like that. I would never have believed, he thought, that anybody but a Jew could pull that much feeling out of a violin.

Colette was sitting there admiring the sure touch of Ken's accompaniment. Slowly her attention turned to the pure tones of the violin. Hal Evans listened more and more intently as a melody line vibrated some remotely responsive chord of memory… Jubilo…Jubilo. Where had he heard that tune before? It was back under the old oak tree. On a warm summer evening, listening to the Baptist choir. In some strange way it was dominated by the soprano section, for the music was high-pitched. Then in a moment of silence after Kay finished he found himself in the high school auditorium.

Faithful to Mr. Weinberger's instructions Kay lowered her violin and stood facing the audience. He had told her to bow when the applause started and to walk slowly offstage by the exit near the piano, so she and Ken could go out together. If there were sufficient applause she should come back, bringing Ken with her to bow a second time.

Kay had the directions well in mind, but there was not a sound. It could not have been that bad, she thought. What should she do now? She hesitated a moment and turned to exit. She was moving across the stage when a storm of applause broke out.

"Child," Ken said when she came up to him, "if you are going to play like that, don't ever ask me to accompany you again. Next time I just want to sit and listen."

"Oh, thank you, Mr. Wilson. And thank you so much for playing."

"Honey, stay in love with that violin and you'll really be going places."

But she was less and less sure of where she was going as the days passed.

Kay was sitting in the French classroom long after school was out. The building was quiet and there was nothing to disturb her concentration, yet she found herself unable to study. For some time she had been having periods of nausea and she was frightened. Maybe the baby was dead inside her as punishment for what she had done. She had nobody to talk with about her condition. She was nervous these days and easily moved to tears. The only thing she could enjoy was playing the violin.

In the calm of twilight she could hear the boys shouting as they came into the dressing room downstairs. A few minutes later she heard someone bounding up the stairs and Tony appeared at the door.

"Hi, beautiful. Improving your mind?"

"I just can't keep my attention on studying."

"Nothing to worry about. I've been that way all my life. Say." Tony looked at her. "You are pale as a ghost. You sick or something?"

"I'm O.K."

"Listen, Kay, the All-Star track meet has been set up a week. We're supposed to leave Thursday evening on the 8:30 train."

"But, Tony. That's when I have my appointment. That's when...well, you know what."

"Maybe we can change our appointment. The old lady won't mind. I sure want to go to that track meet. I don't want Chuck Mason to go in my place. I may be able to take first medal."

"We can't change that, Tony. My folks will be gone this week end and I will never have another chance like that. Besides, this just won't wait any longer."

"Yeah. Guess that's right. I'll stay here then."

"Oh, you can go if you want to. You don't have to stay for that."

"Cripes, Kay." He looked relieved. "Maybe Jack could go with you. He could take you down in his dad's car and check on you Saturday morning."

"Oh no."

"I know you don't like him but he's really a good egg. He'd be glad to do it."

"No. I don't want Jack in on this."

"Well, you can't go alone, that's a cinch. Guess I'll have to stay." Tony traced a line on the floor with the toe of his shoe.

"You don't *have* to stay. And I don't have to go alone. Martha would go with me I'm sure."

"Cripes, that's an idea. She'd probably be more help than I would. I can give you the thirty thousand francs Thursday. Sure you wouldn't mind?"

"No. I can ask Martha." She had no intention of putting Martha on the spot.

"You'll be at Martha's?"

"Yes, I'll be there. That's fine."

"Come on. I'll take you home on the bus."

"No. Go ahead. I want to stay here and study some more. I'm way behind in French."

"Cripes, Kay. You're sore because I'm going away. Come on. I want to take you home."

"No, really. I want to study."

"Honest?"

"Honest," she said.

He came over to give her an awkward kiss.

"Bus leaves in five minutes, every body out," she heard Coach Parsons calling out downstairs. A few minutes later he shouted into the corridor. "Building clear, everybody out. Last bus leaving."

Kay heard it pull out of the loading area with a grinding of gears, and the building was quiet. She planned to take the city bus home, anyway. She just couldn't face all those kids right now.

Kay put her head on the desk and started to cry. Oh, Tony, how could you? And for a stupid track meet. Sure, he would have stayed if she had insisted but it's no good that way. He should have wanted to stay. Couldn't he see that? Maybe this was just the beginning of her punishment. She had known that God would punish her but somehow she never suspected He could be such a terrible master.

She was still there with her head on the desk when a French cleaning woman came in.

"*Vous êtes malade, ma petite?*"

"*Non, madame,*" Kay replied.

234

She gathered up her books and papers. The woman began to sweep the floor.

"*Histoire d'amour?*" she asked.

"*Oui. Histoire d'amour.*" Kay tried to smile.

As she departed she turned to look at the woman.

"*Au revoir, madame.*"

"*Au revoir, mademoiselle. Bonne chance.*"

Chapter 33

"How did it go at the club last night, Ken?" Bill paused in the kitchen door to exchange greetings with Ken before leaving for school.

"I didn't play at the club last night."

"Oh?"

"I was with Marguerite. Larry shipped out yesterday."

"That's terrible. Their baby isn't even six months old."

"His name is Paul. That's about his age."

"When are they leaving?"

"They aren't." Ken leaned back in his chair and looked at Bill. "They won't let her go."

"What? Who won't let them go?"

"I don't know exactly. I guess it's the United States government."

"Why, for heaven's sake. She's his wife. They have a child."

"They said it was because her uncle is a Communist so they refused her a visa. Her brother is in the party. She couldn't pass a security investigation. Of course that's just an excuse."

"What do you mean?"

"I believe the real reason is because Larry is black and his wife is white. That's what."

"I doubt that, Ken. We can be pretty silly about Communism. But it's hard to believe they would break up a family."

Bill poured a cup of coffee and sat down at the table.

Ken looked at him. "Marguerite is absolutely out of her mind. Larry has a three-year hitch left and they can't do a thing about it. Some

237

stupid goddamn chaplain told her if she loved Larry she would let him go because they would never be happy in America. He told her their kids would be crucified."

"Good God!"

"I lived a long time last night. It made me see a lot of things I guess I really knew but didn't want to face."

Bill couldn't think of a thing to say.

"I've been working on a concerto." Ken was swinging his cup around watching the swirling coffee. "But my real ambition has been to do an opera. Believe it or not, Bill, the theme of my opera was to be an American Negro married to a Southern white girl in Paris."

"Like Larry except that his wife is French."

"Exactly. And that makes it worse. I couldn't have dreamed up anything more tragic." Ken put his cup down. "When I came to Paris I felt like a human being for the first time in my whole life. It was great to go into a shop—to go anywhere and not worry about what color I am. I knew I would always love Paris but in the back of my mind was the dream of going home a success. Maybe I thought living here would rub some of the black off—inside me, I mean—so it would be different when I went home."

"Well, you're developing your musical career."

"I was going to write the great American opera and go home in triumph. Make all the spots in Harlem before a trip home to Michigan. Everyone would turn out to see the native son composer. My mother would be dressed up with a flowered hat as she sat with me on a platform while Mr. Willis, the mayor, made a speech to a town decked out like the Fourth of July, every store on Main Street flying the flag."

Ken grasped both ends of a croissant and ripped it in two.

"I don't ever want to see the flag again. Now I know I'll never go back. Never.""

"Ken, I'm sorry as hell." Bill hated to leave at that moment but he had to get out to school. He stood up and paused awkwardly. "I have to take off, Ken. But I'll come up to the club tonight."

He was out of the door when Ken called.

"Bill."

He stopped on the landing and looked back at the door where Ken was standing.

"I think I ought to tell you, Bill, that some other people were around last night. Marguerite's brother was there and Jean."

"You mean Colette's friend?"

"Yes. The Communists are planning a big demonstration today. They found out the U.S. is building dormitories for a boarding school. I think the American School is one of the places where they will march. Sorry I didn't tell you that first thing, but I guess there's nothing anybody can do about it."

"Thanks, Ken." Bill was halfway down the first flight of stairs when a thought occurred to him and he called back, "Ken, was Colette there last night?"

"Yes, she was."

In his haste Bill ran a red light getting to school that morning. But he was too late. The street in front of the school was jammed with cars of every description: trucks, staff cars, Army and French police cars and covered blue trucks of the *Compagnie Républicaine de Sécurité*. The main gate had been sealed off by a cordon of M.P.'s, Canvas-covered American troop trucks were filled with soldiers sitting impassively on the side benches.

A policeman flagged Bill down and after inspecting his identification suggested that he park his car in a side street.

Picking his way through the crowd toward the gate, Bill noticed an American officer with a bull horn walking up and down the fence shouting, "American personnel, stay back, stay back. The French police are in charge."

The demonstrators were young, probably students, Bill thought. A few of them gathered in front of Chez Maurice and started chanting *"Amérique c'est la guerre"*, "Americans go home." As French police rushed upon them, swinging their clubs, the group seemed to vanish. They were no longer there but other young people on the opposite corner took up the chanting. The police wheeled and chased back across the street where others were chanting in unison. Police dashed here and there chasing the students who dispersed and reassembled with amazing rapidity.

Bill could see a strategy in the demonstration. The movements were not entirely random. Students running from the police darted into the street slowing passing automobiles and forcing them to stop.

With traffic halted the crossroads in every direction were a mass of immobilized vehicles giving the demonstrators a jungle of passageways among the cars to escape the police. Stranded motorists descended from their cars further complicating the work of the police. Bill sensed that many of the spectators were sympathetic to the demonstrators.

The French police nabbed protestors, men and women alike. Bill watched a policeman hit a girl with his stick before he delivered her to the men throwing captives into the paddy wagon (*le panier à salade*). A man on crutches bearing a sign *Ancien Combatant*, caught the attention of a policeman who snatched his sign knocking him off balance. Before he fell the *gendarme* rapped him smartly on the head. Bill turned away.

Groups of high school students unloaded from buses were being held behind the fence by M.P.s. Some of them from later buses were caught in the traffic outside the fence. They poured out to mingle with police, Army, and spectators before anyone could take charge of them. A group led by Jack Brewster heading for the center of action drew Bill's attention. As he rushed out to stop them he was struck on the shoulder and felt a grip of iron on his arm. A policeman pulled him toward the corner.

"*Allez-vous-en.*" He shoved Bill toward the entrance of *Chez Maurice.*

Rattled by the experience Bill realized that he should be inside the gate, taking charge of the school building. He was admitted after a scrutiny of his identity card and as he neared the front door a great shout went up from the crowd.

"Here they come."

A body of demonstrators had broken through the unguarded fence on the far side of the athletic field. Marching four abreast in a winding column they headed for the school building. At the campus entrance confusion reigned. American personnel had been instructed to stand back and were awaiting further instructions. French police were hesitant to enter the grounds of an American military installation. So they massed in front of the gate. The French troops poured in when somebody ordered the gates opened. They rushed to meet columns of demonstrators. From an upstairs window Bill saw the first shock of encounter.

He rushed through the building and on the rear stairway he met Hal who seemed to have things under control.

"Seniors aren't in the building because they don't have exams today. Most of the other students are here now."

On the main floor Bill and Hal found Murphy occupying their office.

"The Army is in charge during this emergency. Nobody is to use the telephone. Keep all students and civilians inside this building until you get further orders."

Bill picked up the telephone and pulled it away as Murphy lunged for it. He turned his back. Cradling the instrument in one arm he lifted the receiver and stuck his finger into one hole of the dial but he couldn't think of anyone to call on the spur of the moment. He slammed the phone down on his desk.

Murphy laughed and strode out of the office.

Bill heard shouts from the front of the building where French police were battling waves of demonstrators. He pushed past the protesting M.P.'s who tried to hold everybody back. As he searched among the marchers he saw a familiar figure, the one perhaps he had unconsciously been looking for.

A slender man with a shock of dark hair stood on something that raised him a meter or so above the crowd. He was back a few yards surrounded by demonstrators whom he seemed to be directing. It was Jean, all right.

As Bill watched, a wedge of police broke through the ring surrounding Jean. He raised his elbows in defense as an agent de police came up to grab him. Another cop swung at him from the front. He raised his club high and brought it down with all his force on the side of Jean's head. Jean pitched forward full length on the ground.

To Bill's amazement Jean arose, blood streaming over his face as he turned toward his followers, urging them forward. With renewed vigor they charged into the police. Other people momentarily blocked Bill's view. The next thing he saw was Jean's limp body being carried to a waiting police wagon.

By one o'clock the mid-day sun shone out of a clear sky on a peaceful school and the stretch of suburban road along the front entrance.

When Colette had learned of the demonstration the night before she thought of calling Bill. But it completely slipped her mind as she tried to comfort Marguerite, who was wild with grief in the hopelessness of her situation.

Setting out for school before her usual time Colette thought she would be able to warn Bill before the action started. She knew he always came early. But the school was already sealed off when she arrived. She tried to insist, but the American M.P. at the gate would not let her enter.

"Sorry, Miss, I got orders not to let any French nationals except military come through this gate."

"But I work here. I am a teacher."

"Sorry. I can't let you in."

"Can you call Mr. Helmer for me? He is director of the school."

"I got orders not to leave this gate."

"What can I do?"

"You'll have to see the commanding officer. Sorry."

She went into Chez Maurice and sat at a table watching out of the front window of the café for Bill until the crowd blocked her view. Then she stood at the edge of the road scanning people coming up to the gate.

By eight thirty when the skirmishing with the police had started, she decided she had missed Bill. With no conscious sense of purpose she turned her back on the crowd and climbed the hill over looking *la Porte Saint Cloud*, away from the school. Near the crest of the hill she turned to watch the scene below.

Colette saw the main body of demonstrators going along the athletic field fence before the police were aware of the maneuver. She watched the column march across the playing field. She turned and walked on without waiting to see the fighting. She had seen demonstrations, too many of them, and had no desire to watch the outcome. Walking along she tried not to think at all. But her attempt to get some order into her thoughts was also unsuccessful.

She was dressed for teaching and before long her feet started to hurt as she moved along the paved road in the morning sun. By the time she passed through the *Val d'Or* to the river near the *Pont de Suresnes* her feet were raw, shooting pain up her legs. Perspiration dripped from her face and ran under her blouse as she drove herself on until she reached the *berge* of the Seine. Removing her shoes she sat down and watched the boats go by on the river.

Early in the afternoon she rose to her feet and put on her shoes. She limped along *le quai Louis Bleriot* for blocks before she came to a Belt Line bus stop and waited.

As she neared the entrance to her apartment building Colette's legs ached so intensely that she could feel the pain creeping up to her shoulders. She had almost mastered the turbulence of her thoughts by concentrating on the hot bath she was going to enjoy. She would fill the tub to the brim with hot water and soak.

But she never reached her apartment. Crossing the lobby she was aware of a figure sitting on the stairs with her head in her hands. She waited politely a moment to see if the woman would move. Then the girl raised her head and looked at Colette. The red, swollen face was twisted into such a grim expression that it was a moment before recognition came.

"Marguerite." Colette dropped her bag and held out both hands.

Ignoring the outstretched hands the girl rose slowly to her feet and looked at Colette with a strange expression.

"You worked today?"

"No."

"Were you there? Did you see what happened?"

"What do you mean?" Colette felt a stab of fear.

"I think they may have killed him."

"Who?" It was a whisper.

"Jean. Standing right there I saw the whole thing."

"What happened to Jean? Where is he?"

Colette leaned against the wall of the stairway, feeling sick.

"There were a dozen police and I think every one hit him. He was wonderful. He got up and tried to keep going but they hit him again and again. There was blood all over. Oh, Colette."

Marguerite was weeping and threw her arms around Colette, holding her tight.

Colette held her a moment, stroking her hair and then gently pushed away.

"Do you know where he is?"

"Yes, in the hospital. He is in the…"
But Colette was pulling her along by the arm.
"Come on. We will find a taxi."

Part Four: Final Examinations

Chapter 34

On the early afternoon of a sunny day in May a young woman coming out of the Latin Quarter entered *la rue St. Jacques*. She turned right and followed the sloping street toward the Seine. Dressed in a white jacket and light blue skirt and carrying a medium-sized shoulder bag, she moved along at a slow pace.

Saturday afternoon traffic was light but the streets were crowded with pedestrians, mostly students and tourists. The girl stopped at *la rue Soufflot* to let cars pass by before crossing. At *la rue Cujas* she changed direction and walked briskly to the left between rows of closed shops and storage buildings down the deserted street, turning north again toward the river on *la rue de la Sorbonne*. The massive university building dwarfed a dimly lighted passageway.

A lively crowd filled the outdoor café at *Place de la Sorbonne*. The girl paused to listen to a young man with a guitar, playing the songs of George Brassens. Some spectators were humming along with words from *Le Petit Cheval Blanc*. On the corner of the square at *le boulevard Saint Michel* young people were listening to a speaker deploring the influence of American capitalism on French culture.

Where the boulevard intersected *la Rue des Ecoles* she stopped by a kiosk to rest for a time on a wooden bench. Across from her a thin, dark woman sat on the sidewalk holding an infant, her small cardboard box in front of her.

After a time the girl arose from her bench and continued down the boulevard after placing a handful of coins in the woman's box.

Traffic was heavier at *le boulevard Saint Germain* where pedestrians were gathering into a mass of people before rushing across as the lights changed.

A lady selling lilies of the valley on the sidewalk looked at the girl and smiled as she held out a bouquet.

"*Non, merci Madame.*"

"*Vous avez l'air triste, ma petite.* These will bring a smile" She pinned a bouquet on the girl's jacket and refused the coins the girl held out. "*Cadeau de printemps pour une belle fille.*"

"*Merci, Madame. Vous êtes très gentille.*"

At *la Place Saint Michel* the girl hesitated for several moments at the entrance to the *Metro* before descending the steps to the station, where she purchased a ticket. She entered a narrow corridor down to the elevators.

With fellow passengers she followed signs: DIRECTION SAINT CLOUD—CLIGNANCOURT. On the platform under the sign Clignancourt she sat down on a wooden bench waiting with a crowd of passengers for the next train.

When the train roared into the station she watched the platform empty as other passengers boarded. She remained as the train pulled out. A late afternoon crowd continued to gather for the next train until the platform was once again crowded.

When the roar of the arriving train sounded in the tunnel the girl sprang up as the crowd surged forward toward the edge of the platform. The headlights of the locomotive emerged from the tunnel and there was a commotion and a cry of voices.

"Stop her. Stop that train. Oh my God."

In a shower of sparks and a shrieking of brakes the train shuddered to a stop with only the first car fully into the station. People were pushing against each other to see what had occurred.

"What happened? Did she fall or did she jump?"

Immediately the Station Master with a helper came forward shouting, "Please get back. Close the gate. No more passengers admitted." Two gendarmes appeared to force the crowd on the platform toward exits at each end of the station.

Stretching yellow ribbons more police roped off the cleared platform as an emergency crew of five men in pale suits arrived with a ladder and battery lights. Their leader rushed to find the Station Master, who was instructing the motorman to unload all his passengers, directing them out through the first car of the train.

"Is the power off?"

"Just a minute," the Station Master was now on the telephone. He turned to the emergency crew chief. "I was just told that it is off. The third rail is safe."

At that moment the station was plunged into semi-darkness. Three men with hand lights and baskets descended the ladder onto the tracks. With a flashlight the Station Master was ruffling through papers at his desk.

After an interval the men came back up with their baskets.

"I think we have all the items we could find," they told their chief. "Now we need the body bag."

Four men carefully raised the bag to the platform to place it on a stretcher. Meanwhile their chief sorted through the baskets after the full lighting flashed on.

"We'll all have to make reports," he told the Station Master and the motorman. "I'll take these papers and get copies of my report to you later today. But I can give you information now. Her handbag is almost intact. We have an identity. The woman is a foreigner."

"You know, I noticed her sitting there and thought she was waiting for someone. She was young. *Une étrangère?* What happens now?"

"We have to make out our reports. The woman is from a military family. I have already called the United States Embassy. They will collect the body. Here are the essentials."

He handed the Station Master a slip of paper:

Name: Katherine May Selner

Nationality: American (U.S.A.)

Age: 18 years

Student, American School

Chapter 35

Dusk creeping across the athletic field softened the outlines of goal posts and the soccer backstop, against the sky. The view from Bill's office window matched the obscurity of his thoughts.

He had just received a call from Peg Callahan.

"The ballots are coming in," she told him. "Looks like a heavy vote. We'll be counting tomorrow night. You coming, Bill?"

"I don't think so, Peg. I've got a lot to do right now."

"Well, I'll be there to see that everything is on the level."

"Good girl, Peg. I'll probably see you tomorrow."

Bill awoke that morning thinking about Kay Selner. Right now the P.T.A. somehow no longer seemed to be important.

The solitude of the deserted building became oppressive. He was tempted to call Colette. Was this desire to escape the loneliness of thinking a sign of ageing? He wondered where Tony was and what he was doing.

Shaken by Kay's death he had no idea of what had actually happened until this afternoon when Martha came into the office. Weighted down by the responsibility of her knowledge, Martha had come to see him. He still didn't know all the details. But from what Martha told him he was able to visualize Kay's terrible conflict.

"She told me that Tony was the only boy friend she ever had, and she was a senior." Martha sat on the edge of her chair. "Her father was so afraid of all the wicked things in Paris that he didn't even want her to go out at night. This would never have happened to Kay if we weren't over here in Europe. I wish we had never come to France. My folks don't like it here. We never wanted to come. I hate France. Why did they send us over here, Mr. Helmer? Why did they send us?"

He wanted to say that it wasn't France that killed Kay, but he kept silent.

"What should I do, Mr. Helmer?" Martha was crying. "I can't tell my folks. They would never understand. I know Kay's parents have no idea what happened or why she did it. What do you think I should do?"

Come on, Mr. Helmer, give the girl some answers. What should she do? The Quartermaster mortician must have known of Kay's condition at death. He evidently had said nothing about it to her parents. Bill wondered why.

Martha appeared calmer when she left but Bill wasn't at all certain he had helped. Funny how we miss the boat, he thought. We don't even touch the kids with our textbooks and tests; we don't know what in the hell is going on, what they are thinking about. We imagine that we are making an essential contribution to our intellectual tradition. What we are really doing is just keeping the kids off the streets.

These youngsters live in a world that may be blown to hell any moment, a world where half of the population is starving to death and the other half is busy lynching or exploiting each other. And what do we do to our high schools? We run students through a set of exercises after which some of them are stamped as certified for college so they can go on and study to earn enough money to buy all different colored cars with a lot of horsepower.

He recalled that Colette had told him that we hardly scratch the surface the way we teach literature. Well, that's true of the whole damned school system. We only skim the surface and never risk removing the veneer of complacency at being freedom-loving Americans protecting the whole world from the forces of evil. We're afraid to admit that we are just the same grab-bag assortment of men and women as every other nation on earth.

He picked up the telephone and dialed.

"Hello," said a voice at the other end.

"Hello. Mrs. Mosca?"

"Yes."

"This is Bill Helmer at the high school. I wanted to ask about Tony."

"I'm so glad you called, Mr. Helmer. I'm worried sick about him. I know this is the last week with tests and all, but I just haven't the heart to make him go. Is he missing something he can't make up?"

"I'm not concerned about his school work at the moment. He can take care of that later. The important thing is how he is taking all this."

"He feels terrible of course. Hasn't eaten anything to speak of since he came home from Germany. He just sits around and tortures himself by thinking about it. Just now I got him to go out and buy some things for supper. It's the first time he's gone out of the house since...well, since he found out about it."

"Does he talk about it much?"

"Not now, but he did tell me everything. Do you know what really happened, Mr. Helmer?"

"I think I know most of the story. Martha came in to talk with me this afternoon. Poor kid, she couldn't keep it on her conscience any longer."

"I know how she feels. I'll have this on my conscience as long as I live. I keep asking myself, why didn't Tony tell me about this before? Why didn't he tell me, Mr. Helmer? I'm not so mean that he couldn't tell me about it." She was crying.

"You should not blame yourself, Mrs. Mosca. Children don't often come to us with their most important problems, even to their parents."

"But why? It's terrible. I feel that I really don't know him, my own child. I feel so guilty."

"As far as that goes, we should all feel guilty. We're sometimes pretty smug, we teachers and parents, about how important we are and how much good we do. We don't usually have to face up to our failures."

"She was such a lovely child. I just can't feel in my heart that they did anything so terribly wrong."

"I hardly think we're in a position to set ourselves up as judges of what is right and wrong," he said, "and there isn't much point in worrying over past mistakes. The future is the important thing right now. We can work on that together."

"Yes. You're right about that."

"Please let me know if I can do anything to help. At least you can tell Tony not to worry about his school work."

"Oh, thank you. You don't know how much we appreciate that, Mr. Helmer." She was silent a moment and then she asked, "Have you talked with the Selners yet? Do they know the story?"

"That is the very question I've been avoiding. No, they haven't called me and I haven't talked with them. Apparently Quartermaster mortuary services didn't say anything about Kay being pregnant. I am quite sure they don't know."

"Well, I thought about calling them but I didn't. And I won't. Maybe it isn't very Christian of me, Mr. Helmer, but I can't help feeling bitter toward those people."

"I see."

"I am willing to take my responsibility but it seems to me that they have a load of it on their backs. She was such a sweet child and I'm sure she wouldn't have done it if they…well, if they had been more—what should I say—more human?"

"I think they must feel a terrible responsibility."

"Are you going to tell them?"

"To be perfectly honest, Mrs. Mosca, I haven't decided yet."

"What do you think is the right thing to do?"

"I don't know."

"Well, Mr. Helmer, you're probably busy so I won't keep you. I can't tell you how much Tony's father and I appreciate all you've done for us."

"I've done so tragically little. Anyway, call me if I can help. Goodbye, Mrs. Mosca."

All right, there it is Helmer. You're the one who has to decide. Let's look at it this way: what will you accomplish by telling the Selners about their daughter? Will it make things easier for them, or worse? How will her father take it? Maybe it will soften him up, make him more understanding.

He sat staring out the window as the dusk thickened into darkness, obliterating the playground and turning the sky deep purple. Perhaps the best thing to do would be to talk with Kay's father and feel him out.

He could decide on the spur of the moment whether or not to tell him. He would trust his intuition to find the right thing to say.

Bill reached for the telephone.

Chapter 36

Dressed only in pajama bottoms Bill straggled into the living room and sank onto the sofa.

"You look fagged this morning." Ken greeted him from an armchair.

"Morning, Ken. You're up early."

"Up?" Ken stretched. "I haven't been down yet. But what are you doing at this hour. It's only five-thirty."

"Have to be at school early. Today is the last day."

"Boy, you look like I feel."

"I had a hard day yesterday. Worked late."

"Was the riot pretty bad?"

"Terrible and it couldn't have happened at a worse time."

"Did you see the papers? I picked up a couple." Ken tossed the newspapers over to Bill. "Your school made the front page. Congratulations."

"Thank you." Bill scanned the news write-ups. "These stories aren't accurate." He threw down the papers in disgust. "Ken, I saw Jean yesterday in the demonstration. He was severely beaten by the French police."

"They can be merciless."

"Brutal as hell. It was sickening."

"I tried calling Marguerite last night from the club but nobody was home. The kid must be at her mother's house."

"I couldn't get Colette either. She wasn't at school yesterday. I'm worried about her."

"I'm concerned about you, Bill. You're working too hard. Better take a hot shower. I'll make a pot of coffee and fry some eggs."

After breakfast Bill folded a double-breasted suit and a white shirt neatly over his arm.

"You going to impress Colette by wearing two suits a day?" Ken asked.

"I don't have time to come home and change before the commencement ceremony tonight."

"You making a speech?"

"No, but I'll introduce the speaker and present the diplomas. There will be a reception for the seniors afterward."

"You should take it easier, Bill." Ken yawned. "Like me. I'm going to sleep for years."

Next week I can take it easy, Bill thought as he drove along. I can have some time to be with Colette. She worried him lately but he couldn't do much about it. Recently at dinner together she acted strangely.

During summer break away from school they could be together more often. At just the right moment he could pin her down He had fouled up the first time, asking her in a third-rate hotel room. Next time he would do it properly. This cheered him up. Arriving at school he was surprised to find Peg Callahan in his office.

"Morning, Bill."

"Hi, Peg. Seeing you makes it worth while to get here early."

"I thought you would be interested in an election report."

"How did the balloting go?"

"We agreed to extend the deadline for a final count. There was a heavy vote and ballots were still coming in last night."

"Where are they?"

"That was funny, Bill. Nobody trusted anybody else to keep the ballots. We finally asked the Sergeant-Major to put them in the headquarters safe, in care of the Old Man."

"That's a good idea. Was Selner there last night? He wouldn't talk to me on the phone."

"No. I heard on the q.t. that he has asked for a transfer Stateside. He'll get it of course. That is a sad story."

"What a year this has been."

"It's been a horrible year, Bill. Tom thinks Chaplain Selner was mistaken when he originally signed up with the military. I'll let you know when the balloting is done."

"Frankly, Peg, I'm tired at this point. It would be a relief to get a dignified job, like doorman at the American Embassy."

"Don't let me down. The council meeting is Monday and we will be all right. I will phone you tomorrow."

Bill found a stack of diplomas on his desk with a note from the counselor asking him to sign them. He had just finished when she came in.

"Did you check the diplomas against the list of graduates?" she asked.

"No. I just signed the damned things. Did you check them?"

"Yes. One is missing."

"That so? Which one?"

"Tony Mosca."

"Why isn't Tony's diploma there?"

"Mr. Jackson refused to give Tony a credit in his second semester of English. Tony was out of school for almost a week during final exams."

"I told his mother not to worry about it. Didn't he take make-up exams?"

"Yes, along with some other students. He completed his English finals but he was late turning in a theme. Second semester Mr. Jackson required a theme that he said was an important requirement. He set a deadline date and told the students no papers would be accepted after that date. Tony handed in his theme a week late."

"I'll see Jackson first thing."

"I already talked with him. Let me warn you that he is stubborn. Mr. Jackson is using one of your favorite phrases, Bill. He is determined in Tony's case to maintain standards."

"The bastard," Bill said. "Excuse me, Mary."

"That's all right." She picked up the diplomas. "It's exactly the way I feel about it."

"Good morning, Mr. Helmer," Henry Jackson said when he came in a few moments later. "The counselor said you wanted to see me."

"Have a chair, Henry. I need to talk with you about Tony Mosca. I notice that his name was not on the list of graduates. Mary tells me he flunked English,"

"That is correct. He failed to turn in a major assignment within the allotted time. Senior students must learn that a deadline date is exactly that. They had almost two months of advance warning."

"Henry, you knew about Tony and Kay Selner, didn't you?"

"I suppose her death was a shock to the boy."

"It was more than that. There was a connection that I don't feel free to talk about, but the boy had reason to be upset. I talked with his mother on the phone and assured her that Tony would be able to make up the work he missed during the week following Kay's death."

"He could have finished the theme at home and sent it to school. I don't care what connection he had with Kay Selner. In my opinion he had no valid excuse."

"Apart from the theme, how was Mosca's work for the semester in your class?"

"Fair," Jackson said. "Not bad but not nearly as good as the work he should do."

"And he completed everything but the theme?"

"Yes, but the theme is precisely the question. If we don't set date limits and then respect them, how can we maintain standards and help students develop self-discipline?"

"I guess I've done a lot of talking this year, Henry, about maintaining standards. I appreciate your support of the idea, but it seems to me that standards and rules must take account of human values. What good would the school accomplish by forcing Tony Mosca to go an additional year for a credit in English? It could do a great deal of harm."

"I'm afraid we don't see eye to eye on that, Mr. Helmer."

"Henry, I'd like to ask you to reconsider and give Mosca's paper whatever grade you think it deserves, taking into account to be sure, that it was submitted late."

"I don't care to do that. He needs a lesson in discipline more than anybody I know. I intend to see that he gets it."

"Your deadline date, Henry, is an administrative rule of classroom procedure," Bill said. "Rules of procedure are made by the teacher but are subject to coordination and control by the office. If necessary I will stand on administrative prerogative and request an extension of the deadline for Mosca's theme."

"In other words, you are ordering me to pass the boy."

"I wouldn't put it that way. Let's say I am requesting you to accept the paper. No matter what grade the paper merits, the general average of his semester work should pull him through."

"All right. I wash my hands of the whole thing. I try to maintain standards and get no support. I'll give you the theme and you can do what you want with it."

"Oh, no. I'm exercising my administrative prerogative."

Jackson sat there as he kept turning this over in his mind. The office was so quiet you could hear the sharp click, click of Maria's typewriter through the wall and the thump of its carriage returning after each line.

"Mr. Helmer, I'm not sure you have the authority to do that."

"I have the authority all right, Henry. I can, if you wish, show you the paragraph in the Administrative Regulations."

"All right. You win. I'll tell the counselor to give him a D-minus in English. But I'm doing it under protest."

"Henry, what I said about the regulations was true. I'm within my legal rights. But that is pure chicken shit. This is the first time I've thrown the rulebook at somebody. It's a spineless way to duck an issue. If it makes you feel any better, I ordered you to pass Mosca. That was the real problem. I'm willing to take full responsibility."

"You may have to."

Chapter 37

On the last day of school Bill had scarcely settled down from his encounter with Henry Jackson when Jack Brewster, looking ill at ease, came into the office.

"Morning, Jack. I thought I'd seen the back of you after final exams."

"Got a minute, Mr. Helmer?"

"Sit down, Jack. Don't tell me you flunked something."

"No. This is serious."

"You in trouble?"

"Yeah, but not what you're thinking." Jack was playing with a cigarette, tossing and catching it. "Mr. Helmer, what do you think I should do?"

"What do you mean?"

"Just last week I realized that I got no idea what I want to do now that I'm through school."

"Have you talked this over with Miss Serinac?"

"Yeah. But she's a woman and doesn't understand."

"Have you thought about what you want to do?"

"To be honest, I haven't. For the last five years, maybe the last ten I've been fighting against the idea of going to West Point, which my old man wanted me to do."

"So you won't go?"

"You kidding? With my grades I don't think even the general could get me in. But I wouldn't go anyway. I don't ever want to see another military uniform in my whole life."

"Have you talked with your father about this?"

"Naw. He's too busy squiring Congressmen around and flying to Washington. Funny, I don't really know my dad. He's a good troop, I guess. He's given me about as much money as I wanted and he's always on my side when I get in trouble. But I just can't talk with him about anything serious."

"You want to get into college, Jack?"

"I don't know what I want to do."

"You've wasted a hell of a lot of time in high school but I think you have a good mind and you've certainly had some experience living in Paris."

"Don't rub it in."

"I am serious. Experience in living is an important part of education, maybe the most important part. I'll admit that you have been a pain in the neck for me but I have a hunch that you are intelligent. You speak French well. You are an independent type and probably a natural born leader. You have some good qualities."

"You really think so, Mr. Helmer? Nobody ever said that. Maybe I should go to college."

"Will you be here this summer?"

"Yeah. I got no plans at all."

"Come in this summer, Jack, and we'll talk about it. I'll be glad to help you if I can after you make a decision that you should make entirely on your own."

"Thanks. I'll get in touch."

During the morning Mrs. Mosca telephoned to say that Tony refused to be in the Commencement exercises. His parents felt he should be graduated with his classmates and have the best memories possible of his last days in high school. Finally he agreed to talk with Mr. Helmer about it.

"I know how busy you are," Mrs. Mosca said, "but could you see Tony today?"

"Send him up early this afternoon."

"Do I have to go to Commencement to get my diploma?" Tony asked when he came into the office.

"No, Tony, you don't, but your parents feel you should."

"Cripes, that settles it then. I think graduation ceremonies are silly, anyway. It would be different if Kay were here. But I can't...well, I just couldn't do it, that's all."

"Yes, Tony. It would be a difficult thing to do."

"Cripes, Mr. Helmer, do you think I ought to go through that whole business tonight?"

"I don't know. That's for you to decide, Tony. Commencement is a timeworn ritual. You see, the ceremony is not so much for the students as for the parents. It's a sad time for parents when their children grow up and leave home. Graduation is a symbol of that. Your parents would be pleased to have you graduated with your class."

"Cripes, they don't know how I feel. You think I ought to do it then?"

"I won't say what you should do, but I would counsel you not to make your decision entirely on the basis of your feelings. Think of your parents. They're pretty nice people, you know. I want you to think about them when you make up your mind.

Tony sat for a time in silence.

"Yeah. My folks have really been swell. I'll think about it. Maybe I'll do it then."

"It's up to you but think it over carefully."

"Gee, thanks, Mr. Helmer. I'll do it, but it'll really be rough."

Anxious as Bill was to talk with Colette he had no chance to see her during the entire day. Security officers had finally found time to complete a report on the demonstration at the school. They streamed through his office asking questions. They wanted to know the number of absent students, the precise time each teacher arrived, and why Mrs. Stepanovic, a foreign national from Poland, had been allowed to remain at the installation during a military emergency. Bill couldn't have survived without Maria. He had no idea how she had come to work.

By evening he surmised that they had taken hundreds of pages of statements, all of them probably as vague and meaningless as his own. He had eaten no lunch and only had time to duck into the faculty men's room to change clothes for the graduation ceremony after a quick snack at the café across the street.

'As he sat on the stage that night he was aware that he was watching the completion of a cycle he had seen many times before, looking at similar graduating classes, listening to similar speeches.

"Never believe for a minute, young men and women," the speaker was saying, "that the things you have been taught are not true. In the infinite wisdom of your seventeen or eighteen years you may think that you see great falsehoods and hopeless inconsistencies in the system by which you live. Your education has been the result of your life with those great institutions—the church, the home and the school. You have the precious opportunity to enjoy those bulwarks in the greatest democracy history has ever produced.

"The late President Franklin D. Roosevelt once said, 'To some generations much is given; from some generations much is expected; this generation of Americans has a rendezvous with destiny.' You are not just ordinary young men and women; you are Americans, citizens of the greatest democratic power the world has ever known. Truly, you have a rendezvous with destiny."

Bill tried to catch Hal's eye.

"Give freely of yourselves," the speaker continued, "to support this great system and to defend it with your lives if necessary. As you go from school life into life's school may you be strengthened and comforted by the knowledge that you are on the side of freedom, justice and truth."

Bill took his place beside a small table upon which the diplomas had been stacked. He made the customary appeal that the audience hold their applause until the end and received the customary response, a timid scattering of hand clapping for the first few, prolonged applause for each one as the ceremony continued.

He was falling into a steady rhythm of holding out diplomas and shaking hands. "Patrick Malloy, Charles Mason, Elizabeth Mock, Anthony Mosca... Bill looked up. Tony stood there in his cap and gown, staring straight ahead. Somebody gave him a shove. White-faced he moved across the stage to Bill.

266

"Congratulations, Tony."

"Thanks." Tony stood still with his diploma in hand.

Bill squeezed his shoulder, pushing him toward the door leading off stage.

After the ceremony Bill took refuge in his office to prepare himself for the reception. Somebody knocked on the door and Colette leaned her head into the office.

"I don't feel well, Bill. I'm sorry to leave like this but I must go now."

Colette looked ill, face drawn and white.

"Let me take you home."

"No. Betty Larkin said she would take me."

Bill ran a pocket comb through his hair before he went into the outer office. Then he took a deep breath, pulled the lapels of his jacket smooth and went through the door toward the senior reception.

Henry Jackson, who was waiting in the corridor, watched Bill as he walked away. Minutes later he was talking with a mother in the office.

"Mrs. Breen, I thought you might be interested to know that Mr. Helmer ordered me to pass a senior boy I had failed."

"Really? Who was it, Mr. Jackson?"

"A boy named Anthony Mosca. He failed to complete his work, but the principal ordered me to pass him anyway."

"The P.T.A. Council will be interested in that."

"You understand that I wouldn't want my name used unless absolutely necessary."

"Of course. And I do thank you, Mr. Jackson. The Council doesn't have to say where they got this information. They will certainly want to ask Mr. Helmer about it."

They walked down together along the reception line, congratulating the seniors.

Chapter 38

Bill's hands trembled as he poured a can of beer into a tall glass. Colette had just departed. A short time before he had been delighted when she appeared unexpectedly at his door.

"Darling. What a marvelous surprise."

Taking her into his arms he kissed her. She was stiff and unresponsive.

"Sweetheart, what's wrong?"

"I must talk with you, Bill."

"Well, sit down, darling. I'll get you a drink."

Colette's face was pale. She was dressed in a simple white smock. Bill thought she had never looked so beautiful.

"I haven't seen much of you lately." He handed her a glass of wine.

"Thank you." She put the drink down without tasting it.

"You look tired."

"I am. I have been at the hospital with Jean."

"How is he?"

"He has a concussion. He was unconscious for a long time."

"I'm sorry, honey."

"A policeman must have hit him directly on the head with his club. Oh, how I hate them. I never knew I could hate so much."

"You know, I saw him at school that day. He really has guts."

"He has no fear of the police because he has fought them so many times."

"Have you seen Marguerite?"

"Yes. She also marched that day. She is so unhappy."

"Ken told me about the visa."

"It is a sad world. Perhaps Jean is right that it must be changed completely."

"I hope there is more than one way of changing it. I don't think the Communists have a monopoly on the right answers. Do you?"

"No, certainly not."

"But I'm not interested in politics right now."

"Nor am I. There are more important things."

"Like us, for example."

"Like the way people feel about each other."

"Right now I'm concerned with the way we feel about each other."

"Bill, I have been needing to talk with you. We have been so busy these past weeks."

"I know something is wrong, Darling, but I don't know what. I haven't a clue."

"I must talk of our feelings, of what I feel about you and Jean."

"Jean?" Bill's face tensed. "What does he have to do with it?"

'He is very important to me."

"How important?"

"I love him, Bill."

"So that's why you've been different lately. God, I should have known." He leaned forward as if to diminish the distance between them. "When did you decide this?"

"I have no idea. Perhaps it was when I thought Jean might die. I honestly did not know my true feelings until these past few days."

"Colette, I…I want to be sure you know what you are doing because…well, because I love you."

"I must be honest with you, *chéri*. You have been so important to me. I wish I could say what I feel about you, about this wonderful year."

They sat in silence for a moment.

"I had to come and tell you, Bill. You have been so sweet and…I don't really know how to say it. I think you are …*épatant*. I like you. I like you so much."

"But you don't love me."

"I love Jean. I tried not to love him but I cannot change how I feel."

"Are you sure it isn't pity, Colette? Pity is only one of the sentiments you talked about."

"No." Colette paused. "It is not pity. It is a long story. Jean and my brother Roger fought in the *Résistance* together. Then I lived with Jean. We quarreled and I went to England to get away from him. But you solve nothing by running away."

"No."

"I thought of Jean then as a Communist, a part of an abstract political thing I did not like. In the same way I once thought of you as an American. But that was wrong. I found out you and Jean are not even so very different. We are all just people, men and women."

"But you are in love with Jean?"

"Yes."

Colette stood in the door and held out her hand to tell him goodbye. He clasped her hand in both of his.

"Oh, Bill." She pulled away and ran down the steps.

He watched her out of sight around the turn in the stairs and closed the door.

Bill had gradually developed a habit during the last year of seeing the present in terms of himself and Colette, like two lenses in a pair of glasses. Since Easter he had been making plans with the same double perspective. Now like a myopic with a broken lens he groped for some focus on a future that did not include her. He started pacing through the apartment wondering how it could possibly look the same way it always did after what has just happened.

He was wandering around the living room when the telephone rang.

"Hello, Bill. This is Peg Callahan."

"Hello, Peg."

"Good news," she said. "We have a majority for the P.T.A. Council meeting. We elected three of our candidates, giving us a three to one advantage. The president appoints committee chairmen so we can build up a strong support group next year."

Through a fog of disappointment about Colette the news did not fully register. He silently tried to sort out his thoughts about what this meant.

"Did you hear me, Bill?" It's a great victory."

"Sorry, my mind was completely occupied with something else. So we won. The credit is all yours, Peg."

Bill felt a momentary lifting of spirit thinking of how Murphy would react to the news. But it seemed of minor importance compared with his longing for Colette.

"I just had a brain storm. The old and new councils will meet together. Listen to this. The president will recognize me first at the meeting Monday and I'll present a motion for a vote of confidence in you. Then I'll recommend that a letter be written to dependent school headquarters expressing appreciation of your work at the high school. This puts the opposition on the defensive and it's sure to carry. You'll be there of course."

"Yes. I'll be there."

"You sound strange, Bill. You must be tired."

"I am tired. It's only fair to tell you, Peg, that I have decided to resign. I want that vote of confidence first, but then I'm going to submit my resignation. I don't feel like fighting this battle again."

"Bill, you can't do that. You have done a wonderful job and we want to keep you there, for the good of the school. We need you terribly."

"I'm sorry, Peg. One of these days I want to have dinner with you and Tom and tell you what tremendous people you are. But I'm going to leave. Life is too short to spend in that institution."

"Well, I think I understand how you feel. But I do hope you will change your mind. You will be there Monday?"

"I'll be there."

He felt better when he hung up. At least one decision was out of the way. School would have been difficult enough to face next year and now without Colette it would be impossible. When the doorbell rang he felt a wild surge of hope that she had changed her mind. It was not Colette. Tony Mosca was standing there.

"Oh, hello, Tony."

"Hi, Mr. Helmer."

"Come in. How are you?"

"O.K. I guess."

"Make yourself comfortable. Would you like something to drink? Soda, coffee?"

"I guess I'd like a soda, please."

"Bill brought in a glass of Coca Cola and they sat on opposite sides of the table.

"You know what," Tony blurted out, "I guess you're wondering why I came up here. To tell the truth, I don't know myself. I wanted to be with somebody and I thought of you. I suppose you know about Kay and me."

"I know a little bit about it and I'm glad you wanted to come, Tony."

Slumped in his chair Tony was deep in thought for a moment. Then he asked, "You ever been in love, Mr. Helmer?"

"Yes, Tony, I have."

"Cripes, I didn't ask that to be fresh or anything."

"Of course."

"Then you know what it's like."

"I think I do." Bill lighted a cigarette quickly and smoked in silence.

"We're going back to the States next week." Tony sat forward in his chair and leaned on the table. "I want to stay over here but my folks won't let me. I could go to the University of Maryland branch in Munich."

"Maybe they're right, Tony."

"I'd like to stay here because of Kay."

"I thought she was buried at home."

"Yeah, but as far as I'm concerned Kay will always be in Paris."

"And what about next year?"

"I don't know what I want to do. I just want Kay. But I suppose there isn't much use thinking about that. You know, I was looking at my diploma yesterday. I guess it doesn't mean anything. I don't really know much right now and I can't even think of anything I want to know."

"You might get a job and work for a year, Tony. But if you decide to take a shot at college I don't think you'll have any trouble."

"That's not what I mean. I used to pretend to Kay that I was somebody who knew the score about life and everything. And she believed me. I don't really know anything at all."

"I'm not sure, Tony, that any of us know a hell of a lot about what the score is. Maybe not being so damned sure we know the answers is a good place to start learning."

"I should've have started sooner. If I hadn't gone to that track meet in Germany Kay would be alive today."

"That's possible." Bill looked at Tony. "But it isn't certain. Kay's death was the result of a lot of things that are wrong in this world. It would be foolish for you to take all the blame and it wouldn't change anything now. I'm sure Kay wouldn't want you to go through life torturing yourself by feeling guilty."

"I guess you're right. Cripes, there's something really wrong with this whole set-up, but I don't know what it is."

"Why is that?"

"Take Kay, for instance. She did everything you're supposed to do. She never told a lie, would never cheat on an exam, always wanted to do her share. Look what happened to her. What's the use of doing things right?"

"A year ago I could have given you some cocky answers to that. Now I'm not so sure. This year I'm asking some of the same questions."

"Somebody must know the answers."

"Everybody has answers," Bill said. "The Communists have answers; the Christians have answers; teachers have them. For years they've been asking all the questions but only the ones they have answers for. It is time for you to start asking your own questions."

"So I'm on my own. Cripes, how do you know where to start?"

"You start by rejecting all the ready-to-wear ideas; by recognizing that we're all just men, not fallen angels, or exploited victims of an economic system or..."

Tony looked startled at this outburst.

"Sorry, I'm lecturing."

"Go ahead, Mr. Helmer."

"You might start with what Mr. Evans calls the Big Lie. By looking under the surface, by studying what people do rather than what they say. This you can do wherever you are—in or out of college."

They sat there in silence.

"Cripes, it's almost dark." Tony stood up. "You know, Mr. Helmer, it always makes me feel better to talk with you."

"That's a nice thing to say, Tony."

"This may sound goopy but I just want to tell you thanks for everything. You're a cool principal." Tony hesitated at the door. "The kids at school know about you and Captain Murphy. You're a good fighter, really a fighter; Well, thanks and so long."

"Good luck. And Tony I want to hear from you."

"A real fighter?" Bill sat down at the table. The idea pleased him. He thought over the events of the past year. Unexpectedly he saw himself, his ideas, his job, in a new perspective. He was right in fighting for changes at the school. But haggling with Murphy and tightening the screws for higher academic standards was not the important thing. Colette was right. It only scratched the surface.

Training citizens was what the military community expected the Paris High School to do. It was supposed to package, grade-label student units stamped "Made in U.S.A." That was all wrong

We have to start asking new questions, he thought. What is our school all about? Why are we here In Europe? If we think our system is best why are we afraid to learn all we can about Communism, or Socialism, or new ideas? Why do we treat people like Ken and Larry as inferior human beings? Why is somebody like Marguerite refused a visa?

That approach would be a rough go but Bill could try. He could take them on, by God, and when they got him he could put up a good fight and not worry if his shoes were different. He and Hal and the faculty could develop a curriculum using subject classes as tools to create a better quality of everyday life. He would agree with Murphy that they needed more discipline but it would have to be self-imposed and not military force.

He went to the telephone and dialed.

"Hello, Peg. I called to tell you I've changed my mind. I'm not going to resign. I'm not going to let them run me out of Paris."

"Wonderful. I think this is a real break for the school—for all of us. By the way Captain Murphy just phoned to check on the meeting. He doesn't want to miss it."

"I'll bet he doesn't."

"He suggested that we meet in the military office this time."

"The hell he did. We'll meet in the library like we always do. I'll tell Maria to have it set up Monday morning."

"Good." Peg laughed.

Hanging up the telephone, Bill walked over by the window to watch a tugboat towing against the river's current a huge barge loaded with coal. Near the rear cabin a woman wearing a red bandana was hanging her washing on a line stretched across the deck. By her side a little girl clutched her mother's long skirt.

The child looked up at Bill's window. She smiled and waved. Bill leaned out of the window and waved back. He blew her a kiss before she disappeared under the arch of *le Pont Marie*.

Chapter 39

Hal Evans rose from the bench by the bus stop and stretched his arms. He could feel an impression of the stone wall against his back as he reached for a cigarette. Damn! Crushing the empty package he threw it into the street.

Across the way a crescent moon hung low over the row of gray stone houses. As Hal was surveying the street, one front window, then another liqhted up.

He crossed the road to start his tour once again. It had become a reflex, from the bench by the gate to the vacant lot on the corner and back again to the bench by the gate. He could probably do it blindfolded.

Following the cinder sidewalk he tried to review the day's events. There was a strange discontinuity about today. He had no clear memory of what had happened before the telephone call. Thinking back he couldn't even recall what he was doing when the office phone rang. Maria must have been out for the moment because he had answered.

"*Allo.* Monsieur Evans, *est-il là, s'il vous plaît?*"

"Speaking," Hal recognized the voice immediately.

"*Monsieur Evans,* we have located the concierge."

"Where?"

"In the suburb of *Montrouge, monsieur.*"

"Give me the address. I'll go out to see him today."

"Just a moment, please. We have already contacted him."

"Yes?"

"The young lady called Zizi came to bring him a gift last New Year's day. She gave him an address but he has not gone to see her since."

"Well, give me the address."

"Patience, Monsieur Evans, if you please. Our man has checked the address. We have a delicate problem and we want your instructions."

"Yes, yes."

"The concierge at this address is difficult. She will not admit that the girl lives there. It would be simple to force the issue by inquiring at the *commissariat de police* to see if she is registered. But it might make trouble for your friend. We have no interest in doing that."

"Of course not. Give me the address and I'll go."

"Our man has run a surveillance of the house since about one o'clock. He thinks she did not come home for lunch. Do you want him to remain?"

"Tell him I'll be right there."

Hal wondered vaguely if he'd said "thank you" as he hung up.

The concierge *was* difficult.

"*Zizi. Non, monsieur.*"

"Perhaps another name? About so tall." Hal held out his hand. "Dark hair."

The woman shook her head.

"*Un peu timide mais gentille.* Beautiful smile." Hal looked at her eagerly but she shook her head again.

"But I am certain this is the address."

"I have no tenant by that name, monsieur."

"Goddammit, she's got to be here."

"You are from the police, monsieur?"

"*Non madame.* I am a friend of Mademoiselle Zizi."

"I am sorry, monsieur. I have work to do." She closed the door.

"I should have strangled that old hag on the spot." But as Hal thought it over maybe the old girl was trying to protect Zizi, or maybe she was telling the truth. This could be just another false alarm. But if Zizi did give this address she must have lived here at one time. Why didn't the concierge say so?

Hunched over on the stone bench he shivered. He had come directly from school in his nylon summer suit and was cold. An unexpected realization that his teeth were chattering made the noise reverberate like thunder in his head. He was frightened as he had never been before. What if Zizi is married? What if she comes home with a man? Hal would certainly look silly sitting there waiting for her.

Hal had scrutinized every bus that stopped. But the driver of the last one said there would be no more bus runs to *Montrouge* until the following morning.

A noise in the street brought him to his feet. It was a workman with his bicycle. Hal passed by casually, studying him as he opened the gate. This man appeared to be about fifty—certainly too old for Zizi. Hal went back to his bench. What if Zizi had a family? Hal tried to visualize her carrying...

The footsteps were almost upon him before he was aware of them. Jumping to his feet he stepped out on the sidewalk squarely in the path of the oncoming woman.

"*Imbecile!*" The long loaf of bread she carried under her arm was broken. She had dropped her net shopping bag full of groceries.

"*Excusez-moi, madame.*" Hal picked up the bag and handed it to her. "*Il n'y a pas de mal?*"

"*Il faut faire attention, monsieur.*" She turned and hurried away.

Hal stepped into the middle of the street and looked up at the house. A light went on in the second floor window and he wondered if it could be Zizi's. There might be a back entrance. The detective had assured him that there was none but he could have missed it. If she didn't come in another half hour he would force his way into the house. He sat down again on the bench.

The footsteps echoed sharply some distance away. They were on the other side of the street and Hal watched intently. A shadowy figure hurried along the wall and Hal had just decided that it would continue down the street when the girl turned and crossed toward the gate. She was wearing a white sweater and she had long hair that fell to her shoulders. She seemed young—too young for Zizi. But she was carrying something that looked like an easel. He stood up and stepped out just as she reached the gate.

"Zizi," he said. "Zizi."

The girl drew back against the gatepost.

"Oh God." She dropped her easel and reached out to touch the lapels of his coat. "Oh God."

Hal put his arm around her and led her over to the bench. He had rehearsed this a thousand times. Now all he could say was "Zizi" over and over again. He took her face between his hands.

"Why didn't you answer my letters?"

"Letters?"

"Of course. You didn't get them. But the Christmas cards?"

"I had one card from you. I lost it when we moved. Elsa and I had to leave quickly."

"Zizi..." He was having difficulty breathing. "Zizi, you...aren't, married or anything?"

"No. I knew you would come back."

"The hell you did. What made you so sure?"

"You said that when you left."

He took her into his arms and pulled her onto his lap, but he didn't kiss her right away. Instead he held her tight against his chest. They sat there until some of the lights went out in the gray stone houses and the crescent moon had moved eastward.

Hal held her at arm's length.

"Zizi, I don't know what to say next."

"I do." She arose and pulled at his hand. "I am starving. Let us eat."

"You haven't changed a bit." Hal hadn't laughed like that for a long time.

"I still get hungry."

"Tonight, *chérie*, we'll drink the best champagne we can find. We're going to the *Tour d'Argent* and look out at Paris while we eat."

"We are not. We are going to my room. Now I have a two-burner alcohol stove."

It isn't easy to hug a girl, pick up an easel, and open a gate at the same time. But Hal managed.

About the Author

Richard Johnston, Ed.D., grew up in an itinerant working family in the Pacific Northwest. His father, a socialist, devoted his energy to organizing fellow laborers into unions. He dreamed of creating a happier world through union brotherhood.

In a variety of rural schools Richard settled for passing grades while reading adventure books like *Mantrap* by Sinclair Lewis. A student at Eastern Washington College of Education, he served as sports editor of the journal and helped to earn his way as a stringer for daily papers in Spokane, Washington. During World War II Richard was assigned to infantry training at Camp Roberts, California, before being transferred to study in the U.S. Army Counterintelligence Corps School located at Holabird Signal Depot in Baltimore, Maryland. Later he joined the faculty to teach in that school for the duration of the war.

At Columbia University he met and married photographer Mary Alice Boyce. After finishing their studies in New York they used their remaining G.I. Bill entitlement to study at the Sorbonne in Paris. When those funds were exhausted Richard found employment with the U.S. Army Dependents School system. They remained in Paris for eight years.

Back in the U.S. Richard was a professor in three state universities before becoming a founding faculty member of an experimental Public Affairs school, Sangamon State University (now a part of the University of Illinois) in Springfield. There, intrigued by the possibility of democratizing education through the relatively new Community College movement, he edited Community College Frontiers, a quarterly publication (1976-1982). His articles and book reviews have been published in national and international journals.

Living now in Colorado Richard enjoys writing, and hiking with his wife on mountains trails.

Printed in the United States
73945LV00003B/253-273